LOVERS OF THE DAMNED

DEMON'S *Mate*

COLETTE RIVERA

Love isn't for the Fallen

ISBN

Print: 978-1-991284-05-1

Kindle: 978-1-991284-06-8

Dear reader,

This book deals with adult themes and is intended for mature audiences. I'd like to note that one of the main characters has a sexual assault in his backstory, and while this is not a major aspect of the book, it affects him, including one instance where he is triggered during consensual sex. There is also an on-page run-in between the main character and the perpetrator. Further content guidance for this book can be found in the final paragraph of this note. Please take care and use your discretion.

This book is part of a series with an overarching plot, though each book features a different couple. The romance stands alone and ends in a happily ever after, but every question you have about the external story and the world may not be answered by the end. Therefore, you can expect a minor, series-related cliffhanger.

Content & Trigger Warnings: (may contain spoilers) References to a character's past interactions with homophobic family members. A character with an abusive father and other abusive family members—all instances of abuse are in the past. On-page confrontation with abusive father. A character with sexual assault in their backstory, an on-page instance where they are triggered during consensual sex, and an on-page run-in with the perpetrator. Witches who worship Satan. Romanticized stalking between main characters: one main character is influenced by a magical connection they don't fully understand, prompting stalking behavior. On-page blood magic rituals. Past nonconsensual blood draining for magic purposes. On-page attempted and failed kidnapping of a main character as well as an on-page successful kidnapping—by antagonists, not the love interest. Magical and physical violence. On-page and off-page killing of antagonists. Blood-drinking demons—similar to vampires. Sexual content: intended for mature audiences.

LOVERS OF THE DAMNED

DEMON'S Mate

COLETTE RIVERA

1

HARPER

Harper Nightingale had to escape his coven. Everything was stacked against him, but he had to get out. Another second longer, and he might implode.

Harper closed the door to his studio apartment and locked it, risking a glance down the hall. The witch spying on him was nowhere in sight, but there was always someone. Adjusting his backpack, Harper walked away as if it were a perfectly normal morning.

He wouldn't be here by the time next weekend rolled around. No matter what. Things were about to get so much worse.

He put one foot in front of the other.

Just get to the library. Pretend today is the same as every other Saturday.

Harper forced a carefully bored expression as he descended the stairs, clenching his fist so he wouldn't reach for the potion in his pocket. He knew it was there. There was no need to check and risk drawing attention.

He exited the apartment complex on the outskirts of Shearwater Landing. When Harper was first sent to the city by the sea, his father told him he'd be living there alone.

He bit the inside of his cheek. How had he ever been gullible enough to believe that?

Harper let out a measured breath. It didn't matter. He would never fall for one of Arthur Nightingale's lies again.

His skin itched as he made his way down the quiet street. The witch following him wasn't far behind, his magical presence looming in the back of Harper's mind.

Now that Harper knew to look out for someone tailing him, he always checked. One of Arthur's men stalked him everywhere he went, and at least half a dozen of them lived in the apartment complex with him.

When he'd first arrived in the city a year ago on his mission to hunt the Hounds of Hell, he hadn't noticed anything amiss. Stupid. He was so stupid for believing his father trusted him and was giving him a chance to improve his rank. Harper clenched his fist harder and pushed the regret away. There was no changing the past.

But he hadn't even discovered his stalkers on his own. It was as embarrassing as being duped in the first place. He'd believed he was beyond his coven's reach, and when he'd taken the chance to go out to a club one night, a familiar witch had appeared seemingly out of nowhere and stopped him.

Why had his father bothered pretending to give Harper a longer leash, only to reassert his complete control? Was it just to fuck with him? Demoralize him? The witch had dragged Harper back to his apartment, spouting Arthur's familiar homophobic bullshit and ranting about Harper's "questionable" behavior.

He was never beyond his father's reach.

Harper's blood boiled at the memory, but he kept his pace

even as he walked past shops and a small park toward the nearest subway station.

After that night, Harper's coven kept up the illusion he was on his own, never letting him catch a glimpse of them around the complex or town, but everywhere Harper went, someone followed, their presence detectable through their magic.

Except for one witch, who seemed uninterested in participating in Arthur's mind games. That, or the witch was lazy. Harper caught him following all the time, and he'd take advantage of the witch's apparent apathy toward his task. At last.

After months of careful planning and preparation, Harper was going to disappear. And not a moment too soon.

He reached the subway station and waited for a train, idly scrolling on his phone and pretending his stomach wasn't in knots. He was too tall to be inconspicuous, but he'd gotten over that a long time ago.

Harper was lean and lanky. He looked like a nondescript office worker in drab slacks and a button-down that washed out his pale skin, but dressing how he wanted wasn't a luxury he'd ever had.

When he'd first been sent on his mission, he'd wondered why his father had him living in one of the city's outermost suburbs since he had to travel into the heart of Shearwater Landing to make any progress with his hunt. Once he'd realized his building was infested with coven members, he suspected he'd been placed in the suburbs to isolate him and make him easier to keep track of because he had to get on the train to go anywhere of consequence.

An unpleasant chill prickled down Harper's spine. *Focus.*

He boarded a train headed for downtown Shearwater Landing. The car jolted forward, the motion turning his knotted stomach. He breathed through his mouth, trying not to smell the stale air, and willed time to speed up.

Harper's stomach roiled as he rode into the city. His palms prickled with sweat, begging to be wiped on his slacks. He held them still, better to not give away his nerves. He couldn't risk anything tipping off his tail. The witch had to think today was like any other day.

Harper discreetly surveyed the train car. It wasn't crowded, and his tail wasn't in the car with him, but he knew exactly where Harper was. His coven tracked him via magic and his phone's location.

It made disappearing complicated. Harper cursed his inability to use magic directly against his coven. It wasn't fair. He hated how helpless it made him. If only he could knock his stalker out and run.

He was powerful in his own right, but blood loyalty to his family prevented him from using magic directly against any Nightingales who outranked him or any unrelated coven members who had been sworn in above him. Of course Harper held the lowest rank in his coven. He'd never win in a fight against any Nightingale, let alone his father, whose position as coven leader gave him power over everyone.

A phantom pain pulsed through Harper's wrist and elbow, reminding him he couldn't even defend himself against his father, let alone attack or challenge him. Harper's stomach heaved and he swallowed back bile, focusing on the subway car floor until he blocked out the dark images looming in the back of his mind.

Finally, the train reached Harper's stop, and he got off. His legs weren't much steadier on the unmoving ground than in the rocky car. He stumbled and knocked into someone.

"Sorry."

The man didn't acknowledge him, and soon, he was out of sight.

People bushed past Harper in all directions, talking on

phones and to one another. He climbed the stairs to street level and let the city sounds wash over him. Car horns, music, bikes whizzing past.

Cities were nothing like the remote mountain compound where Harper had grown up. They were full of distractions, keeping everything that lurked in his head at bay.

His back straight, Harper walked as casually as he could through the downtown shopping district toward Old Town. Tall buildings shaded the street, keeping the summer morning cool. Harper suppressed a shiver. He swore he could still feel the motion of the train car.

He was so close. His muscles ached with the urge to run, but that would give him away and ruin everything.

Patience was key. He could do this. He'd been sneaking around the city for more than half a year, and this was the last time he'd have to do it before he was free.

As he went, the buildings got smaller and less modern. The library was in one of the oldest parts of the city, an area he frequented as part of his hunt. Not that he'd had much success tracking the Hounds of Hell, a failure his father had punished him for repeatedly.

Harper ground his teeth. Don't think about it.

The walk seemed to take forever. Harper's heart pounded like he'd been running after all, sweat dampening the back of his neck.

At last, he arrived and ascended the many stone steps leading to the grand library. His tail never followed him inside the historic building. Or at least the sloppy man following him today never did.

Harper glanced behind him as he held the front door for an older woman, catching a glimpse of his stalker sitting outside a coffee shop across the open plaza.

He entered the library and returned the books he'd checked

out previously, leaving his bag nearly empty. He hadn't wanted to look suspicious leaving his apartment weighed down with too many things, but it wasn't like he'd miss anything he left behind.

After the books were returned, Harper hurried down the building's rear stairs, pulling his phone from his pocket and turning it off as he entered the basement. There were plenty of books down here, as well as a few reading rooms. Harper had turned off his phone every time he'd come into the basement over the last eight months, leading the men following him to believe he had no reception down here.

At first, when Harper had done this, he'd spent the entire day in the basement reading as a test to see what response the lost phone signal would receive. His more diligent stalkers had checked up on him when they'd lost sight of his phone's location, but after weeks of them always finding Harper in the basement, they stopped checking.

The man at the coffee shop waiting for him certainly wouldn't come to find him—he never had before—and this was key to giving Harper a head start.

He walked quickly through the stacks to a *Staff Only* door. After checking no one was around, he slipped through the door and into a narrow hallway, heading straight to a supply closet a few doors down.

Inside, he flipped on the light and shifted boxes of cleaning products around until he came to the one at the back where he'd stashed some things. Grabbing his bundle, he flicked off the light and hurried farther down the hall to the staff restroom.

Harper set his bundle on the restroom counter and shucked off his backpack. He stripped out of his ugly office clothes and pulled on the jeans and T-shirt he'd stashed, transferring the potion to his new pocket.

The clothes were no more his style than what he'd been wearing, but at least they were casual. He pulled on a baseball cap and checked himself in the mirror. Most of his brown hair was covered. He'd let it grow long, and some of it stuck out around his ears, but it was good enough. The last touch was a pair of thick-framed glasses.

Harper opened his backpack and pulled at a loose thread in the lining, ripping the seam. When the hole was big enough, he reached his hand in and pulled out a leather bracelet and his secret debit card.

Stooping, he secured the bracelet around his ankle. The spell trapped in the leather tingled against his skin as it masked his magic from any witches he might pass on the street.

He'd tested the bracelet many times and was certain the man tailing him today wouldn't notice the disappearance of his magic. He'd never acted like he'd noticed before, leading Harper to believe this guy didn't track his magic closely.

The bracelet wasn't foolproof. Anyone magical who thoroughly assessed him would be able to break past its enchantment, but it was good enough for this stage of the plan. He didn't want anyone casually noticing a witch sneaking around when there was a chance it could get back to his coven.

Harper grabbed his ID and stuffed his discarded clothes and backpack—including his turned-off phone and wallet—into the trash can. He took the spare cell phone he'd stashed with the clothes, slipped it into his pocket with his ID, and carefully exited the restroom.

The hallway was still empty as he walked quickly to the employee exit at the end, where he'd snuck out before. He opened the door and stepped into an alley, resisting the urge to glance at the single security camera. It was unlikely to catch his face with the hat on.

Harper measured his steps as he walked, shoes scuffing the old paving stones. It was less of a risk to run now, but it would be smarter to act normal—draw no attention—he had to be smart in order to not screw this up.

More sweat prickled his skin and a wave of nausea made him glad he'd skipped breakfast. Almost there. He just had to stay calm and get through this. Which was easy. This was the last time he'd have to sneak out of the library. Everything was fine.

Exiting the alley, Harper turned in the opposite direction he'd come from and headed down the street.

He'd debated leaving Shearwater Landing as soon as he disappeared, but the logistics were near impossible. He'd had to sever all connections with his coven, meaning he had no money —his money had been connected to his father—no job, and no support system.

Growing up isolated in the Nightingale Coven meant he had no friends and anyone he'd met while hunting demons in Shearwater Landing would have been noted by his stalkers, so he hadn't bothered cultivating friendships. If Harper left the city, he would be unprepared to live wherever he ended up, so he'd built something here—slowly and secretly.

Every Saturday the lazy man followed him, Harper had slipped on his bracelet and left the library to create a new life.

He was a potions master. Mixing magic and earthly elements was where his greatest powers lay. It was why he'd been sent to hunt the Hounds of Hell, even though his father preferred to keep him close. Harper hadn't met a potion he couldn't brew, and so, on one of his reconnaissance missions through the city over six months ago, he'd used his potion skills to get himself a job.

Sort of.

Utilizing the empty drawers in his dresser, he'd brewed popular potions that sold easily in the magical market. Most humans didn't believe in magic, but that didn't mean witches and vampires didn't have their own world hidden in plain sight. Harper had found a hole-in-the-wall apothecary in the Banks that sold potions and had approached the owner—disguised as a human with his leather bracelet—and sold his potions, pretending to be in the employ of a reclusive witch.

He'd done this repeatedly, slowly saving and depositing the money he earned into a bank account he'd opened without his father's knowledge.

So Harper had an income, even though anything connected to the magical community carried the risk of being discovered by his coven. At least the owner of the apothecary was a lone witch, not associated with any coven, and extremely unlikely to cross paths with any of the Nightingales.

Staying in Shearwater Landing after his escape was likely foolish, but Harper would leave once he could afford it and had a job lined up elsewhere. It was a big city with a population of over a million people. Surely, he could slip into the crowd and, with magic on his side, never be found again.

A month ago, Harper found a room to rent in an apartment near the apothecary in the Banks, a less affluent part of the city by the river, near the Docks and all the old canneries.

Harper had never been to the Docks or the Banks as part of his hunt. He'd never been near the river or the port at its mouth. He hadn't even been very far into the Arts District that separated the nicer part of the city from the rest.

He wasn't planning on going anywhere near the neighborhoods he used to frequent or the ones he went to occasionally, like the upscale waterfront to the north, just to be safe. Harper might not leave his new apartment much at all, at least at first. Why risk it more than he had to?

He just wanted to be safe and free from his old life.

Harper left the library and Old Town behind and headed into the Arts District, passing the university. The back of his neck tingled from the sweat dampening his skin...but was it more than that? Was someone watching him, or was he being paranoid?

Glancing around, nothing caught his eye. He cast a detection spell, sending his magic out around him, looking for anyone else who possessed magic. There wasn't even the faintest hint. There couldn't be a witch following him and his father would never stoop to employing a human. Regarding humans as less than was despicable, but at least his father's prejudice worked in Harper's favor.

He was in the clear, the same as he had been every other time he'd snuck out of the library. Harper sped up, walking faster, neck prickling relentlessly.

He was further from his old life and closer to freedom than ever. Everything in his plan was falling into place. Everything he'd set up over the last half-year was paying off. So why was his heart pounding like it might all go wrong?

This moment was twenty-four years in the making. The most important thing he'd done in his life. He should be happy. Relieved.

He was sick to his stomach.

Harper ducked into a convenience store and went to the restroom. He heaved a breath and instantly regretted it. The air was foul. Fuck, he might actually be sick.

He doubled over, closed his eyes, and sucked breaths in and out through his mouth. Sweat broke out on his forehead. He was almost there. No one was following him. He shouldn't be this much of a mess when nothing was going wrong.

Maybe he needed to complete the last step of his plan. Fuck, that better help, or he was going to bolt out of the restroom and do something stupid.

Harper straightened and pulled the potion from his pocket, his trick to truly disappearing. He unstopped the vial and swallowed its contents in one mouthful. The liquid fizzed all the way down his throat and he winced at the bitter taste.

But he didn't throw up.

A chill coursed through Harper as the potion suppressed the magic in his blood. He would still be able to use magic, but while the suppressant flowed through his bloodstream, no one would be able to tell he was a witch, no matter how hard they inspected him. No one would be able to track him with magic either. Even someone with his hair or blood, like his father, couldn't use magic to find him as long as the suppressant remained in his system.

The dose he'd taken would last twenty-four hours. He'd have to brew more potion and take it religiously to remain magically invisible. It was a complicated concoction, intricate and risky to mess up, considering how much power it took to create.

Thank Satan potions were his calling.

Harper left the convenience store and the fresh air hit him like a shot of coffee. His stomach settled and he continued toward the Banks, only slightly sweaty.

He was free.

They wouldn't find him. He was nothing but another lone witch in the city by the sea. And he deserved this, dammit. Harper had gone through Hell to get here. Not literally, but his upbringing had to be comparable to the actual Realm of the Damned.

An unwanted memory popped into his head: his arms and legs tied down, his blood draining away before he was left alone, locked in the cold cellar all night. Nausea returned, but Harper stubbornly swallowed it.

He clenched his fist so tight his nails dug into his palm.

His father claimed their coven served Lucifer in everything they did and that every bit of suffering showed Satan their loyalty, but really, the coven served Arthur Nightingale, and Harper was done with all of it, Satan be damned.

Like he wasn't already.

The only thing Harper wasn't giving up was his hunt. He'd track down Lucifer's Dogs, the Hounds of Hell, just like his father wanted, but he wasn't doing it in the name of the Nightingale Coven or Lucifer. He never had been.

He had his own agenda.

2

———

ASH

Ash landed on top of the Shearwater Landing library, dropping into a crouch and gripping the top of the sloping roof as he folded his wings against his back. The sun warmed his bare chest, a slight sea breeze tickling his skin and ruffling his feathers.

Ash scowled. Who'd have thought he'd be back in this place after what, a century? Maybe more?

At least the library was familiar. Most of the plaza below was recognizable, but it had changed since he'd last been here.

Ash scanned the area with his demon sense. The only magical being in the vicinity was a witch sitting at a café on the other side of the fountain. Hardly worth sounding the alarm over.

No one could know demons were back in Shearwater Landing, but the witch wasn't a threat. An illusion crafted by his demon power rendered Ash completely invisible, and there was no way the witch could detect Ash's magic.

Ash's tail twitched. He had to put it away, horns and wings as well, but suppressing his true form bothered him more than it used to. Avoiding humans was preferable, and his last thirty years had been close to human-free. However, tracking Dante through the streets would be easier than flying around, perching on rooftops.

At least demons passed for human more easily than other magical beings. With his disguise in place, he could walk right up to the witch at the café and he'd have no idea what kind of power stood before him.

Ash leaped into the air, spreading his white-tipped black wings. He circled the library and came to land in a narrow alley out back. The old paving stones looked original, just as unchanged as the grand building behind him.

A strange scent filled his nose, like fresh mountain air and flowers. Ash breathed deeply, reminded of home. How was it possible for an alleyway to smell this good? Was there a florist nearby?

It didn't matter. With a shudder, Ash pulled his demonic features inside himself. His skin itched and burned as his wings disappeared into his flesh, forming large tattoos spanning his whole back. His horns and tail did the same, the tattoos hidden by his hair and pants.

Being incomplete grated, the tattoos tingling, almost nagging at him, telling him it had been too long since he'd put his features away. There was nothing he could do about it. Ash wouldn't be in this city if he had a choice. Unfortunately, he couldn't let his preference for isolation prevent him from warning Dante and Onyx.

At least Dante being easy to find was in his favor. He'd have to remind Dante it was in their enemy's favor as well.

He stalked out of the alley, the scent of mountain air and flowers tempting him in the opposite direction of the plaza. He shook it off. Why were his baser senses suddenly dominating him? The last thing he needed was flowers, so it shouldn't have felt wrong to walk away from the alluring scent, but it did.

Maybe this was what he got for avoiding cities. One whiff of flowers, and he was pining for his mountain home. And solitude.

People stared at Ash as he entered the crowd of morning shoppers in the plaza. Right. He should have brought a shirt. He never wore one at his isolated hunting lodge. They just didn't work with wings.

Grumbling, he ducked into a souvenir shop and was briefly relieved to see a display of black T-shirts until he noticed they were adorned with the city crest and a large illustration of a flying sooty shearwater. An almost inaudible growl left Ash's throat as he grabbed the largest shirt and brought it to the counter.

The woman at the register eyed him, brow raised, but didn't comment on his lack of clothing. Once Ash paid, he pulled on the T-shirt. It was too tight for his broad chest and thick biceps, but at least no one would be staring because he wasn't properly dressed.

He exited the shop and crossed the plaza to the fountain in the center. It hadn't changed. Fish and more damn shearwaters spouted water out of their mouths just as Ash remembered. He turned his back on the fountain and inspected the buildings around him.

Which direction had Dante's home been in? Something would jog his memory eventually.

It wasn't likely Dante lived in the same place he had a century ago, but he was bound to be here somewhere, and Ash needed a location to start his search. Tracking was easiest if he had a fresh sense of a being's magic.

A whiff of that floral mountain air drifted by on a breeze

and Ash whipped his head in that direction, frowning. The scent wasn't as strong as in the alley and faded quickly.

Oh well. He'd be home in the mountains as soon as possible, and everything would smell as sweet as whatever flowers lurked nearby.

Ash surveyed the area. That narrow street to the west was vaguely familiar. Maybe. He headed toward it.

The street was lined with modern shops and restaurants, but the paving stones were old like the ones in the alley behind the library. If only Ash could recognize the exact stones he used to walk along.

He let his instincts guide him until he had the urge to turn left down another narrow street. These buildings were older, and while the ground floors had been renovated, the floors above were familiar. Or weren't they?

When you remembered cities that had been gone for more than a thousand years, it was hard to be sure. There were too many memories. Usually, Ash kept the past where it belonged, but it was finally catching up to him.

Two centuries of freedom wasn't long now that it might be coming to an end.

He shoved his hands in his pockets and wandered on. Dante's place had to be around one of these old corners—well, old for this city at least. The West Coast of North America didn't have old buildings compared to other parts of the world, and nowhere in the Human Realm had old buildings compared to the Eternal Realm.

What did the Eternal Realm look like these days? Ash shook his head. He'd never find out, damned as he was. Why bother thinking about it?

He kept walking.

Halfway down the block, Ash stopped short, an image leaping from the depths of his mind. This was it. The worn stone building looked pretty much exactly as it had. There weren't even shops on the ground floor.

Ash crossed his arms and glowered at the building from the sidewalk across the narrow street. Dante's scent was undetectable, so he hadn't been here in at least a year.

He scrutinized the structure with his demon sense. No magic? Really? Then why wasn't the place inhabited by humans? He delved deeper, letting his most primal instincts, the part of him that was pure magic, come to the surface.

Yes, there it was. A spell. It was skillfully masked, so at least Dante wasn't being careless. Ash hadn't expected any less. Dante had always been responsible. However, it'd have been more prudent to sell the building, leaving no magic behind, no matter how well hidden, and let some human take the place over.

A dark-gray bird landed on the building's awning and tilted its head, looking at Ash. His blood heated as his demon fire flared. Damn shearwaters. They didn't usually fly this far into the city. Not like seagulls did.

Shearwaters were seabirds and naturally stuck to the coastline, spending most of their lives migrating around the globe's oceans. Except for the shearwaters here. They'd always behaved strangely, and it was no surprise to see one this far from the water. But it was annoying.

At least it was summer, when the birds were meant to be in this part of the world, and not winter, when they were supposed to be breeding in the Southern Hemisphere. The infernal things caused confusion among marine biologists, who couldn't figure out why the sooty shearwaters of Shearwater Landing defied the migratory patterns of the rest of their species.

Ash knew exactly why, not that any biologist would believe him. He waited as the bird eyed him with a keenness that didn't quite pass as natural.

Suddenly, the bird took flight, dark-gray wings flapping as it rose into the sky.

Maybe Ash should have stayed invisible so he could have followed it without the people on the street noticing. It would have saved him from buying this silly shirt, but he hated walking through crowds when no one could see him. It was hard not to bump into people, and his intimidating height and build meant that when he was visible, people naturally made way for him.

As arrogant as it was, he preferred it that way.

Ash scanned the sky, the bird almost out of sight. He could find a place to disappear and follow the bird. Maybe behind Dante's house?

"What are you scowling about?" asked a familiar voice.

Ash turned. Dante leaned against a lamppost, grinning.

"I'm not scowling."

Dante laughed. "Sure you're not, brother."

They were brothers by choice, not blood. Hearing the familiar term shouldn't have stirred up feelings, but Ash's chest warmed. Almost like he'd been lonely. "I see you're as chipper as ever."

"Why wouldn't I be?" Dante cocked his head tauntingly. He had thick, curly black hair and black eyes that looked truly terrifying when they glowed, even with his more delicate face.

Ash and Dante shared the same brown skin, but that was it. Dante was slightly shorter and less bulky. Though, to be fair, everyone was less bulky than Ash, whose dark-brown hair only had a slight wave—barely noticeable when it was short—and whose brown eyes were dominated by a burnt-orange coloring.

"You didn't feel it?" Ash asked.

Dante's smooth brow furrowed.

Out of their group of three, bringing bad news always seemed to fall to Ash, but that didn't mean he liked it. He let his deepening frown and silence do the work for him. They may have been apart for decades, but after thousands of years together, they didn't always need words to communicate.

Dante's face fell, and Ash hated being the one to dim his light, no matter how necessary. Dante pushed off the lamp post. "Shall we go somewhere to catch up?"

Ash nodded. "Somewhere private."

3

———

HARPER

As Harper reached the Banks, he cast out his magic, checking he wasn't being followed. He was still in the clear.

He picked up his pace. So close. He was so fucking close.

Passing a row of restaurants, the scents of spices and baking bread filled the air. Harper's breaths came easier, his chest no longer as tight as it had been.

Harper continued toward the river. There was less green space in this part of the city. There weren't many trees planted along the sidewalks, but the buildings weren't as massive as the ones downtown. The neighborhood felt lived in and well-loved by the people, even if the state of the buildings varied, some seeming abandoned.

A coffee roaster bathed the whole block in a rich aroma. Harper's stomach growled. Now that he wasn't on the verge of being sick, he was starving. Too bad he had no food at his new apartment.

On the next block, Harper passed a cute coffee shop with a long line and people filling all the mismatched chairs and tables on the sidewalk. There wasn't time to go in now, though Harper had wanted to check out the place since he'd first seen it the day he'd rented his apartment. But the coffee shop wasn't important. He needed to get to his destination. He needed to be safe, even though making it didn't guarantee anything.

He stopped in a corner store and bought a loaf of bread and peanut butter. Better than nothing. He'd save his money for a coffee when he had a better chance of enjoying it without distractions.

Harper's new apartment building was smaller than his old complex and housed no witches. He'd checked, and unless someone was masking their magic as thoroughly as him, he was in the clear.

The building could use a fresh coat of paint, but how it looked wasn't important. It was on a street without any shops or restaurants. Only other apartments and a warehouse.

Harper didn't want to live somewhere with a lot of foot traffic or cafés where it would be natural for people to hang around. He didn't want anyone who might come looking for him to be able to blend into a crowd.

The street was quiet for a Saturday, and as he approached his building, tension released from Harper's shoulders. He keyed in the code to the front door and slipped inside, clutching the bread tightly.

He was home, or hopefully, this place would turn into a home. Hopefully, he'd finally be safe.

Harper climbed the stairs to the top floor.

There were three other doors next to his on the landing. He glanced around, listening, but didn't hear anyone in the apartments. He pulled off his shoe and fished out the key inside. It would be nice not to walk around with it underfoot. He'd been too paranoid about someone from the coven finding it to ever leave it anywhere.

He'd cast protections on the apartment when he'd stopped by a couple of weeks ago, then masked the spells. Now that he was here to settle in, he could strengthen his spells regularly using his blood. He'd be as safe as he could be given everything.

Shoving his foot back in the shoe, Harper unlocked the door and it creaked open. No other sounds came from inside, but that wasn't unexpected. His roommate usually worked on Saturdays.

Sure enough, Ollie Hudson, a human about Harper's age who already lived here, was nowhere to be seen. He'd seemed friendly when they'd met, and it would be nice to finally live with someone who wasn't from his coven. Harper could stop hiding every last thing about himself. Maybe he'd even figure out who he was now that he was free.

There was a Pride flag in one of the windows. Harper stared at it, standing there in clothes he didn't like and a stupid base-ball hat. His stomach swooped, and he smiled.

He'd found the listing on a local LGBTQ+ forum and had mentioned to Ollie that he was gay when they'd met. All Ollie had said was, "Cool, me too." Harper couldn't stop thinking about it.

Harper took his food to his room. It was already furnished with a bed, side table, and dresser and had a window looking out onto the street below. Harper had been collecting things he needed to start his new life since he'd rented the room, dropping off clothes he'd thrifted on Saturdays and having other items delivered.

He was glad Ollie hadn't asked too many questions about his strange moving methods.

After checking that everything was as he'd left it—his new potion-making equipment was safely tucked away in a magically locked box—Harper sat on the bed.

He ached to lie down and sleep. How good would it feel to not be conscious?

But his stomach rumbled, so he opened the bread and

grabbed a slice. Using the knife from his potion kit, he spread the peanut butter and ate.

His new life wasn't that exciting but Harper didn't want excitement. He wanted stability and independence and for no one to leach his blood, stealing it for their own magical use. You know, the simple things.

Was he finally safe?

Had he reached a place where he could build his own life and have a real future? He wished he could say yes definitively, but the threat of his coven loomed.

What if they found him?

All Harper wanted was to be around people who accepted him. People who wouldn't betray him. It felt impossible. Everything in his past told him it would never happen, but here, with a random human and his rainbow flag, maybe it wasn't so outlandish.

HARPER JOLTED at a sound outside his bedroom. He was flat on his back, legs hanging off the mattress. The peanut butter and bread lay open beside him. He must have fallen asleep.

He sat up and moved the food to his side table. Shit, how long had he been out? The sun seemed low in the sky, like it was about to set. He'd meant to get so many things done that afternoon, yet he'd achieved nothing.

Harper ran a hand through his hair. No need to panic. He had room for deviations from his plan now.

He adjusted his fake glasses. Ollie had seen him wearing them, so it was best to keep pretending. Besides, he liked how they framed his narrow features. He was ditching the baseball caps though. They really weren't his thing.

Speaking of *his thing*, Harper got up, opened his dresser,

and pulled out a box of black hair dye. He'd always wanted to dye his hair, and while he was partly motivated to change his appearance to make it less likely he'd get recognized around the city, he'd look good with darker hair.

Picturing a change in style lightened the weight in his chest.

There were so many new things he could do now. He could do anything he wanted as long as it didn't put him at risk of capture.

His coven would know he was missing by now. What were they doing? Had they found his discarded clothes in the library? Was his father flying out from Colorado? Harper shuddered. He didn't have to worry about it. He'd never have to see his father again.

Harper opened his bedroom door. He should say hi to his roommate and not hide, but he hesitated. He'd never had friends. What if Ollie found him annoying, or they had nothing in common?

He inched into the living room where Ollie was curled up on the couch, looking at his phone, lips turned downward. As soon as he noticed Harper, he perked up.

"Hi." Ollie beamed, showing off a perfect smile. He had a round face and curly blond hair. "I was wondering if you were here. You all moved in?"

"Yeah. Sorry, I was sleeping." Wait. Why was he apologizing?

"Makes sense. I bet moving was tiring. I mean, all those stairs." Ollie made a sympathetic face. "It's why I never want to move out of this place. Imagine lugging everything back down again." He set his phone on the coffee table, his gaze landing on Harper's hands. "What's that?"

Harper looked at the box of dye. He'd forgotten he had it. "I was going to dye my hair."

Ollie wrinkled his nose.

Harper's chest tightened. Maybe Ollie didn't want the dye to mess up the bathroom. He should have considered that. "I don't have to," he added quickly. "It was just a silly idea."

Ollie's brow furrowed. "I mean... Go for it if you want. I just can't in good conscience let you use *that* without offering my help." He smiled.

"Help?" Harper felt like he'd missed a step. He'd overreacted. There was no reason to be afraid of Ollie's disapproval. Ollie wasn't his father or anyone from his coven. He wouldn't judge or try to control Harper. "What do you mean help?"

"I'm a hair stylist, remember?" Ollie shook his head, lips twitching. "Please let me do your hair instead. It'll look so much better than *that*." He pointed at the box.

Harper's cheeks heated. "You don't have to. It's fine." He couldn't afford to get his hair done on his current budget.

"But why be fine when you could be amazing? You'll look stunning with darker hair."

How was Harper supposed to respond? People weren't normally this friendly. "Uh?"

"Sorry. Am I being weird?" Ollie cringed. "I'm just so glad you're here. It's been too quiet by myself, but if I'm freaking you out, I can back off. What you do with your hair is up to you."

"No, it's okay." Harper was being rude. He had to relax. This was his chance to finally make a friend and do all the friend stuff he'd longed for. "You're probably right about this not looking any good. I'm bound to mess it up." Harper's hand tightened on the box. "But anything else is out of my budget."

"Oh." Ollie hummed in understanding. "Don't worry about that. We can go to the salon when I'm not working, and as long as you cover the cost of the dye, I won't charge you."

Was this typical getting-to-know-your-roommate behavior?

Ollie seemed just as eager to be friends as Harper was. He must have been really lonely in the apartment by himself. Why else would he make such an effort to be nice when they didn't know each other? Or maybe Ollie wasn't being overly nice, and Harper just didn't know how to interact with kind people.

"That sounds really great," Harper admitted.

Ollie's grin widened. "Perfect. Let's go."

"Now?" Sweat broke out on Harper's palms. He wasn't ready to leave the apartment.

Ollie stood from the couch, pocketing his phone. "We might as well get your makeover going. I wasn't exactly looking forward to sitting around all evening. Now we've got something fun to do."

Harper stopped himself from fidgeting under Ollie's gaze. Satandamnit, why was he so awkward? "Are you sure you don't mind? You were just at work."

"Na, not at all. Let's do it. Then we can get dinner on the way home. There are some quality takeout places on the way that I'll have to show you since you're new to the neighborhood." Ollie grabbed a light jacket off the armchair, looking expectantly at Harper.

He was shorter and dressed in all black, his long-sleeve button-down rolled up to the elbows with the top few buttons at the collar left undone. He looked good, stylish, like someone with his own personality who knew who he was.

Would Harper have his own style one day? Maybe even a personality that felt authentic rather than like a mask? Fuck, he hoped so.

Screw it, he was leaving the apartment even if he hadn't planned to so soon. He wanted this experience, bonding with his roommate.

Harper ducked into his room to grab a hoodie and followed Ollie out of the building.

As they walked, Ollie chatted about his job and his colleagues. It sounded like he was pretty happy at the salon.

Harper magically scanned people as they walked, looking for witches, and even when he didn't detect any—or any vampires because the difference between the two wasn't immediately obvious when vampires could move around during the day—he didn't relax.

How could he? He may never relax again at this rate, let alone on a nice summer evening with crowds of people out enjoying themselves. Every corner they passed, he expected someone to jump out.

The salon was in a busy part of the Banks Harper hadn't been to before, near lots of restaurants and bars. At least the salon itself was dark and quiet inside.

Ollie let them into the large, open-plan space, switching on the lights and illuminating the high ceilings and exposed brick walls. He led Harper over to his station, and they talked about colors, highlights, and lowlights before Ollie went to mix the dye.

Harper eyed the large front windows and all the people beyond, but no one passing by paid the salon any attention. There still weren't any witches around. Everything was fine.

The sky turned orange, casting everything in a soft glow.

"You okay?"

Harper startled, heart pounding, and nearly jolted out of his seat. It was just Ollie returning with his supplies. Harper gripped the armrests to steady himself. "Yeah, fine."

Ollie paused. "Jumping out of your skin doesn't exactly inspire confidence in your answer."

Harper froze. Was Ollie mad at him or making fun of him? Maybe he couldn't do this friend thing after all.

"You seemed tense walking over here. Is everything all right?" Ollie went on, his tone kind and maybe even concerned. "Sorry, I don't mean to pry."

Good, Ollie wasn't mad. Harper tried to shake it off. He

didn't want Ollie thinking anything was odd about him, but he didn't want to have to wear a mask all the time either. "I was just worried we'd run into someone, but it's fine. I'm having a weird day, that's all."

"Okay." Ollie gave him a small smile. "If you need anything, let me know."

Yeah, there was no way he was asking human Ollie to help him avoid the Nightingale Coven, but he appreciated the offer. "Sure, thanks."

Ollie started sectioning off Harper's hair, placing the foils, and brushing on the dye. The contact sent tingles over Harper's scalp. Ollie caught his eye in the mirror. "If it's an ex you're worried about seeing, I totally get it."

Harper shifted in his seat. He didn't have any exes. "It's not that. Um...it's more a family thing."

"Gotcha." Ollie frowned. "Do you mind taking off your glasses?"

Harper did so, folding them and putting them on the counter in front of the mirror. "Are you avoiding your ex?" he asked, hoping to turn the conversation back to Ollie.

"Yeah. He used to live with me. We started off as roommates, and then... Well, you know. It was a mistake." Ollie made a face. "I'm never letting that happen again. I'm just glad he was the one to move out."

Harper nodded like he might understand from personal experience. His stomach twisted. He'd never had a boyfriend, but technically, he was betrothed.

Damnation. Even thinking the word made him want to hyperventilate. He refused to accept being engaged without his consent, no matter what his father had organized. The betrothal didn't count.

Arthur Nightingale knew Harper was gay and didn't accept him. That had never been more apparent than the day he'd declared Harper was going to marry some woman named Aurora from the Thornfield Coven.

Harper had never even met her. The Thornfields were a Shearwater Landing coven, and if they were on good terms with the Nightingales, Harper didn't trust them.

Arthur had always talked about Harper carrying on their family line. They were supposedly descended from the first witch and Lucifer himself. Never mind that Harper had cousins and tons of other relatives, *he* had to father children with a witch from a good bloodline to carry on the Nightingale name.

He had no idea if he wanted kids, but he'd never have a wife. Back when he was still trying to appease his father, improve his rank, and earn love, Harper had suggested surrogacy as a way of continuing the family. But Arthur hadn't wanted to hear it.

The topic hadn't come up in a while, and not at all since Harper had started his hunt. Then, two weeks ago, Harper's father had called to say Harper had a fiancée and her family was expecting him at their compound for an engagement party in three weeks.

Harper had seen red. His father's complete disregard for him had hurt and enraged him, even though it was nothing new. But he hadn't argued. His escape plan had already been set, so he'd lied and agreed to meet Aurora without a fight.

He hoped the woman wasn't looking forward to the marriage any more than Harper was. And if she was, oh well, she'd move on, he was sure.

Now that Harper was free, he could find a boyfriend. Was that too ambitious? Something casual might be better to start with.

He hadn't been in the right headspace to put himself out there for a long time, even if he'd had the chance—which he hadn't while constrained by his coven—but the idea of meeting guys and hooking up didn't stress him out anymore. Not like it had after his assault. Now, two years later, his life was just starting in so many respects, and Harper was itching to embrace all of it.

Harper longed for a partner, someone he could share everything with and love with all his heart. Someone safe who he belonged with and trusted. But he'd never trusted anyone.

Maybe he'd figure out how after his coven was out of his life for good.

"I'm sorry you guys had a bad breakup," Harper told Ollie. "I promise I won't try to date you."

Ollie laughed. "Perfect. Sounds like we'll get along great."

Harper smiled. He hoped so.

4

———

ASH

"Lucifer has left the Realm of the Damned."

Dante stood in grim silence before eventually saying, "And you know this how?"

Ash turned to face the sea. They were on Dante's balcony, off the back of his house built on top of the cliff north of the city. His whole property was protected by a powerful illusion, rendering the building and anyone in it invisible, allowing Ash and Dante to have their demon forms displayed freely.

"I know the same way I've always been able to sense these things. My connection to the Realm of the Damned and the magic trapping us there changed when we escaped but didn't break entirely. No demons have left the Realm since we did. Until now."

Dante gripped the railing, his soot-colored wings flexing and sparkling with a hint of silver. "But how do you know it was Lucifer and not someone else? Every demon wants to escape. That's why Lucifer had to imprison us there in the first place."

"Only he and the three of us have a connection to the magic sealing off the Realm of the Damned. You know that. Our escape didn't break the seal. Everyone is still imprisoned there, leaving only Lucifer able to follow us, using the same method we did to escape."

Dante tucked his wings against his back as the wind picked up. "Yes, I know. But why follow now? It's been over two hundred years since we broke free."

"I don't know." Ash dropped his head between his shoulders, arms outstretched as he braced himself on the rail.

Ash, Dante, and Onyx had been imprisoned in the Realm of the Damned for centuries, along with every other demon who'd fallen from the Eternal Realm. It wasn't the Eternals who'd trapped them, but Lucifer. Lucifer, who had once been their friend—their brother—until somewhere along the way, he'd turned Ash, Dante, and Onyx into his dogs, forced to do his bidding and subjected to his control.

Lucifer had stolen some of Ash's, Dante's, and Onyx's magic to create the seal that trapped all demons in the Realm of the Damned. When they'd finally escaped, Ash had predicted Lucifer wouldn't follow them to the Human Realm, not wanting the rest of the Realm to know his loyal dogs had abandoned him. And it seemed he'd been right.

Until now.

"Something must have changed," Ash said, lifting his head. "Who knows what's going on in the Realm now. Lucifer couldn't have hidden our absence forever."

"He can't drag us back." Dante's eyes flashed with black fire. "There are three of us and one of him. He only got one over on us before because we trusted him. That mistake won't be made twice."

"True, but we have to be careful. You shouldn't still be here, Dante. You need to live somewhere less conspicuous." Ash leveled a stern look at his old friend.

Dante scoffed. "I'm not hiding. Shearwater Landing is mine. The birds will warn me if Lucifer is coming."

"You're placing a lot of trust in your shearwaters." Ash tried not to let anger get the better of him, but Dante and his connection to the shearwaters was too much of a giveaway that there was magic in the city. Magic too great to belong to any witch or vampire.

Lucifer would know a demon was here. It was foolish.

"Yes, well, not all of us want to live alone in the woods, Ash."

Ash grunted. There was no need to defend his lifestyle. It suited him. End of story.

"I *know* this is the city," Dante said in a softer tone. "I'm not leaving until I find him."

Ash's anger fled and his heart ached. Dante had never given up hope. It broke Ash. He'd given up a millennia and a half ago. How did Dante do it?

The wind off the ocean caressed Ash's face and he closed his eyes, trying to hold the memories back. The past felt less distant than it had in a long time. This never happened at his hunting lodge.

In what was arguably ancient history, he, Dante, Onyx, and Lucifer had been beings of the Eternal Realm. They and others of their kind were known as Eternals, the guardians of magic and human souls in the afterlife. There was no Realm of the Damned back then, just the Human Realm and the one of magic.

Life had been good but not perfect. The Eternal Realm was ruled by a council, who had absolute power over the guardianship of the two realms and the balance between them. Part of guarding that balance was granting Eternals their mates.

Each Eternal had a fated mate, but only the council could bring mates together and gift pairs the right to produce offspring.

Being immortal, the Eternals in charge rarely changed.

Some Eternals requested their mates only to be denied by the council and told to come back in the distant future.

Many Eternals didn't think the system was fair and grew tired of waiting. Lucifer had been among them. He had been denied repeatedly, as had his younger brother Onyx, Ash, and Dante. No explanation was ever given and the loneliness made time stretch agonizingly, leaving them not knowing if they'd ever be granted their other halves.

Lucifer believed the council didn't have to grant mates and that individuals could find their fated loves themselves. Some successfully mated Eternals had sworn they'd found the fated connection without the council's help, discovering their mates among the human souls occupying the Eternal Realm. They'd then requested approval to be mated and were granted. The council denied this, but of course, they would when it challenged their absolute power over the process.

The council didn't control fate itself. They only had the power to see fated connections between beings. But why should anyone have to wait to be granted a mate when the connection already existed? Not all mated pairs wanted children, and offspring could be granted separately if desired, allowing the balance between Eternal and human lives to be guarded.

Ash had agreed with Lucifer, and so had many others. Some had waited thousands of years for their mates and were ready to take things into their own hands.

And it had seemed possible.

Eternals could be fated to mate between themselves or with human souls, granting those souls eternal life and a permanent place in the Eternal Realm when they mated. The process allowed the human soul to leave the cycle of reincarnation that governed human life and thus needed to be guarded. According to the council.

But this meant that if an Eternal was confident their mate

wasn't another Eternal, they were either somewhere in the Eternal Realm as a soul or on Earth, living as a human.

Lucifer believed all their mates were out there, in one Realm or the other. The connection was already there, waiting to be recognized. Their mates could be found and the bond formed outside the council's control. They just had to search, and if they felt no connection in the Eternal Realm, their mate must be on Earth.

Why wait for their mate to enter the afterlife and then for the council's approval—risking their mate reincarnating and starting the cycle over—when they could travel to Earth and find their mates themselves?

The only problem was that Eternals were not permitted to enter the Human Realm. Magic and mortality were separate, offset to balance one another. If any of them fell to Earth, they would not be allowed back into the Eternal Realm. But why would they need to return? Wouldn't it be better to live in a land where they could search for their mates, claim them, and live happily forever?

There had been no reason not to go.

Ash had secretly and naïvely believed that once they fell and found their mates, they might one day be allowed to return to the Eternal Realm. Once their quest was proven to be purely motivated by love. It was silly, but Ash had been relatively young back then.

He followed Lucifer to Earth, at his side as his right-hand man and best friend, with Onyx and Dante completing their inner circle. The four loyal friends had been committed to helping all Eternals find their mates. But when they got to the Human Realm, they couldn't find them.

No one had expected it to be instant. They searched for generations as souls cycled in and out of the Human Realm, but hundreds of years passed, and none who had fallen were mated.

No matter how they searched, they couldn't find their fated loves.

Humans who saw them in their true forms called them demons, and the Eternal Realm made it clear they would never be welcomed back. They were stuck in the mortal world forever, and some of the Fallen began to whisper that the council had trapped their mates in the afterlife, preventing them from reincarnating, to punish the Fallen.

They would never find fated love. Lucifer had led them to eternal loneliness.

Their plan had been flawed. In hindsight, the council retaliating and keeping their mates captive was an obvious move, even if it challenged the council's claim that everything they did was meant to look after the balance between realms and preserve the natural cycle of life. The Fallen would never find their mates, and they would never return home.

Ash gave up. What was the point of hope? He resolved to stick with his chosen brothers and make the most of their grim situation. But Dante and Lucifer kept searching, faith unwavering, dragging Ash and Onyx around the globe. That had been bad enough, but then things got so much worse.

Ash sighed.

Even now, Dante hadn't given up. He was convinced he'd find his mate in Shearwater Landing, of all damn places. Ash wanted to shake sense into him. They were never going to find their mates. They didn't exist in the Human Realm and never would. And if by some miracle they did, after everything, Ash and the rest of them wouldn't deserve them anyway.

There was a time when Ash deserved love, but that was before he and all the Fallen had been damned. They truly were demons, no longer eternal guardians of magic and nature's balance. Things had been irreversibly damaged when they'd let magic infect the Human Realm.

Ash never had children with a human, but other fallen Eternals had. Lucifer was the first to father a half-human child, even though he had convinced them all they could find their mates on Earth. He was the first to give up in an irrevocable way, lying and saying he was still searching.

That first child had damned them all. They were born the first witch, the first human to possess magic.

Magic wasn't meant to exist outside the Eternal Realm or to taint Earth's natural order. Mortality and magic were supposed to be separate, and when the council discovered the existence of witches—their population growing as more Eternals had children with humans, and those half-humans sired a second generation—the council damned them all.

The magic in a witch's blood made it impossible for their souls to reincarnate after death. Magic was something only Eternals, who lived forever, were supposed to possess. The balance of magic and mortality had been broken, leaving witches no longer able to participate in the natural cycle of life, so the council banned all humans with magic from the Eternal Realm.

And so the Realm of the Damned was born, a Hell for all magical humans to spend their afterlife in, separated from their nonmagical loved ones forever.

The Realm of the Damned grew crowded with souls who couldn't cycle back to Earth, and magic twisted in the Human Realm as witches looked for immortality and a way to escape damnation.

It was all their fault. Ash's fault for convincing others to follow Lucifer. Lucifer's fault for having that first child. Never finding their mates was their punishment for ruining the balance of magic in the universe.

"He isn't here," Ash said to Dante, trying to be kind but needing to be firm. "We can't stay waiting around forever. Lucifer will know we're here—I'm sure he's heard of your birds and will know what it means—I won't let him drag us back to Hell. If we leave now, you can return to Shearwater Landing once we've dealt with Luc."

"No." Dante's fingers flexed on the railing. "I can feel it. We're close. I'm not leaving until I find him."

Ash detected a deep sorrow in Dante's stubborn words, which was much harder to argue with. He rubbed absently at his chest, just over his heart. "Then what do we do about Lucifer? If you won't leave, we have to do something."

Dante turned, facing Ash and resting an elbow on the railing, a hint of surprise in his raised brows like he'd expected Ash to continue hounding him for not leaving the city. But Ash wouldn't be the one who broke Dante, no matter how many problems his hope caused.

Dante's gaze turned calculated. "Lucifer might be coming here to look for us, but he won't find anything. This house is close to impenetrable, and I won't investigate any new triggers to the magic on my old place. It will be a dead end. I only showed up to meet you because my birds told me you were in the city. If you lend a hand in bolstering the illusions and protections here, Luc won't be able to get in on his own. He's not stronger than the two of us combined."

"We don't know he's alone," Ash reminded Dante.

Dante's tail flicked. "Then we better get Onyx."

"You know where he is?" Ash suspected tracking down Lucifer's younger brother would be much harder than finding Dante.

"Yes," Dante grumbled, almost a growl. "He's here in Shearwater Landing."

"Here? Why?" Wasn't this city too boring for Onyx?

"I have no idea. It's not like we see much of each other."

"Right." Onyx had always been hard to get a handle on. "We'll go find him and make a plan. Lucifer might not realize I sensed his entrance into the Human Realm, so hopefully, we can get ahead of him."

Dante smiled, letting his fangs descend. His eyes blazed. "I wouldn't mind capturing him for a change."

They had to neutralize Lucifer somehow, and even though Eternals and demons could be destroyed, Ash didn't think they'd kill him. "Imprisoning him would be satisfying," he admitted.

Ash wanted to steal Lucifer's power as Lucifer had done to him, Dante, and Onyx. He might never have a mate, but he could find satisfaction in turning the tables on his enemy.

This could be good. As long as they weren't being foolish by staying here. Lucifer always seemed to have some trick up his sleeve.

5

___

ASH

"An art gallery?" Ash stared at the pristine, modern building Dante had taken him to in the Arts District. Since when had Onyx been interested in art?

Dante didn't seem phased, but then he'd known about this place for more than a minute. "It's become one of the most prestigious in the city." If Ash didn't know better, Dante sounded impressed.

Dante opened the door, and Ash followed him into Gallery Four.

The front room was cavernous, with the ceiling extending past the lofted second story. A small plinth sat in the center of the foyer, holding an abstract sculpture. Two large paintings hung on opposing walls, with a sleek reception desk situated behind, sectioning off more gallery space at the back of the building.

Onyx was not at the desk.

"May I help you, gentlemen?" asked a rather short man with perfectly done silver hair.

Ash stepped forward. "We're looking for Onyx."

"Onyx?" The man stiffened. "And who, may I ask, is inquiring?"

Ash gave Dante a sidelong look. He'd better deal with this. Ash didn't have the patience. He could blame it on living out in the woods alone for too long, but waiting over two millennia for his mate had worn his patience away.

Dante approached the silver-haired man and began reminiscing about an opening Onyx had apparently organized several years ago that had debuted a now-famous artist. It was like Ash had stepped into another world.

At least Onyx was channeling his energy into something productive and seemingly legal this time.

After a few moments, the gallery curator departed up the stairs, presumably to find Onyx, though not before he wrinkled his nose at Ash's touristy shearwater shirt. He came back down minutes later.

"You may go up," he said to Dante.

"Thank you," Dante replied graciously. Ash climbed the stairs without acknowledging the man.

At the top, Onyx leaned against an open doorway at the back of the equally cavernous second story. He was smaller than Ash or Dante in height and weight and looked alarmingly human.

Onyx wore jeans and a T-shirt, but unlike Ash, his looked expensive and painfully fashionable. Onyx's pale skin glowed like he'd fed recently, and he'd dyed his hair to match the deep blue of his eyes and wings. Not that his wings were on display, of course.

"Ash and Dante," Onyx cooed in a sing-song voice. "What have you come to hassle me about this time?"

Ash bristled. "We don't hassle you."

Onyx raised a brow.

Okay, fine, but the hassling was always warranted. "Have

you done something we should know about?" Ash braced for the answer.

"Of course not," Onyx purred.

Ash didn't believe him. He was nothing but trouble. However, that wasn't why they were here. "Do you have somewhere we can talk? That man from downstairs is probably listening in."

"Follow me." Onyx turned down the hall he'd been blocking and led them to a room at the back. "Would you like something to drink? Ash, it might help with your crankiness."

Dante unsuccessfully stifled a snort.

Ash glared at him. "I'm fine. I eat regularly."

Demons had to drink blood to maintain their immortality in the Human Realm, another hitch in Lucifer's plan no one had known about ahead of time. Ash didn't cast illusions to feed on innocent, unsuspecting humans, and he often couldn't be bothered finding a willing member of the magic community to source blood from, so he was constantly pushing how long he could go without feeding. But he wasn't telling Onyx that.

Onyx opened a small fridge hidden in the wood paneling of an ornate bookcase on the side of the room. "Really, Ash, let me pour you a glass. It's bagged."

"Stolen then." Ash wasn't surprised.

"No, we buy it," Dante cut in. "Or at least I do."

Onyx huffed. "I'm not a thief."

Both Ash and Dante gave him a look.

"Anymore," Onyx amended. "Besides, I only steal fun things like jewels."

Ash ignored the comment. Dealing with Onyx was like trying to befriend a feral animal. You couldn't give him an inch of wiggle room, or you'd get bitten. "We need to talk."

Onyx closed the fridge, his eyes flashing with blue fire. "I'm sure we do. I mean, why else would you have left your isolation cave?"

"My what?" Ash crossed his arms and loomed imposingly. "I don't live in a cave."

Onyx laughed. "You sure? You're seeming very caveman."

Ash shouldn't let him get under his skin. Onyx was only trying to annoy him, and giving Onyx what he wanted led to even worse behavior. Ash needed to try harder to be friendly and forget the thousands of years of animosity between them, but it was nearly impossible.

"Oh, come on, Ash." Dante elbowed him in the arm. "You live in the woods. It's close enough. And maybe if you visited every few years, we wouldn't make such a big deal out of seeing you."

Ash grunted in acknowledgment. Dante might have a point.

Onyx flopped languidly into a chair behind a desk as sleek as the one downstairs. "What's up? I've got a lot going on, so you better get to the point."

Dante sat in the leather seat opposite the desk. Ash remained standing. "We have bad news," Dante said carefully.

"So dour." Onyx wrinkled his nose. "But I'd already guessed as much given..." He gestured to Ash.

"Lucifer has left the Realm of the Damned," Ash began before relaying everything he and Dante discussed.

Onyx's playful mood soured, his mouth tightening into a thin line. "Really, you two are going after him? What happened to getting free and living our lives? Forgetting about all of it."

"We can't forget Luc if he's coming for us." Ash refrained from mentioning they could ignore Lucifer if they hid somewhere other than Shearwater Landing and stopped calling attention to themselves by enchanting the wildlife, but he didn't want to keep hounding Dante. There was no point. Onyx might be feral, but Dante was an immovable stone.

"Haven't you considered Lucifer could have new minions?" Onyx flicked his wrist dismissively at the other two. "A new inner circle to leach power from? He isn't going to come after us alone. We won't have the upper hand. Seriously, do you know him *at all*?"

"Then what do you think we should do about it?" Ash challenged.

Onyx sneered. "*We?* Nothing. You and Dante? I don't know. Not my problem."

Ash ground his teeth. "Aren't you even the least bit worried?"

"Why would I be? When has Lucifer ever cared what I've done?" Onyx's voice turned as cold as his blue fire. "He lets me get away with anything. He'll always forgive me. No matter what I do. Escaping the Realm of the Damned will be no different."

It was true. Onyx could cut off Lucifer's wings and Lucifer wouldn't be nearly as angry as he'd be if someone else attacked him.

"Let him come," Onyx spat like he was shooting venom. You'd almost think he hated Lucifer for letting him get away.

Ash rubbed his temple. He'd been in the middle of Luc and Onyx's squabbles for eons. No one could deny that Ash and Luc had been close, but Onyx seemed to think Luc loved Ash more than him and treated Ash more like a brother, even though Onyx was Luc's blood.

"We aren't just going to sit around waiting for him," Dante said, breaking the tension. "Come on, Onyx, you don't want him dragging you back to the Realm of the Damned. He won't let us stay here, not even you."

Onyx chewed his lower lip. "Doesn't mean I want to get involved in whatever the two of you are cooking up."

Onyx always tried to get out of helping, no matter what the

problem was, but then, why had he settled in Shearwater Land-ing, so close to Dante? Shouldn't Onyx be on the other side of the world where no one would bother him?

"Are you going to leave town and hide if you don't want to help?" Dante asked.

"No." Onyx's mouth dropped open, eyes flashing. "I've worked my ass off for this gallery. I'm not leaving it behind."

"Then we need a plan." Ash braced his hands on Onyx's desk, leaning forward. "If the two of you refuse to leave, we need to do something. Otherwise, we might as well walk back to the Realm of the Damned and lock ourselves in."

"Fine." Onyx glanced up, eyes glinting. "But I want some-thing out of you first."

"Of course you do," Ash muttered.

"Both of you." Onyx cut his gaze to Dante.

"And what do you want?" Dante asked with a sigh.

Onyx flashed his fangs. Nothing good was about to come out of his mouth.

6

HARPER

Harper stared at the fountain in the plaza in front of the library. It was a gray day, but the water still glittered. A chill ran down his spine. He swore eyes were on him even though none of the people walking by could see him.

He was invisible, not even really there.

A man checked his pocket watch a few feet away. Beyond him, a boy sold newspapers, shouting the headlines. Harper couldn't hear him. There was no sound in the memories of the past since stone couldn't hear.

Harper concentrated on the people, looking for anyone that stood out. Beings with magic glowed faintly. Harper had seen several on his last trip. Demons were supposed to be blinding. That was how he'd know when he finally found one.

No one was even shimmering today.

Harper flicked his wrist and the scene before him sped up, people bustling by at double, then triple speed. He had no idea how long he stood there, but when a headache started behind his temple, he still hadn't seen anything useful.

Harper closed his eyes and muttered an incantation. He gasped, blinked, and his bedroom ceiling appeared. He pushed himself up, his mattress dipping. A glance at the door assured him it was still closed. He'd locked it magically. There was no way he'd risk Ollie coming in while he was on his hunt.

But Ollie had been out with a friend all afternoon, and the apartment was still quiet. Harper sat up and gulped the water he'd left on his bedside table, trying to wash the taste of stone from his tongue.

Once the water was gone, he packed his potion kit away, cleaning the glass vials and beakers with magic as he went. He checked his bag of ground stone. There was still way more than he wanted to look through.

Hunting the Hounds of Hell wasn't as glamorous as it sounded. The Nightingale Coven was confident the Hounds had been in Shearwater Landing in the early nineteen hundreds due mostly to strange reports about seabirds. The coven suspected the Hounds, or at least one of them, was still here for the same reason. However, knowing they were in the city wasn't much help.

No witch had any hope of tracking a demon with magic. Demons were much more powerful and could mask themselves completely from other magical beings. The Nightingales also had no idea what any of the Hounds looked like, which was understandable when they'd spent close to a thousand years in Hell before returning to this world.

So how was Harper supposed to find them? By sifting through the past.

His potion expertise allowed him to brew a complex concoction, unlocking stone memory. Harper had collected bits of paving stone from the plaza in front of the library, all of which had been laid when that part of the city was built, back when the demons were thought to have first settled here.

Brewing and ingesting the potion allowed Harper to look into the past and see everything the stones had seen. A stone's vision was pure and unaffected by illusion, making any magical being visible, even if they had been masking their magic when the stone originally saw them.

Harper was looking for the Hounds one hundred years ago, trusting that the glow of a demon would be impossible to miss among lesser beings. Unfortunately, he couldn't use the stone to look through anything more modern. Recent memories were too fresh to have fully incorporated into the mineral structure.

He'd had no luck in the last year. The monotony sucked, and so did the potion's taste, but he had to find the Hounds. He couldn't let the Nightingale Coven find them.

Harper ate a peanut butter sandwich to wash away the remaining taste of old stone, staring out the window at the setting sun.

Would he be able to win the Hounds over after he found them? *If* he found them, because it was starting to feel impossible.

Even if he spotted them in the past, it would be a lot of work to follow them through time. What if, in tailing them to find their home, the demons passed through a part of the city that had been completely rebuilt? He'd lose the trail.

That was a problem for another day.

If Harper ever found them, he'd tell the Hounds exactly what his coven had planned. It was a risk—not knowing how the Hounds would react—and a betrayal to Lucifer, whom Harper had sworn to serve, but Harper held no faith in that oath. He didn't serve the Devil, his coven, or their aims.

Supposedly, the Hounds had escaped Hell, and Lucifer wanted them back. Arthur Nightingale wanted to deliver the Hounds to Lucifer to show his devotion and earn favor. Not that Arthur had ever met Lucifer. Satan didn't bother with witches on Earth, as far as Harper could tell, but many of them still served him. They had Lucifer to thank for their power, so it made some sense.

But Harper was done with that life and ready to sell out his coven to the Hounds—if he found them. He'd show the Hounds he was on their side, let them know witches were using the past to hunt them in Lucifer's name, and hopefully, they would appreciate the warning and leave the city.

In Harper's wildest fantasies, the Hounds took him under their protection for warning them, and he was able to destroy his coven with their help. But that was never going to happen. It was a nice dream. Something to comfort him during the nights when he couldn't sleep.

Even if he never found the Hounds, Harper had to make sure his father didn't either and never gained anything from Lucifer. He couldn't be allowed any more power.

Harper might be unable to ruin his father with the blood loyalty binding him, but he could stop things from getting worse. He already had. Now that Harper was beyond Arthur's reach, he'd lose some of his power regardless of what happened with the Hounds. From now on, Harper would be the only one using his blood to strengthen spells.

Harper shivered at the memory of being tied down and having his blood drained. He hated his rare power. If he'd been average, his father would have left him alone. Sometimes, he'd been left so weak that he swore he'd been on the verge of death, and he'd been helpless to do anything about it. All that power in his blood, yet he'd still been trapped, as weak as a human against Arthur Nightingale.

Something sticky spilled over Harper's fist. He looked down at the crushed remainder of his sandwich, peanut butter everywhere.

"Gross." He grabbed a tissue and wiped it up.

The front door slammed shut, and Harper jolted. His

potion stuff was hidden, but he didn't want Ollie to see the mess of peanut butter and now tissue that was all over his hand. He quickly dashed to the bathroom and cleaned himself off.

Harper entered the living room, finding Ollie's friend with him. He looked about their age, with curly brown hair, light-brown skin, and a similar style to Ollie. Harper fisted the hem of his boring T-shirt.

"Oh, Harper, hey. Come meet Dex." Ollie waved Harper farther into the living room.

Dex lifted his chin in Harper's direction. "Hey, man." He had the most stunning gray eyes. They fixed on Harper and it was like the guy was x-raying him.

A quick scan revealed Dex wasn't a witch or vampire. "Hi." Harper double-checked there was no lingering peanut butter on his hand before shaking Dex's.

"You should come out with us tonight." Dex glanced at Ollie, who nodded.

Harper perched on the arm of the couch. "Out where?"

"There's a new gay club opening." Ollie practically bounced with excitement.

Dex unlocked his phone and checked something. "My cousin is DJ-ing and put me on the list. I'll be able to get you in no problem."

The sandwich churned in Harper's gut. "A club on a Sunday?" That seemed weird, right?

"It's an exclusive opening. Don't worry, it'll be packed," Ollie assured him. "It's perfect since Dex and I don't have work tomorrow. And you don't either, right? We're going to watch a movie then get ready. You in?"

"Um... Where is it?" Leaving the neighborhood wasn't a good idea, and neither was going on the subway. It felt like pushing his luck.

"It's in the Docks, near the old Rivermouth Cannery," Dex said without looking up from his phone.

That was fine. Not this neighborhood, but only the next one over, and Harper had never been there before. No one would have any reason to look for him there. Still, it would be safer to stay home. He'd brewed enough of his magic-suppressing potion to last a few days, but he could use the evening to brew more, or he could get started on the potions he sold to The Herb Emporium.

"It's okay if you're not into clubbing," Ollie said. "We won't be offended if you say no."

It was the perfect out, except Harper found himself saying, "I've actually never been to a club."

"Really?" Ollie seemed excited by this for some reason. "But you'd want to go?"

"Yeah."

Dex looked up from his phone, studying Harper. "What's holding you back? There's plenty of great spots around the city."

"I haven't lived here long." Harper hadn't told Ollie he'd been in the city for a year and didn't plan to. "I lived with some, um, pretty strict family before this."

Dex nodded.

"You should definitely come with us." Ollie flashed an encouraging smile.

Fuck, it was tempting. He'd love to go to a gay club, dance with guys, and maybe even go home with someone. When he'd tried to go out before—in a hot new outfit and everything—his coven had stopped him, and he'd worried he would never get the chance again.

If he'd been off to do anything else that night, finding out how trapped he was wouldn't have hurt nearly as much. Whenever Harper had expressed himself or did anything his father deemed feminine or, Satan forbid, *gay*, he would lecture

Harper, punish him, shame him. Trying to go out that night had been no different, even with his father several states away.

His face flamed and his gut twisted just thinking about it. Wasn't the point of running away to be free of all that shit, do what he wanted, be who he was, try new things, and not live in fear? He couldn't let paranoia stop him from going out when the risk was low. He'd even have people to go with.

Harper wanted new experiences. He wanted to dance like he never had, check out hot guys, and broaden his knowledge in every way. He wanted to be like everyone else.

He couldn't stop the smile that stretched his lips. "Count me in."

HARPER SCRAMBLED out of the rideshare after Ollie and Dex. They were in a mostly deserted part of the Docks, full of old warehouses and the closed cannery. The building in front of them was lit up in a multicolor display. Music pulsed from inside and a line wound down the otherwise quiet block.

It seemed like a strange place for a club, but what did Harper know.

Dex led the way to the bouncer at the door. He gave his name and the guy checked their IDs before letting them in.

A thrill went through Harper as the heat of the club hit. After the year he'd had, it was like walking into another world.

It was a good thing Harper had borrowed some clothes from Ollie. He didn't have anything cute in his limited wardrobe. Ollie had lent him a tank and a pair of black shorts, which were ideal for the hot club. The shorts were tiny and hugged Harper's body, making his ass look better than should've been possible.

"Drinks?" Ollie shouted over the music.

Dex nodded enthusiastically, and they pushed into the

crowd. Ollie reached back and grabbed Harper's hand, pulling him along so they didn't get separated.

Harper stumbled, his palm pressed against Ollie's.

It was such a casual, friendly gesture. One it seemed Ollie hadn't thought twice about, but Harper had never held hands with anyone like this. It felt so good that he didn't even register the people they pushed through on their way to the bar.

Harper didn't like Ollie in a romantic way, which almost made the physical contact more jarring. There'd been no casual affection in his life, or any affection, really. Ollie's soft palm made him realize how little other people had touched him other than to hurt him. How nice was it to feel connected to someone this way?

They reached the bar and Dex leaned forward, waiting for a bartender to look in his direction.

Ollie dropped Harper's hand. "What do you want to drink?"

Harper crouched to be heard over the noise. "Nothing for me." He wasn't letting anything lower his inhibitions.

"Okay." Ollie passed his answer on to Dex, along with his drink order.

For once, it wasn't annoying to be tall. Harper took in the club as the other two got their drinks. Lights flashed in the far corner of the large open space. The DJ must be over there, where everyone was dancing, and there was a second bar to the left, next to a platform with dancers covered in body paint.

A loft ran along one edge of the club—some sort of VIP area, maybe? Harper couldn't see the people up there with the lights flashing below, but as he looked, he got an odd feeling, a prickling of anticipation like something was waiting for him.

He cast out his magic, inspecting the loft. No other magic registered, so he wasn't sure what put him on edge other than paranoia. He pushed it away.

Ollie and Dex threw back a shot each. "Another!" Ollie slammed his shot glass on the bar and Dex handed him a second one. He downed it. "I'm so glad you came out with us, Harper."

"Yeah?" Harper couldn't help smiling. Ollie's dimpled grin was infectious.

Ollie slung an arm around Harper's waist. "Yeah, and I'm happy you moved in with me and that *you're* my new roommate."

Harper laughed. "I'm glad you're my roommate too."

Ollie squeezed him. "Yay. You're so sweet. And respectful. And nothing like my last roommate." He frowned.

Ollie seemed a bit drunk. He and Dex had a drink at home before leaving, but Harper didn't think that made anything he was saying untrue. It was a relief Ollie liked having him around.

"I got lucky finding your place for rent," Harper said. "I think it's going to be good."

Ollie's smile returned. "It is." He grabbed Dex and pulled him and Harper toward the dancefloor.

Harper didn't know how to dance, but who cared? His insides bubbled, and he couldn't stop smiling.

When they reached the dancing crowd, Ollie and Dex pressed close together, arms slung easily around each other like they'd done this countless times.

Ollie pulled Harper in. "Dance with us."

Harper pressed against Ollie's back, moving with them. He laughed. The way they were touching seemed suggestive, but there was no heat between the three of them. It was fun, and Harper liked being close to someone he felt comfortable with, with no pressure put on what they were doing.

Ollie turned around, putting his back to Dex, who crowded in, his hands on Ollie's hips. Ollie gazed up at Harper. "Having fun?"

"Yeah." Harper grinned as Ollie wrapped his arms around

him, the heat of his friend's hand on the back of his neck warming him in a way he hadn't known he needed.

It was exhilarating to be out and surrounded by queer men, some of whom were giving the three of them hungry looks. Harper wanted to broaden his sexual experience and get over the hurdle of hooking up for the first time in a long time, but that wasn't all he wanted. That wasn't the only way he could embrace being himself. He was glad he wasn't here alone and hadn't realized how good it would feel to have queer friends, even brand-new ones he'd only just started getting to know.

Honestly, the night couldn't get any better.

7

___

ASH

ASH SCOWLED DOWN at the club. Of course this was what Onyx wanted in exchange for cooperating.

Dante elbowed him. "It's not so bad."

"It's a waste of time." Ash turned his back on the room below and scanned the VIP area. Onyx sat between two bulky, bare-chested humans who had their hands all over him. "He doesn't even care that we're here."

"So what? Tomorrow, we'll sit down and figure out what our next move is." Dante passed Ash a small vial Onyx had given him. "You could use some fun. When was the last time you left your cabin?"

"Hunting lodge," Ash corrected, passing the vial back.

Demons couldn't get intoxicated the way humans could. The vial held a strong potion that would do the trick, but Ash wasn't interested. They might have decided to wait until tomorrow to make their plan, but they were still being hunted. Lucifer wasn't going to wait for them to have a night out if he happened to find them at the club.

Dante unstopped the vial and took a sip. "So, when was the

last time you left your hunting lodge and found someone to keep you company?"

Too long to admit. Not as long as Dante, who'd decided to wait for his mate a century ago. But the last thing Ash wanted to talk about was mates. He grunted.

Dante stared, expression flat. "Not even a single word in response? Wow. Sounds like some *stress relief* would do you good." He waggled his eyebrows.

"Maybe," Ash admitted, turning back toward the club. There was no denying the tension he'd been carrying around.

A whiff of floral mountain air caught his attention. How odd. It was exactly the same as the scent from the plaza and so subtle he shouldn't have noticed it in a club, even with his demon sense. There was no mistaking it for a nearby florist this time. Did the scent belong to a person?

Now, that was intriguing. "You know what? You're right, Dante. I'm going to go dance."

Dante's eyes widened, obviously having expected Ash to stick to brooding. "Great. I'll keep an eye on Onyx."

Ash huffed. "Good luck with that."

He descended the stairs and circled the club, catching a whiff of the floral scent here and there. Damn, what direction was it coming from?

Ash brought his baser instincts forward. When he caught the scent again, he let his body take the lead, his brain in the back seat. His spine tingled. Fuck, he wanted a taste. The scent wasn't enough.

He prowled the club, scanning the men around him. Who the hell smelled like flowers and home?

"Hey, Daddy," a slim brunet called.

Ash gave him an up-nod. He wasn't the source of the smell.

"You looking for someone?" the man asked, lashes fluttering.

"Yes, sorry. Have a good night." Ash moved on.

He'd gotten rid of his shearwater shirt, but the button-down he'd borrowed from Dante was too tight, making it seem like he was about to burst from the fabric. Clearly, men found his look appealing.

A mix of cologne and body odor overwhelmed his senses, completely obscuring the subtle scent he craved. Damn. Would he find it again? Ash stood still, demon sense tingling, searching.

Nothing. What if the scent—the man—left? His pulse thudded. Ash needed release. He was too worked up to ignore his desire. He circled the club again but couldn't catch any hint of flowers. Maybe he should forget about it and return to the man who'd approached him.

A laugh rang out over a brief lull in the music, calling to him like a siren song. Ash pushed toward the main bar in time to see a tall, slim man and his two shorter friends slip into the crowd on the opposite side of the room.

He followed on instinct, easily keeping track of the taller man's dark hair as it bobbed above the people around him.

Ash liked a tall lover, someone who wasn't completely dwarfed by his own excessive height.

He caught a whiff of mountain air. Could it be the man's scent?

The tall man and his friends stopped once they reached the dancefloor. Another waft of flowers and fresh air hit Ash. He knew in his gut it came from the man. His demon sense practically screamed it at him.

He'd found him.

Ash hadn't ever met someone with such strong pheromones, let alone a human, and a brief inspection revealed the man had no magic. Fascinating. Ash held back and took in his quarry, humming appreciatively at all the pale skin on display. If the man's shorts were any shorter, his round ass cheeks would be showing.

Ash's gaze roved lazily up the man's body, something catching in his chest as he got a better look at his face, with high cheekbones and a soft pink smile. That grin couldn't have been prompted by anything short of genuine happiness. Ash's whole body warmed. He liked the look of joy more than he should have.

The man adjusted his glasses and began dancing stiffly. He seemed to be enjoying himself if his unwavering smile was any indication. As Ash watched, the man relaxed, flowing more easily with the music.

He was lovely. The urge to get closer tugged at Ash's chest.

One of the man's friends—the blond—pulled him close, and they danced together.

A growl rumbled in the back of Ash's throat. He wanted his hands on those narrow hips, those long legs wrapped around him as he licked the arch of that sweet neck and plundered those pretty lips.

He moved closer. Would the young man's skin taste like fresh mountain air? Ash bet his cum was sweeter than any other. His mouth watered, spine and hidden tail tingling. Damn, when was the last time he'd been this lost to his instincts?

Visions flickered across his mind. Hands on soft skin, their mouths tangled together, his wings beating, tail thrashing, as Ash thrust into tight heat, that round ass bouncing. He'd claim this man. Satisfy him until he couldn't think, fill him and make him his.

Yes. Mine.

Ash stopped, taking a ragged breath.

Where had that come from? Claim him? What in damnation was wrong with him? He wasn't sentimental about fucking. Ash wanted to have sex, to get off with this gorgeous man, not *keep* him.

It had been too long since he'd gotten laid. Fuck, he was going soft. Like Dante.

Someone pushed past Ash. Bodies pressed around him, but he hadn't noticed until now. He watched the three men dance, the crowd pulsing around them. Should he approach the man with the floral scent? His gut said yes, demon sense purring with need, but he needed to engage his brain.

There didn't seem to be much sexual chemistry between the man and his blond friend. Hopefully, he'd be looking for someone to go home with, and that someone would be Ash. If he was rejected, Ash might never leave his hunting lodge again.

The brown-haired friend turned away from the other two to dance with someone else, and as if on cue, two more men approached, separating Ash's man from the blond.

Time to make his move.

Ash pushed closer. His tall, beautiful man danced less enthusiastically with his new partner as if he was unsure of the change or uninterested. Ash frowned at his discomfort. His blond friend must have noticed too because he broke away from his dance partner to check on him before pulling him away. The two joined the guy the blond had started dancing with, and the abandoned man turned away, seemingly unbothered.

Ash let them settle into the new configuration. The blond was sandwiched between the new man and Ash's breath of fresh mountain air, who seemed to relax again, cradling his friend's hips as they all writhed with the music.

Would he welcome Ash's advance? Maybe this man wasn't interested in dancing with people he didn't know.

Disappointment mixed with something like sadness in Ash's chest. Why did he care? The club was full of attractive men.

He should walk away. He'd let his instincts rule him too much. They were affecting his reactions and emotions.

Ash didn't need emotions coming into play when he had sex.

But he didn't leave. After a few minutes, Ash moved closer, letting the beat flow through his body as he danced beside the trio, and fuck, it felt right. He had to be here. Everywhere else, with anyone else, was wrong.

The man's scent enveloped him. Fresh florals and crisp, cold air.

He turned and caught Ash's eye. His stare lingered, trailing over Ash, and his cheeks darkened.

Ash's chest swelled and he shifted closer. "May I join you?"

The man's lashes fluttered, his glasses slipping. He barely had to look up to meet Ash's gaze, and fuck, if that wasn't hot. He nodded. "Sure." His voice rang out softly, inaudible over the music if not for Ash's enhanced hearing.

Ash stepped closer, positioning himself behind the man. He leaned in to speak in his ear. "How's this?"

In answer, the man pressed back, his round ass so perfectly cupped by his short-shorts pressing against Ash's groin. Ash rumbled a low, satisfied sound and placed his hands on the man's hips, moving with him as he danced with his friend.

Ash's nose lingered behind the man's ear, the fresh scent of bluebells washing over him. So that was the flower he couldn't quite pick out before. The rich scent went straight to his head. He gripped the man's waist tighter as arousal tingled within him.

My flower.

With a jolt, Ash pulled his face from the man's hair. It was a good thing he hadn't had that potion. He was acting drunk enough as it was. Dante was right. It had been too long. That was the only explanation for his strange sentimental mood and giving pet names to strangers.

He pushed visions of fucking *his flower* in a sunlit field

aside and concentrated on the noise of the club and the press of the ass rubbing against his dick. Fuck, Ash could do this all night. He loved the teasing feeling, slowly coaxing him to hardness.

The man in Ash's arms faltered in his rhythmic writhing and spun around away from his friend. He pressed his hands against Ash's chest, gripping Ash's shirt, his wide eyes framed by long dark lashes. His glasses slipped down his nose, but he didn't seem to notice.

Was this in response to feeling Ash's hardening cock? Ash hauled him closer, positioning his dance partner's legs on either side of his thick thighs. The man's erection pressed into Ash's hip.

Ash smiled, and for a second, he had the urge to let his fangs drop.

No. Seriously, what the fuck? Even if the man had been a fellow magical being, Ash wouldn't reveal himself. Not in a club and not in private. What was he thinking? Just enjoy the night. Enjoy him and move on. Then, tomorrow, you'll have a nice memory to get you through dealing with Luc.

Ash cupped his partner's ass with one large hand and moved to the music.

The man gasped and shimmied against Ash, his dark eyes locked on Ash's face as he wound slender fingers around the back of Ash's neck.

The scent of bluebells swirled around Ash, strangling his senses.

His partner's cheeks flamed and his mouth parted as he moved, pressing closer to Ash. Ash brought his other hand to that perfect ass and squeezed. His partner moaned, fingers flexing on the back of Ash's neck.

"What's your name?" Ash purred in his ear.

He shivered. "Harper."

The name fit, sweet like his scent but with a sharpness to match his gorgeous face. Perfect. Lovely.

"I'm Ash," he said, pulling back and locking eyes with Harper.

He didn't seem to know what to say to that. In fact, Harper looked dazed.

Ash's cock hardened further, straining against his jeans. Harper pressed impossibly closer and Ash guided him, rolling his hips to the beat.

Harper's eyes fluttered closed and his head tilted back, exposing his neck. Mm. What if Ash sunk his fangs into that sweet flesh? Just a taste. Harper's fresh scent intensified, and Ash's mouth watered. Shit. Maybe he should have fed when Onyx offered yesterday.

Harper stiffened in Ash's arms and pushed back, putting space between them. Ash let him go, his chest tightening at the loss. Had he made Harper uncomfortable, given away his beastly thoughts in his expression?

Harper averted his eyes. "Maybe we should go somewhere...?" He blinked, gaze darting around.

So he wasn't uncomfortable. Ash grinned.

Getting out of here was a great idea. But why had Harper moved away so suddenly if nothing was wrong? His scent faded, which was interesting. It was almost like his arousal had peaked. Like Harper had been close to coming before he'd pulled back, just rubbing against Ash fully clothed.

Ash swallowed a growl before it could pass his lips. "Where would you like to go?"

Harper bit his lip. "My place?"

"Perfect." Ash pulled him close again, burying his nose behind Harper's ear. He couldn't help it. "Tell your friends where you're going, and I'll meet you outside." He released Harper and walked away.

Look at him, practicing restraint.

He itched to throw Harper over his shoulder and carry him out of the club, but that wasn't appropriate. Harper needed space and the opportunity to change his mind. Ash never wanted to pressure anyone, but sometimes, his intimidating stature did, regardless of his intent.

So he left, hoping Harper would follow.

8

———

HARPER

After a quick chat with Ollie, Harper left the dancefloor. His heart pounded. Fuck, his cock ached, frustratingly constrained by his tiny shorts.

He'd never felt anything like this.

Harper wasn't totally inexperienced, but he'd had no idea attraction could feel like his world had been turned upside down, consumed by one hard, imposing man.

What a man.

How was it possible that such a hot guy had approached Harper, of all people, looking at him like he wanted to eat him.

Not literally. Ash wasn't a vampire. Harper had checked for any signs of magic, and yes, he was masking himself, but magical beings rarely went to the lengths he did or had the ability to brew the suppression potion. He was confident Ash was human.

Harper pushed the club door open and stepped into the mild summer night. Ash stood a few feet away, occupied by his phone.

Harper approached. "Hey." He wasn't sure what else to say. When they'd been all over each other, it had felt natural. Talking was a lot harder.

"Harper." Ash gave an almost predatory smile, but there was nothing menacing in his rich brown gaze. Yeah, he wanted to *devour* Harper. "I was just organizing a car. What's your address?"

That was easy. Harper relayed it, shifting on his feet as Ash typed it into the phone.

Harper's arousal calmed down, replaced by a strange, achy longing that tugged at the center of his chest. He didn't want to fuck this up. He'd felt so good in Ash's arms, almost calm, carefree, and like nothing could get to him. It didn't make sense because they didn't know each other, but Harper needed more of whatever that feeling was.

They waited for the car in silence. Harper wanted to wrap himself around the bigger man, but it'd be weird to do that out on the street, right?

The car arrived and they climbed in. Ash's fingers tapped restlessly against his leg as they drove. Was he dying to get his hands back on Harper or getting bored? Should Harper have been doing something and not just sitting here? Was he not being sexy? How could you even be sexy sitting in a car? Fuck.

When they arrived, Harper jumped out and quickly led Ash into his building and up the many flights of stairs.

He pulled his key out of his pocket to unlock the door and Ash pressed against his back. Something inside Harper unwound. He leaned into Ash, warmth radiating from Ash deep into Harper's soul.

"Get the door open, sweet. Then I'm going to ravage you," Ash rumbled in his ear, sending chills up and down Harper's spine.

Harper got the door open as fast as he could. Ash nudged him playfully inside. Harper's world spun, and he found himself up against the wall.

Ash's muscled body and hard cock pressed into him. Pleasurable chills gave way to goosebumps as Harper's skin tingled. Fuck, it was like he'd been lit on fire or shocked by electricity or something.

He hadn't fucked up after all.

Ash's gaze seemed to smolder, the brown of his eyes almost golden orange as they locked on Harper's lips. "Is kissing on the table?"

"Yeah." Harper nodded frantically. He'd never been kissed. He'd given a few blowjobs, but he'd never had anyone's lips on his, never had anyone reciprocate or touch him intimately. Being denied something as simple as a kiss—let alone anything more—had hurt, even if Harper pretended it hadn't at the time. Now, a fire burned inside him. *Please.* He needed Ash to kiss him so badly it was embarrassing.

Ash captured Harper's mouth with his, hot and wet, and Harper whimpered. Ash worked him open roughly, his lips commanding Harper's, overpowering him. Harper gave in willingly. He sagged in Ash's arms, letting Ash take him how he wanted.

A rich, smoky scent filled Harper's nose. Ash must be wearing a cologne he hadn't noticed in the club. It made Harper's senses tingle and spark, and he wildly hoped the scent would rub off on him, mark him so he could keep a bit of Ash forever.

Ash pushed his tongue into Harper's mouth and he swore he tasted spiced smoke, sweet like cinnamon. The kiss deepened, and Harper tangled his tongue with Ash's, releasing a humiliating array of sounds. Ash swallowed them like he thrived off Harper's moans, his strong hands coursing through Harper's hair and running down his back.

Satan, he really was devouring Harper.

Ash's hands found their way to Harper's ass and squeezed, lifting him. Harper gasped and wrapped his legs around Ash.

Fuck he was strong. Harper wasn't exactly small at six feet tall, no matter how scrawny he was. Ash didn't even seem to strain. He just gripped Harper's ass and thrust against him, bringing their hard cocks together, frustratingly separated by their clothes.

Harper cried out, breaking the fiery kiss, and gasped for air. He was going to come if they kept doing this. He'd almost come in the club. His limited, one-sided experience hadn't prepared him for what it was like to be touched this way. It was so much hotter than he'd imagined it would be.

"Want me to fuck you against the wall?" Ash asked, his voice so deep and rumbly that it vibrated through Harper.

Harper whimpered, unable to speak.

Ash held him firm and waited, rubbing his nose over Harper's cheek, not pushing for an answer or going ahead with anything.

He liked that Ash didn't take silence for permission. It was a low bar, but it still warmed him, and in a much softer way than the heat of Ash's lips had.

Harper's mind cleared. He pushed away unwanted memories of the scraps of barely-there affection and lies given to him previously and focused on the strong arms around him. "Um. Maybe we could go into the living room?"

Ash hummed an agreeable sound and carried Harper down the hall. Harper clung to Ash's broad shoulders, ducking under the doorway.

What did Harper want to happen next? He was intimidated by anal sex. Just the thought made him want to hide. Yes, he had fantasies about being fucked, but he wasn't ready to go there tonight. He didn't want to tell Ash, or any one-time hookup, that he'd never done it before. Having to talk about anything sounded terrible.

When they were lost in touching each other, everything was easy. It was so much better than having time to think.

In the living room, Harper assumed Ash would set him down on the couch, but instead, Ash sat, keeping Harper situated on his lap, his hands remaining on Harper's ass, squeezing him.

Harper let out a small, breathy sound, rolling his hips, and let go of his uncertainty as he focused on how good everything felt.

Ash studied him, not saying anything or leaning in for another kiss. His mesmerizing dark eyes took Harper in, and Harper squirmed. How was it possible to be even more desperate now than before?

Ash's full lips twitched.

Damnation, he was gorgeous, his build thick and defined. Harper's hands itched to undo the buttons of his shirt and explore.

"What would you like tonight, sweet?" Ash asked.

Harper's cheeks flamed at the endearment, his heart thudding like the pet name meant something more than Ash wanting to get into his pants. "Can I take this off?" Harper trailed a finger along Ash's shirt buttons.

"Please. Can I take your shirt off too?"

Harper shivered. "Okay."

Ash pulled Harper's tank over his head and tossed it away. His large, callused hands spread over Harper's stomach and worked their way up until his thumbs brushed Harper's nipples.

Harper gasped, remembering he was supposed to be stripping Ash, and got to work exposing beautiful brown skin and dark curly chest hair.

Ash tweaked Harper's nipples and Harper's mind blanked. It was like the tender nubs were directly connected to his cock. He'd had no idea.

Ash rolled each nipple between a thumb and forefinger, watching Harper closely. Harper let out a strangled moan, unable to break Ash's stare. Ash rumbled in approval and pinched.

Fuck. Harper was on the verge of coming again.

"What else do you want, hm?" Ash murmured, almost a purr, as he wound his hands around Harper's body, planting them back on his ass like they belonged there.

Right. He had to answer, or it seemed Ash would keep asking.

He didn't want Ash to fuck him, or he did—the idea made him want to sob with a mixture of arousal and longing—but not tonight. If this wasn't a one-time thing, then maybe he'd feel comfortable enough going there for the first time.

Harper leaned in and whispered in Ash's ear, "I want to suck your cock."

Ash growled, like, full-on growled, sending a thrill through Harper. Who'd have thought *he* could make a man like Ash lose control?

"I'd love that," Ash rumbled, releasing Harper's ass from his possessive grip. "I'm negative, but I've got a condom if you'd prefer."

Harper shifted in Ash's lap. "I'm cool with no condom. I'm negative too."

Witches were also less prone to human infections due to the magic in their blood. It wasn't impossible for Harper to get an STI, but he had an advantage. Not that he could say any of that when Ash was human.

Ash brushed his thumb over Harper's kiss-swollen bottom lip. "You want to taste me, flower?"

Harper's breath caught. Flower? What the hell was that, and why did it make him melt? "Y-yeah, I want to taste you."

Ash grinned wickedly. "Then I won't make you wait."

No, there was no reason to wait.

Harper slid off Ash's lap onto the floor. As he reached for Ash's zipper, butterflies churned inside him. He pretended not to notice. There was no reason to be nervous. He knew what he was doing. Okay, maybe that was overselling it. At least giving blowjobs was the one thing he had experience with. It was why he'd wanted to suck Ash off in the first place.

Harper undid Ash's jeans, and Ash pulled his cock free. Harper's mouth watered. Ash's dick was proportional to the rest of him. Fuck, Harper was going to choke on it. His stomach clenched in a whirlpool of feelings as the ache between his legs grew.

He wrapped his hand around Ash's thick shaft and stroked him. Precum leaked from Ash's slit, and Harper leaned forward, lapping it up. Was that too tentative? He hadn't done this in a while and needed to work up to it.

He licked again. Ash was tangy and surprisingly sweet, his precum leaving a lingering hint of something smoky behind, almost like his cologne.

Harper's eyes fluttered closed as he flattened his tongue over Ash's cockhead. More. He needed more. Ash tasted so good.

Ash rumbled an approving sound, one of his hands resting in Harper's hair, then stroking through it. Harper leaned into the light touch, cupping Ash's heavy balls and wrapping his lips around his cock, groaning as Ash's taste intensified. Harper sucked on Ash's tip. Ash tightened his hand in Harper's hair, his grip firm.

Harper tensed, every one of his muscles locking up.

What if Ash thrust forward, holding him in place so he couldn't get away? *No.* Harper didn't want that. His stomach clenched. *Please, not again.* He couldn't. This was supposed to be something he chose, not... He had to get away.

"Sorry," Ash murmured, quickly releasing his grip on Harper. "Do you not want me to touch you?"

Harper released Ash's cock from his hand and mouth and glanced up. Shame flooded him from head to toe. His pulse raced. He blinked. Focused.

He wasn't being assaulted. That was in his past. Nothing bad was happening. This was fine. Harper clung to the present. He was with Ash, the hot guy from the club, not the man he'd first fooled around with who'd refused to kiss him, not the other man who'd held him down against his will. This could still be something good and had nothing to do with what came before.

Ash patiently waited for Harper to answer his question.

"You can touch me," Harper said, voice softer than he liked.

Fuck. He didn't want to do this if Ash wouldn't touch him. He liked Ash's hands on him. He needed Ash's touch. One sexual partner who had avoided touching him intimately was more than enough, especially now he knew what the other side felt like.

"I liked your hand running through my hair."

Ash stroked Harper's cheek. "I liked that too. Is there anything you don't like?"

Harper leaned into the caress. "I don't like being forced. I'd rather be in control."

Something dark passed over Ash's face. "Someone's forced you?"

Harper's mouth dropped open. What a fuck up. He hadn't meant to reveal anything, but it was pretty obvious he was referring to an assault, wasn't it?

"I'd never force you to do anything," Ash continued, saving Harper from speaking. "I'll ask you before doing anything. Okay, Harper?" He waited, gazing expectantly down at Harper, brow furrowed.

Harper nodded.

Ash smiled, this time much more sweetly, his lush lips quirking and eyes lightening, crinkling around the edges. "I like the idea of you being in control and doing what you want with me."

Heat spread through Harper's chest, and he was glad to move on. "Me too. I just want to make you feel good."

Ash stroked his cheek again. "You will, sweet. You already have. But I want to make you feel good too."

Harper's heart burst, something weirdly tender passing between them, considering he was on his knees for a guy whose last name he didn't even know.

He seized the good feeling and dove back in, wrapping his lips around Ash's cock, taking more of him in this time, and coaxing him back to full hardness. Ash ran his hand through Harper's hair, and Harper trusted him not to grab and hold him down. He believed Ash wouldn't hurt him.

Harper worked his tongue, getting lost in the full feeling of taking Ash's big cock. He touched and sucked and moaned, not caring what kind of slurping noises he made. He'd never enjoyed giving head like this. Ash's taste, his rumbling satisfied noises, his gentle hand teasing Harper's scalp.

Harper took Ash deeper, squeezing his aching erection through his shorts. Dammit, he was close to coming in his underwear.

"Fuck you feel good," Ash groaned, the taste of precum flooding Harper's mouth. "You're so sexy between my legs, flower."

Harper moaned, pleasure shooting through him, his orgasm threatening. He pushed forward, opening his throat the best he could and swallowing around Ash. His lips stretched obscenely, and he imagined he must look...sexy. Ash said he was sexy, and Harper believed it, even as he gagged and had to pull back, eyes watering and spit dripping from his lips.

He attempted to catch his breath, licking up and down Ash's length.

"You're spoiling me." Ash gripped the base of his erection. "Do that one more time, and I'll come down your pretty throat."

Harper's whole face heated. He looked up to find Ash staring at him as intensely as before. "You can come down my throat."

Ash hummed. "I'd love to. Your mouth is perfect, but I'm dying to touch you. I miss having you in my lap."

In his lap? Was Ash going to ask him to ride his cock? Harper was almost tempted until reality came crashing back into him.

"Will you let me play with you?" Ash brushed Harper's spit-slick lips. "Or do you want to stay in control?"

The choice came as a relief. Harper didn't have to call all the shots. He wanted to be touched rather than come in his shorts while giving a blowjob.

"You can play with me. Touch me."

Ash pulled Harper up. His fingers slid up Harper's thighs and under his shorts. "Let's take these off, hm?"

"Please." Harper undid the button and Ash tugged them down. They fell to his ankles.

Ash growled. "What's this?"

Was he talking about the obvious wet spot of precum on Harper's underwear? Harper stammered, "U-uh."

Ash reached around and cupped Harper's bare ass.

"Oh, you mean my thong?" The twist in Harper's gut turned pleasurable. "I couldn't exactly wear boxer briefs with those shorts."

The black thong wasn't anything fancy. Harper had splurged even without getting lace. It had been worth it, walking around wearing something he'd always wanted but hadn't risked buying before his escape.

Ash let out a rumbling laugh. "No, you couldn't wear briefs with those shorts." He hauled Harper onto his lap, their cocks brushing with only the thin layer of fabric between them. "It's hot. You're so sexy, Harper. I want to make you come all over your pretty little underwear."

"Okay," Harper breathed, aching with arousal. He'd sell his soul if Ash asked right now. Being in his lap was that good.

Ash pulled Harper into a searing kiss. Their tongues tangled. Harper rubbed against Ash, shamelessly rolling his hips.

"Touch me," Harper gasped. "I need you to touch me."

Ash pushed the thong out of the way and grasped Harper's dick, his palm rough against Harper's smooth skin. Ash squeezed and stroked.

Harper cried out, leaking precum everywhere. "I need... I need your cock."

"I've got you." Ash pressed his cock against Harper's and clasped them together. "Like this?"

"*Yes.*" Harper thrust, their aligned cocks rubbing, slick with Harper's spit and their combined precum.

He clutched Ash's shoulders and rode him, fucking into Ash's fist, letting out desperate little keening sounds. Ash growled and licked Harper's exposed neck, cupping Harper's ass like he owned it.

Licking turned to sucking as Ash's lips moved up and down Harper's neck. Teeth scraped Harper's pulse point and his orgasm crashed through him. He shouted, digging his fingers into Ash's shoulders, riding him through his pleasure.

Ash growled against Harper's skin, grip tightening on their aligned cocks. "Fuck, Harper. Fuck." Ash thrust and came, his release mixing with Harper's all over Ash's hand, their stomachs, and Harper's underwear.

Fucking hell, that was hot.

Ash panted, his breaths more ragged than before. He licked Harper's neck, murmuring something under his breath.

Harper squirmed, his spent cock oversensitive. Ash released him, wrapping his hand solely around himself. Ash jerked his cock, giving himself a few brutal strokes before a second burst of cum erupted from him.

"Fuck," Ash swore again, sounding even more wrecked.

"That was amazing," Harper sighed, going boneless against him.

Ash buried his face in Harper's neck and breathed in, still panting. Instead of being relaxed now that they'd both gotten off, Ash seemed even more keyed up.

"You good, Ash?"

"Yeah... Fuck." Ash sounded strained. He shifted Harper off his lap and stood swiftly, only half turning back, his open shirt flapping. "Bathroom." He readjusted his pants and walked down the hall.

Before Harper could tell him the bathroom was the other way, the front door opened and closed.

What the fuck?

Harper blinked at the empty room. He pushed his fake glasses up his nose. Had Ash seriously just left? Covered in cum and out of breath?

Harper's overheated body cooled in a flash. He was a sticky mess, his underwear twisted around his balls and shorts hanging off one ankle. He still had his shoes and socks on.

He waited for Ash to come back, their combined cum drying slowly on his skin. Maybe Ash just needed a minute. Maybe he'd come back and explain.

Ash didn't return.

Tears pricked the corners of Harper's eyes, and he brushed them away roughly.

He shouldn't care. This shouldn't hurt. He'd had a hot

hookup. It was what he'd wanted. So what if the guy had literally run away after. It didn't matter that it had taken him years to get to a place where he was comfortable with this again, and *this* was how he was treated.

But it did matter, dammit. Who called a guy flower and didn't even wait to clean up or fix his clothes before leaving?

Harper had been discarded, and it wasn't the first time. It was fucking embarrassing. He got up, gathered his clothes, and went to shower.

9

ASH

Ash slammed Harper's front door and ran up the stairs, casting an illusion over himself as he went. He banged the service door to the roof open and stumbled outside. The night air did nothing to quell the fire within him.

His wings burst forth, tearing his already disheveled shirt. His fangs dropped and his horns shot from his hair, his tail straining against the restriction of his jeans. He tore the pants and the remainder of his shirt off, leaving himself bare.

Tail thrashing, Ash sucked in uneven breaths, his mouth watering at Harper's lingering scent. Fuck, he was covered in cum. Ash grabbed his destroyed clothes and wiped himself clean, but it didn't help.

Harper's sweet scent set his blood boiling.

Claim. Claim. Claim.

Ash burned for Harper.

His demon form had never forced itself to the surface like it was something foreign taking him over. What was happening?

Ash's mind filled with vivid images. He'd mount Harper from behind and fuck him until he was dripping with cum. Sink his teeth into Harper's perfect, sweet neck and make Harper his.

He'd nearly done it just now, bitten him and tasted his blood. Harper had come, spilling his seed on Ash's skin, and Ash had lost all reason. He'd almost done something he couldn't take back.

Fuck, what was wrong with him? This wasn't right.

A small voice inside insisted: *It is right. Nothing is wrong.* Ash had to claim Harper. Mate him. Not just taste his blood but give him his in return. Bind the two of them together and keep Harper. Forever.

Ash's shuddering breaths choked out into nothing. He hadn't thought about the act of mating—in detail—in over a thousand years.

Mating wasn't the same as sex, though it did involve sex. Ash might have had the desire to fuck over the centuries, but mating hadn't appealed at all. Until now. The need to perform the ritual—fuck, feed, claim—sent Ash to his knees. He gouged the roof tiles with his fingers, trying desperately to hold on to something. Anything.

Maybe he should lay Harper out on his back. Spread his legs and fill him while they kissed. That way, Ash could watch Harper writhe and lose himself in pleasure as Ash's cock pumped into him. Yes, that's what Ash wanted: Harper's dark-brown eyes gazing up at him as pleasure flushed his face. Then Ash would bite, mate, and watch his cum drip from Harper's hole.

Mine.

But Harper wasn't his mate. Ash shook himself, withdrawing his fingers from the roof and forcing himself to stand.

It was impossible. None of the Fallen would ever find their mates. It was their punishment and the council wasn't forgiving. Their mates would never be found in the Human Realm. Ash had known that for well over a thousand years. There had never been solid proof that any Eternal could find their fated mate on Earth.

How could Ash forget the facts?

Was it a side effect of seeing Dante for the first time in too long, and confronting Dante's unwavering conviction he'd find his mate? That, plus depriving himself of blood and being a little too horny for the gorgeous man he'd picked up?

Yes, that was all.

Harper's unique scent must have unlocked something in Ash's brain. No, within his baser demon sense. Along with everything else, it was too much. He'd cracked.

The urge to claim Harper faded. Ash's blood cooled, and the night air finally felt refreshing.

Harper wasn't his mate. Of course he wasn't. Ash had never heard of anyone being overcome by the mate connection like this. Eternals didn't go into a frenzy and claim them like crazed beasts the second they found their other half.

Ash needed to get out of here. Fly far away. He crouched, readying to launch off the roof, but he couldn't get his body to cooperate. His wings remained folded against his back and his legs infuriatingly stiff.

He didn't want to leave Harper. Which was stupid. Or maybe not. The way he'd run out had to have confused Harper. Ash's chest tightened. Would Harper be hurt? Fuck. Ash had been worse than rude, but he couldn't go back now, naked, clothes shredded, with his wings out, and apologize.

Ash tried to force his demon features away. They didn't budge. What the hell? They'd never disobeyed him. Putting his wings away was as easy as taking a step.

He tried again. And again.

It took longer than he'd like to admit. By the time he had

command over his wings, it had been far too long to seek Harper out.

Ash remained on the roof, guilt rooting him to the spot. Harper had been open and vulnerable with him, had trusted him, and in return, Ash had walked out on him in the most disrespectful way. For that alone, Ash didn't deserve anything more from Harper.

It was a good thing Harper wasn't his mate. He wouldn't be pleased to see Ash if their paths ever crossed again. Not that they would. Once Ash managed to get off the roof, he'd never go near Harper again.

ASH LANDED on Dante's deck overlooking the city. He managed to get inside and find some clothes before Dante or Onyx spotted him.

The sun rose as Ash moved through the house. He'd sat on Harper's roof feeling like a foolish asshole all night.

Ash ignored the ache in his chest as he entered Dante's kitchen. It was just guilt. He'd fucked up, but there was nothing he could do about it. His feelings had nothing to do with wanting to fly back to the Banks.

Ash opened Dante's fridge and pulled out a bag of blood. The whole feverish episode seemed ridiculous now. He couldn't believe he'd been thinking about mates.

He heated up a mug of blood and downed it, then prepared another. He had to take better care of himself. Be more aware of his mental state and what his demon sense was telling him. If he had, perhaps he could have avoided the mess with Harper.

"Did you work up an appetite last night?" Dante's mirthful voice floated across the kitchen.

Ash set his mug down and turned to face him. "Something like that."

No way in all the realms was he telling Dante what happened. It would only give Dante false hope, and the last thing Ash needed was someone trying to convince him last night's delusions meant something.

"Good. I hope it helped." Dante pulled a box of sugary cereal from a cupboard and poured an obscene amount into a bowl.

Ash wrinkled his nose. "How did it go at the club with Onyx?"

Dante ruffled his wings. His whole house had been built to accommodate demons in their full form, with plenty of space, high ceilings, wide doorways, and large glass-paneled windows that rolled back so they could fly in and out. "About as you'd expect. He went home with that human couple."

"Do you think he'll come back, or will we have to track him down?"

Dante pulled a carton of coconut milk from the fridge. "He'll be here."

Ash doubted it but didn't say anything as he cleaned his mug.

Dante settled on a barstool at the end of the counter and dug into his breakfast. "Help yourself." He raised his bowl.

Ash shook his head. "I don't know how you can eat that."

Dante was like a human child left to their own devices with the amount of sugar he consumed. It was a good thing demons got their nutrition from blood.

Ash scrambled some eggs. They didn't need to eat food to survive. Of the magical beings, only witches did, but most demons enjoyed human food. They even ate in the Eternal Realm.

What did Harper like for breakfast? Ash plated his eggs. What did it matter? He'd never find out.

As they finished eating, a crash came from somewhere at the front of the house. "I'm here," Onyx called.

"Joy," Ash grumbled, even though he was surprised Onyx had followed through on their deal instead of running off and avoiding them.

Dante shot him a glare. "Don't antagonize him."

Onyx burst into the kitchen, still in his club attire. "Full disclosure, I'm drunk." He grabbed the box of cereal Dante had left on the counter and shoved his hand inside.

"Drunk is fine," Dante assured him.

Onyx grinned evilly as he chewed, his blue hair disheveled. He smelled like sex.

Ash eyed Onyx's rumpled shirt. "Where are your wings?"

Onyx gave Ash a pissy look, his pretty face pinching. "Where do you think?"

"Fine. Let me rephrase: why are you hiding your wings when you don't need to?"

Onyx set the cereal down. "Because I don't feel the need to hang around shirtless at every opportunity like you two."

"Okay," Dante cut in, his tone placating. "Why don't we focus on the reason we're all here."

Something nagged at Ash about Onyx's reluctance to let his true form out, but he let Dante change the subject, pointedly ruffling his feathers and earning a bone-chilling glare from Onyx.

"I've been diving into the flock's magic," Dante continued, ignoring them, "and can't find any signs of Lucifer."

Ash turned to face him, the similarity between Dante's wings and the shearwaters' plumage hitting him anew. "Perhaps he's not here yet. And while that's good to know, the shearwaters are what's drawing him to us."

Dante's dark cheeks flushed, his black eyes narrowing. "I'm not leaving, and I'm not apologizing for interacting with the creatures of the city I live in. All you see is a beacon to call Lucifer to us, but can't you acknowledge my birds are an advantage? If we go hide somewhere else, we won't have thousands of eyes watching out for us."

"Yeah, Ash." Onyx crossed his arms, smirking. "Stop being such a pessimistic prick."

"That's not helping," Dante snapped.

"You think I'm here to help?" Onyx scoffed, tossing blue bangs out of his face. "I'm here to watch you two bicker."

Ash didn't believe him. Onyx might be able to get away with a lot, but he wouldn't risk being dragged back to the Realm of the Damned. He was here to help—or to keep himself free, at the very least.

Dante must have thought something similar because he ignored Onyx's comment. "If anyone goes poking around the spells cast on my old place, the birds will notice. And it's not like I'll show up like I did with you, Ash. I can see who's there before I leave my house. Because of the birds."

Ash ground his teeth. "Of course you wouldn't show up there without knowing who was poking around." Dante wasn't stupid. Ash never meant to imply that.

Dante turned to face the massive windows overlooking the deck and city below. "Once we strengthen the protections on this house, we can stay here safely while we use my flock to monitor the city."

Onyx glared at Dante's back. "And what? Be cooped up until my brother comes knocking? No, thank you."

"You don't have to stay with us, Onyx." Dante didn't bother turning around. "If you want to face your brother on your own, that's fine. But if you betray us, we won't hold back."

Onyx's mouth dropped open. "Always so quick to cast me

out. Are you serious? Betray you? My brother can go fuck himself. I'm not doing a thing for him. If he wants you two, then it's my mission in life to ensure he doesn't get you."

The fierceness of his words was almost heartwarming. "So you'll stay with us?" Ash asked.

Onyx cut a sidelong glance at him, chewing his lip. "Fine, whatever. You two are so clingy. But I'm going out whenever I want."

"It's not like we'll stop you as long as you're being smart." Ash didn't plan to stay cooped up in the house either, no matter how lovely it was.

Onyx's eyes blazed for a split second. "I'm always smart." He turned up his nose. "Once we're sure Luc's in the city, we could let him find me as a trap. You still want to imprison him, right?"

"Yes, imprisoning Lucifer will be the only way to get him off our backs," Dante said without hesitation. "A trap could work. Once the shearwaters see what he's up to and who he might have brought with him, we can set it up. However, there is one complication."

Ash knew it. Nothing was simple. "What?"

Dante turned to face them. "Lucifer isn't the only one looking for us."

Onyx laughed, blue eyes flashing. "Um, what?"

"I came across something while sifting through the shearwaters' collective memory." Dante could control the birds and see through their eyes. The enchantment he'd cast also created a collective memory for the flock, which he could tap into. "I don't normally watch the birds too closely. They usually know when something is important enough to pass on to me. This wasn't like that."

"What did you see?" Ash asked.

"Witches are hunting us." Dante frowned, and Onyx

laughed again. Dante ignored him. "The shearwaters didn't recognize what the witches were doing so their hunt fell under the radar, but it seems they're searching for us in the city's stone memory. They've been lurking around old parts of the city, chipping off bits of the buildings and cobbles."

"But they're *witches*," Onyx sneered. "Who cares? What could a witch do to any of us?"

"Hand us over to Lucifer," Ash suggested and Dante nodded his agreement.

Ash had never trusted the sect of witches who worshipped Lucifer. They knew enough of the true history to know Lucifer was their source of magic, but they didn't know everything, and their covens were often the ones causing trouble in the magic world.

"But it's not like the witches have found us," Onyx argued. "So how can they hand us over? Stone memory won't lead them to this house." He gestured around him.

"You're right. It probably won't," Dante agreed, prompting Onyx to smile for a split second. "But I wouldn't trust any witch in the city, just in case."

"Were we ever trusting witches?" Ash didn't mix with other magical beings if he could help it.

Even the witches who didn't worship Lucifer weren't worth dealing with. Many hated demons for being the reason they were banned from their rightful afterlife, even if they had demons to thank for the gift of magic. And vampires were even worse, a bunch of self-important, power-hungry immortals who originated from a group of witches that slayed a demon and drank his blood to gain eternal life.

"We may have trusted witches," Dante said, surprisingly magnanimously, considering no witches were present. "But we won't be now. Shearwater memory can be unreliable in discerning human characteristics. I can't be sure exactly which witches are looking for us, only that some are."

Onyx threw up his hands. "If the birds can't tell people apart, how will they find Lucifer?"

Dante clenched his jaw. "I've imprinted an image of Luc into the flock's collective mind. They know what he looks like and what his magic feels like. If they see our hunters again, they'll be able to show me faces. Looking back through their memory when they didn't know to be keeping their eyes out is what makes things fuzzy."

"Right." Onyx turned away and opened the fridge, clearly done with the conversation.

"It is right." Dante stood straighter. "Just be wary of any witches you meet, even if they can't see through our human illusions and know who we are at a glance. We don't need the trouble of dealing with hunters. Witches have bested demons before, and we don't know if these ones want to hand us over or kill us. Now, let's reinforce the house and discuss what kind of prison we might create for Luc."

Ash had to admit that designing a prison for their dear old friend didn't sound like a bad way to spend the day.

10

HARPER

Harper emerged from his room around midday. He yawned, jaw cracking. Maybe he should go back to bed.

Poor sleep wasn't unusual. Harper spent hours awake in the middle of the night more often than not. That didn't mean Ash costing him sleep didn't sting.

He'd tossed and turned until he'd heard Ollie come home, then listened to Ollie move around the apartment, hoping the sounds of someone else would settle him. It hadn't worked. He'd eventually gotten up and brewed potions just for something to do.

He was paying for it now.

Ollie was curled up in his usual spot on the couch in the living room. "Hey." He gave Harper a tired smile. "There's coffee in the kitchen."

"Thanks." Harper still needed to go grocery shopping. It was lucky Ollie seemed happy to share everything with him.

With a mug of coffee in hand, Harper sat across from Ollie. He sniffed. Was that Ash's spicy cologne? Oh, fuck no. His insides curled and he cringed into his coffee. Something worse than embarrassment tugged at his chest, almost like he longed for Ash's embrace despite his humiliation.

It didn't make sense to be drawn to Ash after the way he'd left, no matter how good kissing and coming with him had felt. How sad was it that even a guy who'd run off like an absolute dick was the best Harper had ever had?

"You good?" Ollie peered over his mug, attention sharp despite appearing hung over. Some of what Harper was feeling must have shown on his face.

"Yeah, I'm fine." Harper tried to act like a guy who *was* perfectly fine. This was how people smiled and talked, right?

Ollie sat up a little straighter, looking less than convinced, worry creasing his brow. "You sure? Was everything good with that guy?"

Harper's face flamed and he looked away as memories from last night flooded his mind. "Yeah," he repeated.

Parts of it were good. Really good. Nothing truly bad had happened, and Harper knew what that was like.

"Last night kind of blew my mind," he admitted, returning Ollie's gaze and choosing to focus on the best parts of the evening, even if it strangled his heart. "I didn't know it could be like that."

"Oh?" Ollie cocked a brow, looking intrigued and maybe a little relieved to hear it had gone well.

Harper ignored his hot face. Was it normal to have amazing sex with someone only to realize they were a jerk? He almost asked. He wanted to talk to Ollie, share some of his experiences so they could get to know each other like real friends.

"Yeah, I, uh, wasn't expecting it to be so..." Nope. He'd burn alive if he continued. "I didn't have a lot of opportunities to meet guys before."

Ollie sipped his coffee. "You said your family was strict?"

Harper nodded. "We lived in an isolated area. Nothing like Shearwater Landing. People didn't visit us often. Anyway...I keep thinking about last night compared to my past experiences. Even the ones that weren't so bad were nothing like it, and now I'm thinking about all the shitty things that happened before."

He didn't add that he was stuck on people who'd hurt him because Ash had made him feel used or that he'd had a flashback in front of Ash. But even that was complicated. Ash had soothed Harper, not making a big deal out of it, which was exactly what he'd needed. If everything else had gone well, Harper didn't think he'd have been so down today or been quite as hung up on the past.

He'd had more than amazing sex with Ash. That was what was so confusing.

Harper had whiplash. He didn't want to remember how safe he'd felt in Ash's arms. He wanted to forget the obviously misplaced feeling and move on. It meant nothing, even if Harper wished it meant something.

If only the encounter had been uncomplicatedly good, he could have one happy memory that wasn't tainted. Shouldn't he be able to have that now that he'd escaped everything crushing him?

It made sense when cruel people discarded him. Like the guy visiting his family's compound from another coven a few years ago, who'd sweet-talked Harper just enough to convince Harper to give him a few blowjobs but had never returned the favor. He'd been Harper's first, and Harper had been naïve, willing to get on his knees and ignore how the guy treated him when they weren't alone. Hell, he'd ignored the fact that the guy didn't touch him other than what was necessary to get his cock in Harper's mouth. Harper had been desperate for anything remotely like affection and had fallen for empty promises.

It hadn't been a great situation, and Harper could now see how that guy's behavior predicted how he'd dismissed him in the end.

What Ash did wasn't like that. Why had he run? Why had he bothered being kind? Was it just so he could use Harper?

Harper's heart skipped, more memories intruding. He didn't want to think about what had happened with that other man—the one who cornered him after the visiting witch tossed him aside—but at the same time, he was sick of not acknowledging it.

"I was assaulted a couple of years ago, and this was the first time I'd been with anyone since," he confessed to Ollie. "I guess I'm just in my head about it this morning."

"Oh, Harper..." Ollie put his mug down and slid along the couch, pulling Harper into a hug. Harper hunched down. It was awkward, but Ollie's touch was soft and soothing.

To Harper's relief, Ollie didn't say anything else. Being comforted rather than questioned gave Harper a sense of validation. He hadn't told anyone before, not counting accidentally revealing it to Ash.

"Thanks," Harper whispered, hoping it conveyed how much he appreciated Ollie.

"Any time." Ollie squeezed before releasing him. "I'm sorry that happened, and I'm always here if you want to talk."

"I don't think I want to say any more about it."

Ollie rested a hand on Harper's knee. "That's okay. Hopefully it helps not holding it in."

"Yeah." Harper was less tense than he'd been. He wasn't suddenly over it, but getting through this conversation felt significant. "You can always talk to me too."

Ollie picked up his mug, saying playfully, "Oh, I don't know if you're ready to hear about my exes. There's no reason to subject you to that." Ollie shuddered dramatically, and Harper laughed.

He welcomed the lightened mood but was serious as he said, "If you need me to, I'll find a way to manage."

Ollie's mug paused on its way to his mouth. "Fuck, you're sweet. You better never move out. I'm going to get addicted to having you here."

"I'm not going anywhere." Harper pushed his plans for leaving Shearwater Landing to the back of his mind.

He didn't *have* to go. Not when he'd stumbled across the best thing to ever happen to him. He needed friends, and his coven had no idea where he was. If he made it undiscovered for the whole six months he needed to save enough to leave, then he'd be in the clear anyway. Right?

Why not stay?

Later that afternoon, Harper left the apartment, his shoulder bag full of the potions he'd brewed in the middle of the night. As he stepped out of his building, he scanned the street and stayed alert for anyone following him, but no nausea or prickling awareness snuck up on him.

He walked without wanting to run, comfortable in his own skin.

Harper had never been relaxed at home, and even after last night's disappointment, he felt better than he ever had around his coven. It had to be down to Ollie.

But he stayed vigilant. He couldn't afford to be sloppy just because he had a safe space.

Harper walked past the coffee shop he kept meaning to visit, disappointed to see it was already closed for the day. Next time, he had to come out earlier and stop in.

He turned away from the dark window and almost ran into a man walking down the sidewalk.

"Whoa, there." The man caught Harper by the shoulders, steadying him briefly before pulling back.

"Sorry." So much for staying vigilant. Harper's heart pounded, but a quick check showed the guy was human.

"No worries." He flashed an almost blinding smile and carried on in the opposite direction.

Harper willed his pulse to calm and continued on.

A few blocks later, he came to The Herb Emporium. Harper looked over his shoulder one last time, and satisfied no one outside was watching him, he entered the narrow shop.

Incense filled the air. A woman browsed candles near the front window but Harper wasn't alarmed to find a witch here. She didn't pay him any attention.

"Hello, Mr. Harper," the man behind the counter called.

Harper approached, careful not to knock into any of the crowded displays. He'd given a fake name—Sam—the first time he'd come here but had blanked on the last name he'd planned to use and had said Harper in a panic. There wasn't anything he could do about the poor disguise now.

"Hi, Nico." Harper smiled as he reached the counter, hoping it looked natural. Nico had asked Harper to call him by his first name rather than Mr. Velázquez, even though he insisted on addressing Harper as mister. It was strange, but Harper went with it.

Nico eyed Harper's shoulder bag as he set it on the counter. He had light-brown skin and rich brown hair and was at least ten years older than Harper. Maybe it was the age difference or knowing he was sneaking around and lying, but Harper always felt like Nico was going to catch him out and be disappointed in Harper's deceit.

Nico pulled a battered notebook from under the counter and opened it to a half-filled page before grabbing a pen out of the pocket of his well-worn apron. "What have you got for me today?"

"The usuals." Harper carefully extracted the vials from his bag and lined them up on the counter.

Nico inspected Harper's potions, making notes in his book. He was as tall as Harper with far more meat on his bones, but Harper didn't think Nico's build was why he found the man intimidating. He'd come to realize Nico was frighteningly observant.

"I've been selling a lot of the alertness enhancer lately." Nico picked up one of Harper's vials and turned it over, watching the potion swirl. "Can you ask your boss to double what he's been making, at least for the next few weeks?" His lips twitched in a tiny, almost-there smile.

It made Harper's skin itch. "Sure. I don't see that being a problem. Do you want the same quantities of everything else?"

Nico studied Harper, seeming to get lost in his thoughts. He blinked. "Yes, that will be fine."

The hairs on the back of Harper's neck rose and he had to resist fidgeting. Was Nico getting suspicious of him? If he was, what was he thinking? Harper wasn't doing anything strange or different today.

"I was wondering if your employer would be interested in expanding the brews he does for me," Nico continued. "The quality of his potions is always exceptionally high. He clearly has talent." He paused, almost like he was waiting for a reaction. "More complex potions sell less frequently, but as I'm sure you're aware, fetch a higher price. If he could do a couple of doses of basic wound healing and nerve pain relief, they're worth triple the current rate he's getting for these." Nico gestured to the vials.

Harper adjusted his glasses. He'd initially avoided making

potions that sold for higher prices because he didn't want his coven to get wind that someone in the city was brewing rare concoctions. However, what Nico had asked for wasn't unique. Nowhere near as complex as the stone memory brew or the magic-suppressing potion Harper was taking.

"Yeah, we can brew those for you."

Nico raised a brow. "You don't need to check with your boss before you commit?"

Harper cursed himself for not phrasing it that way. "He makes those potions on occasion for other people, so I'm sure it will be fine. If not, I'll let you know."

Nico noted something in his book. "Excellent. I set aside the ingredients for you, along with your usual order." He pushed two wrapped packages across the counter.

Potion brewing was more than mixing ingredients. The spells to unlock the hidden properties of natural elements took a lot of power, and there was an element of reading the ingredients, a skill that only potion masters seemed to possess.

Not all witches could brew potions successfully, and Harper tried to count himself lucky for having the gift, even if it came from the strong power in his blood, the thing his father had held him captive and tortured him for.

"Perfect." Harper grabbed the ingredients. "Next time I come in, I'll bring a list of other potions we can do for you. In case you're interested in more variety." Harper hoped so. He couldn't afford to turn down a chance to safely increase his income.

"Great idea." Nico put his notebook away and opened the register, pulling out an envelope of cash.

Harper took the offered envelope. "Thanks. I'll be back in a couple of days to let you know what we can do."

Nico's brows quirked oddly. "See you then, Mr. Harper."

Harper ducked out of the small shop before he could worry

about what Nico was thinking or what that look meant. Everything was fine. These were all good changes to his plan. Improvements. There was no logical reason to worry.

Harper worried anyway. Would he be able to shake the habit soon and be as relaxed everywhere as he was at home? He didn't like the idea of looking over his shoulder his entire life.

11

———

ASH

Two days later, Ash found himself sitting on the roof of the building opposite Harper's apartment. Again. Unsure why he was there.

Lies.

No, it wasn't a lie. He'd needed to get out of the house and away from the other two. He loved his chosen brothers, but there was a reason he lived alone in the woods. Ash needed space and a quiet place to think, like the roof of a random warehouse in the Banks.

Not so random, though, is it?

Ash ground his teeth, cursing his own mind. No, it wasn't random, but it still didn't make sense that he was here, looking into Harper's apartment window, when he could be anywhere else.

He had better things to do. He didn't trust the shearwaters like Dante did and wasn't ready to stake his freedom on the birds warning them of Lucifer's arrival. He should have been doing his own tracking, not sitting here lurking.

But Ash had flown by Harper's apartment the last couple of days, lingering each time. It had become a habit.

He watched Harper hand his blond friend a bowl of what looked like pasta, then cross the living room to close the curtain against the night. Damn.

Ash itched to move closer, to perch invisibly outside Harper's window and listen through the glass. He was being a creep, and the truly frightening thing was how little it bothered him.

Being near Harper felt right. *This* was where Ash was supposed to be.

But he didn't understand why.

The uncontrollable urge to claim Harper hadn't returned. Ash's stalkerish presence wasn't prompted by lust or physical desire. He wasn't craving Harper's blood or overwhelmed with visions of how he might fuck Harper and make him his. It would have made sense if those urges had drawn him here. He didn't understand wanting to be here otherwise.

If he were honest, this deep need to be near Harper was closer to what Ash once imagined the mating connection would be like rather than the frenzy he'd gone into the other night. He hated admitting that, even to himself.

Ash couldn't afford to hope after more than a millennium and a half. It would pull him apart. Hopelessness was safer. He was used to the empty ache and the anger. It was a part of him. He was fine with grumbling at the world and accustomed to being alone.

But the possibility of a partner started to intrude.

What if Ash could face the next thousand years with his mate? He'd been different once, less grouchy and full of dreams, and just like back then, the idea of connecting with someone and sharing everything sparked something in him, blooming deep within and chasing that emptiness away.

He still wanted it. He just wished he didn't.

THE NEXT MORNING, Ash was still on the roof across from Harper's apartment.

During the night, he'd decided all he needed was to see Harper one last time, then he'd leave and not return. Closure would banish the uncomfortable fluttering that had taken up residence in his chest, leaving him free to concentrate on more pressing problems instead of torturing himself by allowing longing for a mate to creep back in.

So, one last look, and that would be the end of this foolishness.

Ash expected Harper to open the curtains to his bedroom, which he'd noticed was next to the living room and conveniently faced the street. However, the morning went on and the curtains stayed shut.

Harper's blond friend left the apartment building at a reasonable hour, but there was no sign of Harper. Ash clenched his fists, glaring at the shuttered window. Had something happened? Was Harper sick? Ash fought the urge to launch across the street, break into the building, and check on him.

At last, Harper exited the apartment building, stepping onto the street and glancing around. Ash's rigid posture sagged. Harper didn't look sick.

His lips were so pink and delicate. Ash's fluttering chest settled into an ache. He rubbed at it. If only he could fly down and speak to Harper, hear his voice. But Harper wouldn't want to see him after the shameful way Ash had left him.

Harper looked over his shoulder, then started down the road. Ash took flight and followed, invisible.

Why hadn't Harper opened his curtains? Was that Harper's usual morning routine? Did he sleep late? The need to know pulsed through Ash, setting his aching chest throbbing. Anything Ash learned about Harper was like a treasure, a spark he could hold on to.

Ash watched from the sky as Harper came to a street corner, had a good look around, and crossed, continuing on toward the river. Maybe finding out where Harper was going would satisfy his need for a tiny bit more of him.

He followed Harper for several blocks. Harper seemed to look over his shoulder and scan the street more often than anyone else out walking. At first, Ash wondered if he was meeting someone, but after this long, it seemed more like Harper was worried he was being followed.

Unease prickled along Ash's skin the longer he watched.

Was someone after Harper? Was he in danger? Ash's demon fire sparked and his fangs dropped. He tasted smoke. No one was allowed to hurt Harper.

Ash scanned Harper's surroundings more carefully. No one around was acting suspicious, but that didn't mean there was no danger. The desire to protect his sweet flower burned brighter than Ash's longing.

Harper needed him.

Ash followed as Harper continued through the Banks. On a street filled with shops, Harper checked his surroundings one last time and disappeared inside a faded green building.

Ash landed on the awning of the store opposite. The faded sign above the door read: *The Herb Emporium.* Ash's brow furrowed. An apothecary?

The shop looked genuine, and sure enough, a lit black candle flickered in the right-hand corner of the window, meaning it was a witch-owned business, not just a human shop selling novelties.

What was a human like Harper doing here? Ash might have believed Harper had gone in out of idle curiosity, except he'd walked in with purpose rather than wandered in while seemingly shopping for other things.

Did Harper know about the magic world?

Excitement bubbled inside Ash, starting deep within and taking hold as pleasurable tingles coursed up and down his spine. His wings flexed and his tail thrashed. If Harper was aware of magic, it wouldn't be such a shock for him to find out Ash was magical. Surely, that opened possibilities for them.

But Ash, Dante, and Onyx had agreed two hundred years ago to never reveal their demon nature to anyone. They couldn't when they were the only demons on Earth. Nothing was worth risking their freedom by revealing where they were hiding when it could get back to Lucifer.

Except for the bloody shearwaters.

Ash ran a hand roughly through his hair and along his horns. Even if he told Harper he was a different magical being, not a demon but a witch or vampire, what would that accomplish? Harper would still be upset about the other night. Ash being magical wouldn't help him win Harper back.

Wait.

Since when was Ash trying to win Harper back? He was supposed to be getting one last look at him before getting on with tracking Lucifer. Fuck.

Ash had gotten his spark, a detail about Harper's life he could take with him, but it wasn't enough. It only ignited his need for more information.

What was a human doing at an apothecary? Did he buy and use the potions shops like that often sold? How had Harper learned about the magic world? Did it have something to do with his potent scent?

Harper exited The Herb Emporium smiling. Ash's chest warmed. He liked when Harper was happy.

Harper glanced skittishly up and down the street, then

hurried back the way he'd come. Ash's good mood shattered. His need for more of Harper wasn't the only reason he was sticking around. He had to protect Harper if he was in trouble.

Ash followed Harper until he ducked into a coffee shop. He perched on a roof a few shops down to wait. There was still no evidence Harper was being followed. By anyone other than Ash, obviously.

But some things were more important than behaving in a socially acceptable manner. Like protecting Harper from *other* stalkers.

No one following Harper right now didn't mean no one was after him. It would take time to figure out what was happening here, and Ash couldn't completely ignore everything in favor of Harper, no matter how much his deepest-seeded desires urged him to.

Ash would just have to juggle this with the Lucifer problem. Surely, he could manage both. He was a legendarily powerful demon, after all.

12

———

HARPER

HARPER PRICKED his pointer finger with a needle and watched his blood well to the surface, forming a dark droplet. He pressed his finger against his thumb and squeezed until the drop swelled.

You didn't need much blood to enhance spells or potions if you did it properly.

Harper let the drop of blood fall into the stone mortar on his dresser. His finger stopped bleeding as soon as he quit squeezing it. That was how small the wound was.

He concentrated on the droplet and recited an incantation rooted in alchemy. The blood transformed to fine dust before his eyes, turning pale as it changed form.

See, this was all you needed.

Not all witches agreed. Witches like his father. They believed transforming the blood took away too much of its power.

Harper had tried to demonstrate that this wasn't the case, showing his father what a pile of dust like this could do. Arthur had chastised him for being disloyal to the coven and Lucifer and for trying to get out of the sacrifice of lending his blood by tricking everyone into thinking a transformed drop had as much magic as pure blood.

"Sacrifice adds power," his father always said.

Harper didn't believe him.

Maybe he had when he was little, but once he was older and practiced enough in the art of potions, he'd known better. Arthur's methods of leaching large amounts of Harper's blood had been about controlling him as much as it had been about gaining access to Harper's magic, even if it was true that not transforming the blood meant you needed more of it to enhance your spells.

How much of his blood did his father have left?

Arthur had traveled to Shearwater Landing several times over the last year to drain Harper. His father once consulted a vampire to help him determine how much he could take without killing Harper and had taken Harper to the limit every time since.

It made Harper sick. His father's greed, his conviction that Harper's only worth was in the power that flowed through him and his ability to carry on the Nightingale name.

Harper shut his memories down. There was no point in dwelling on the past. He was safe now and only used his blood to keep himself so.

Walking around the apartment, Harper sprinkled the dust from the mortar as he recited an incantation to strengthen the protections he had in place. He never used his blood for anything else, not even the stone memory potion or magic suppressant. It wasn't necessary. His affinity for mixing elements was strong enough on its own.

As he performed his spell, the blood sparked and disappeared into the magic shield guarding the apartment.

It was true that not every witch could transform blood like he did. The skill was tied to his potion mastery. His father couldn't do it successfully, but he could have found someone to do it for him, and Harper had offered once he was old enough.

Some covens were more deeply committed to blood-enhanced magic than others. Most covens banned the use of blood unless the situation was life or death. Not all witches were like the Nightingales.

What would Harper's life have been like if he hadn't grown up accustomed to his father chanting incantations while his hands dripped with Harper's blood?

Once he was done strengthening his protections, Harper gathered the potions he'd brewed over the last several days and headed to The Herb Emporium for the third time in less than two weeks.

Checking the street and noting people as he walked had become second nature. As usual, Harper didn't see anything amiss, but his neck prickled and he double-checked over his shoulder.

No one was there, just like when he'd looked a moment ago.

Harper frowned and carried on.

Over the last several days, he'd been plagued by paranoia. He swore it felt like someone was watching him.

The relatively relaxed feeling he'd had when going to The Herb Emporium the day after hooking up with Ash had faded. He'd encountered a few witches on his outings since then, but they were all doing perfectly normal, non-stalking-related things, so Harper wasn't sure what was catching his awareness. At first, he dismissed it as general worry, but after days of uneasiness, he couldn't shake the feeling it was more than that.

Was his coven catching up with him? Had his luck run out? He worried he was missing something the whole walk to the apothecary.

"Mr. Harper," Nico called from the counter at the back of his shop.

"Hi." Harper hurried over, glad the place was otherwise empty.

Nico smiled, eyes flashing with something like amusement. "Always a pleasure to see you. It's been nice having you around more."

"Oh." Harper stumbled over the pleasantry. "Yeah. Um, I'm available more these days."

"Works for me." Nico opened his notebook but didn't look at it, studying Harper instead.

He quickly unloaded his potions, hands trembling. He couldn't help glancing over his shoulder, expecting to see someone peering through the shop window.

There was no one.

"The witch who works with me, making the other potions I sell, is moving," Nico said, causing Harper's head to whip back around. "Soon, I'll be needing a lot more help."

Harper's stomach flipped. This could be a great opportunity to go from making part-time cash to a solid income. "You'll need more potions brewed?"

Nico smiled like he'd noticed the eagerness in Harper's tone. "I will, but not only that, I'll need to fill my in-house position. Kat and sometimes her partner Melanie took care of all my made-to-order brews. It's great having stock behind the counter, but I've always done a good trade in unique mixes."

Harper's heart sank. He could never offer to fill an in-house position when Nico thought he was human.

"Your *employer* might want to consider it. Or"—Nico waved a hand—"anyone else you know who fits the requirements."

Had Nico said the word employer funny, or was it just Harper's imagination? He shifted on his feet. "Yeah...I'll pass it on."

Nico nodded, gaze fixed on Harper's face. "Please do."

Harper finished unloading his bag, keeping his attention on the potion vials.

The way Nico had phrased his request was weird, right? It almost seemed like Nico didn't believe there was an employer and was just humoring Harper, pretending there was.

Satan, did Nico know he was a huge liar?

Harper had the urge to run out of the shop before he was caught but forced himself to stay still. Even if Nico suspected he was lying, he couldn't see past the suppressant Harper was taking. He couldn't know Harper was a witch. Maybe there was no hidden meaning in what Nico had said.

Harper just had to go on as normal and stop overthinking.

Harper closed his bag, fiddling with the top flap. There was nothing he could do about the missed opportunity. He couldn't work here, talking to all kinds of customers about their potion needs and brewing unique mixes when that could easily get back to his coven.

If only things were different.

Nico handed over payment for the potions and a package of new ingredients. "I hope you consider it, Mr. Harper. I won't pry into your, ah, situation with your employer, but just know there are options."

Harper stuffed the bundle into his bag. What did Nico think his situation with his employer was? What options? Did he mean options for Harper?

"Okay, sure." Sweat broke out on Harper's forehead. "The guy I work for definitely has options."

"Yes." Nico pressed his lips together like he was holding something back.

Harper hurried out of the shop.

Harper's stomach hurt as he walked through the Banks. Working with witches had always been risky, but how had Nico figured him out? And he had figured him out, hadn't he? His comments didn't make sense otherwise.

What did Nico mean he wouldn't pry? Was he trying to say he wouldn't interrogate Harper if he admitted there was no employer?

Harper groaned. What did it matter? He couldn't trust Nico and wouldn't go back on his disguise now. He wasn't risking anything getting back to his coven, and a new hire brewing exceptional potions would catch their interest more than a human selling on behalf of a witch.

He'd just have to see what it was like next time he dropped off his brews and go from there. Unless... Should he find another job?

Harper eyed all the shops around him. It was too bad his human employable skills were practically nonexistent.

Seaside Coffee was open when Harper reached it, and he needed a pick-me-up. A nagging voice urged him to save his money, but he didn't want to return to the empty apartment and obsess over the interaction with Nico.

Harper pushed open the coffee shop door. He'd been eyeing this place since he'd first come to this part of the city, and he'd finally gone in the other day. The name was odd, given they weren't near the beach or even the riverfront, but Harper wasn't bothered.

He liked the art on the walls and all the cozy little miss-matched tables packed into the place. Next to the front door was a display of handcrafted mugs and dishes for sale.

Cute. Too bad he couldn't afford stuff like this right now.

"Hey, Harper," a voice called.

He jumped, gripping the strap of his bag tight. Slowly, he turned to see who'd spoken.

"Sorry." Dex smiled from behind the counter, hands up in surrender. "You must have been a million miles away. Didn't mean to scare you."

"That's okay." Harper approached, his heart pounding. "I didn't know you worked here." Dex hadn't been around last time.

Dex shoved his hands in his apron pockets. "I've worked here forever. Did Ollie tell you to come by?"

"No. I just liked the look of the place."

Dex smiled widely, his enigmatic gray eyes lighting. "Sounds like you've got good taste. What can I get for you?"

Harper ordered and took his coffee to a small table beside the counter, right at the back of the room, where he could sit with his back to the wall and see out the front windows.

A prickle of awareness itched along his skin like he was being watched.

He scanned the café, checking if anyone was paying him undue attention. It didn't seem like it.

The person who'd been behind him in line walked past his table toward the restroom. He flashed Harper a smile, and Harper returned it reflexively. He was pretty sure it was the same guy he'd run into the other day.

Was that guy's friendly stare all that had his senses tingling? It'd be good to start recognizing local faces. That way Harper wouldn't have to be so suspicious of every person he encountered.

His posture sagged. Worrying about every little thing was exhausting.

Taking a sip of his sweet hazelnut almond latte, Harper tried to empty his mind. He sipped slowly, casually watching people in the café. The place wasn't packed, but it was an off time of day. A pair Harper guessed were a couple leaned in close to one another at the front of the room, whispering.

Longing stirred in Harper's chest, which was even worse than the paranoia plaguing him.

After his complicated hookup, he was less sure casual sex was his thing. He wanted a partner. It had felt so right kissing Ash, his hard body keeping Harper's world in line. He wanted more of that.

The hollowness in Harper's chest intensified, and he bit the inside of his cheek until he tasted copper. He wasn't going to pine after Ash. He deserved someone who treated him right, not just blew his mind and cast him aside.

Harper had another sip of his coffee.

A tall figure walked in front of the café window and came to the door. Harper paused in the process of setting his cup on the table. As if his thoughts had summoned him, Ash stood in the doorway, his bulky frame taking up too much space.

What were the chances?

Ash glanced around the coffee shop until his eyes landed on Harper. He didn't smile, his square jaw set, a serious furrow in his brow.

An electric tingle went down Harper's spine and he suppressed a shiver.

No. He wasn't reacting that way. He wasn't happy to see Ash and wasn't getting any warm feelings.

Their eyes locked. Ash didn't appear surprised to find himself face-to-face with Harper. It seemed like coming across Harper stirred zero emotion in him, which stung.

Ash entered the coffee shop and came closer, heading toward Harper's table, not the register.

What? No. They weren't going to ignore each other? Harper's pulse quickened. Did he like or hate this twist of fate?

Hate. Definitely hate.

"Harper." Ash nodded in greeting, his voice as deep and melodic as Harper remembered. "I'm glad I ran into you."

Harper set his coffee down at last. "You are?"

Ash's lips twitched downward like he wanted to frown but was trying not to. Harper's cheeks flamed. He didn't want to have this conversation. He'd made peace with never hearing from Ash again.

Hadn't he?

Harper tried to hold on to his embarrassment and anger, but something softer muted his senses. The comfort of Ash's embrace was too easy to remember.

"Yes, I'm glad to see you." Ash pulled out the chair opposite Harper. "May I?" He indicated the seat.

Harper blinked, pushing away the memory of Ash's comfort. He tilted his head, adjusting his glasses and fixing Ash with an unwavering stare. "Why would you want to sit with me?"

Ash took his hand off the chair. "I want to apologize."

Heat burst over Harper's cheeks and traveled down his neck.

Damnation. Harper didn't want to acknowledge how Ash had left him a mess on the couch and didn't want to think about what Ash had seen of him before that. He didn't like how desperate he'd been in front of Ash. Harper didn't want Ash to know he cared.

Ash shifted awkwardly like he didn't know what to do with his hands now that he'd let go of the chair. "I'm sorry for leaving so abruptly. You deserve better than that."

Relief, then anger, swept over Harper. If Ash cared enough to be sorry, why had he run off in the first place? "I do deserve better," Harper made himself say. He could do with the reminder. It didn't always feel true when everyone treated him like he was disposable.

Ash reached a hand toward the chair again, then pulled it back. "Can I make it up to you?"

Oh, hell, was that a note of regret in Ash's tone? Real regret and not just something placating? Ash's golden-brown eyes seemed almost pleading. Or maybe Harper was seeing what he wanted to see. Why would Ash care this much? He hadn't the other night.

"I don't think that's a good idea." The last thing Harper needed was to give someone who'd shown they didn't respect him another shot. Ash would only end up being a dick again, and Harper would have no one but himself to blame for getting hurt once more.

"I see." Ash clenched his fist and opened it. "In that case, please know I'm sorry."

Harper's stomach twisted, his chest constricting so much it hurt. "You could explain what happened." He wanted Ash to be a decent person and for all his misplaced feelings to have meaning. He wanted good things and for people to be kind to him. Fuck, if only this was all a misunderstanding.

"I can't. There's—there's nothing to say." Ash's words were clipped. He turned to go, looking back over his shoulder. "I'm sorry, Harper."

Harper clenched his teeth.

Well, okay then. He'd obviously made the right choice. An apology without an explanation didn't mean a whole hell of a lot, and Harper felt silly for wishing it could all turn out okay when Ash was clearly nothing more than a selfish jerk.

13

———

ASH

Ash strode briskly away from the coffee shop. What was talking to Harper supposed to accomplish? Had he really expected Harper to give him a shot at anything?

The tattoos on his back itched, wings begging to come out.

Harper clearly didn't have any lingering good feelings. Ash's obsession was completely one-sided.

The rejection should have been a relief. Harper feeling nothing supported the fact that they weren't mates. Of course they weren't mates. This should be comforting news—not even news. It should be a comforting *confirmation* of what he had expected.

It only made Ash feel alone.

But Ash liked being alone. It usually relaxed him. His hunting lodge was his favorite place in the world. Why did the reminder make him want to crawl out of his skin?

He found a deserted alley behind a nearby building and walked down it, casting an illusion over himself before removing his shirt and letting his wings free.

Ash launched into the sky. He'd wasted enough time

following Harper around. Maybe some space would allow his need for the young man to die down and be forgotten.

Not that he could leave Harper alone completely. He still had no idea why Harper moved around his neighborhood like he was a wanted man. Ash would still protect him even if nothing more would happen between them.

Even if they weren't mates.

He flew over the city and landed on Dante's deck, where he found Onyx sunning himself on a lounge chair, wearing nothing but a tiny swimsuit. He still didn't have his wings or other demonic features out.

Onyx gave Ash a cursory glance. "You look extra pissy today."

Ash grunted and walked off, not in the mood.

"Excuse me?" Onyx got up and followed.

Ash didn't turn around. "Excuse you, what? I don't have to respond to your annoying little jabs."

Onyx didn't say anything, only followed Ash into the kitchen. Ash ignored the infuriating demon and warmed himself a mug of blood, hoping it would get rid of the restless energy buzzing through him.

Onyx got himself a mug, and Ash reluctantly passed him the blood bag.

"Where've you been?" Onyx asked in a forced-casual tone, like he was trying too hard to seem like he didn't care about the answer.

Onyx hadn't left Dante's house as much as Ash had expected. He'd figured they'd barely see the blue-haired demon, but he almost hadn't gone out at all.

"Scanning the city," Ash replied before draining his mug.

Onyx raised a brow. "Isn't that what the birds are for?"

"I've been doing my own tracking." This was true, even if it wasn't what he'd been doing just now. Ash wasn't telling either of his brothers about Harper.

Ash had a knack for tracking. He'd planned to use his ability to find Onyx before he heard he was in Shearwater Landing. Ash had always been able to track his closest friends more easily than anyone else. Years spent in the presence of one another's magic would do that. But he hadn't been able to get a whiff of Luc's magic.

"Do you think he's getting close?" Onyx asked, setting his half-drank blood aside.

Ash shrugged. "I haven't detected anything helpful."

Onyx's eyes widened.

Ash expected to have picked up at least a hint of Luc's presence if he were heading toward Shearwater Landing. He shrugged. "It's possible he isn't in the area yet."

Ash wouldn't be able to sense Luc's magic if he were too far away. He needed a characteristic to latch onto to track anyone, like a sense of their magic, knowledge of what they looked like, or a fairly good idea of where they were. But even if Luc were outside the city, Ash should have been able to detect a general direction to follow until he got close enough to latch onto Luc's magic and find him.

Had it been too long since Ash had been around Lucifer to get a hold on him, unless he was close?

"Do you think he's up to something else before coming for us?" Onyx asked.

"He could be." The idea was worrying. Ash assumed Lucifer would track them down immediately. If he wasn't coming for them right away, whatever else he was up to had to be important, and nothing important to Lucifer was good.

"I don't like this," Onyx muttered, more serious than Ash had heard him in a while.

"Me either."

14
______

HARPER

Harper didn't leave the apartment for days.

Nico was onto him, and even if Nico had no connection to his coven, Harper's lies had been seen through way too easily.

Maybe he wasn't as safe as he thought.

Someone was watching him. He could fucking feel it. The prickling sense of eyes on him had only grown stronger. He was sure someone was spying on him in the apartment, not just when he was out.

But it made no sense. Someone couldn't be watching him when he was alone at home. No one could see in. There wasn't even an occupied building directly across the street. The warehouse opposite had no windows level with his floor and he'd glanced at the roof often enough to know no one was ever up there.

There was no spell to make a witch invisible, and vampires had to be in close proximity to make their illusion magic work. But no matter how logical his explanations were, he couldn't shake the feeling invisible eyes were on him.

Who the hell was watching? How were they managing it?

His coven wouldn't lurk. They'd recapture him immediately. But aside from his coven, no one had it out for him.

After another failed trip into stone memory, Harper gave up trying to figure out any of his problems and decided to bake cookies. That was a positive activity. Self-care or whatever. And it would be nice to have treats to share when Ollie came home.

Once the cookies were in the oven, Harper checked out the living room window. Was it becoming a compulsion? Seeing nothing there only made his chest tighten. Maybe he should hunker down and do nothing for a week, avoid anything magic-related, and try to live a human life.

Could he get a human job, like at Seaside Coffee with Dex? He'd be terrible at it compared to the other people working there, but it might be the smart thing to do.

He pulled up a website of human job listings to see what a coffee shop might look for in an employee. He didn't expect to get a job with Dex just because they knew each other, but maybe he could ask for help finding something.

Harper browsed the listings, his frown deepening the longer he read. None of these people would want to hire him over a human with experience.

An odd scent caught his attention. *Oh no!* Harper lunged for the kitchen. The cookies!

Harper opened the oven and a plume of smoke wafted out. Grabbing an oven mitt, he extracted the charred cookies and turned on the kitchen fan. Man, there was a lot of smoke.

He rushed to the living room window and opened it. He didn't want the fire alarm going off. Everyone would have to evacuate the building.

He hurried to his room and reached across his dresser to yank that window up too. They were old and only opened a few inches, so not great for getting a strong cross breeze, but it would have to do.

With a sigh, Harper turned back toward the kitchen, knocking into the beakers from his potion kit that he'd left out that morning. They toppled and one rolled off the dresser. He caught the glass before it hit the floor, but in his haste, he hit something with his elbow.

The bag of stone dust fell off the dresser, spilling everywhere.

"Fuck." Harper set the beaker down and fisted his hands in his hair.

Stone dust covered the floor.

The stone had to be pure for the memory potion to work. He couldn't ingest other elements like regular dust or anything floating around the apartment.

He'd just screwed his hunt.

Why had he left the bag out? It was made of enchanted leather and protected the contents from contamination, but he should have locked it up in his magical box.

All the stone he'd chipped from the library plaza, purified, and ground down using an alchemical spell was useless now that it had touched his apartment floor. He couldn't risk trying to get into its memory now that it was contaminated and couldn't repurify it this late in the process.

Harper flopped onto his bed and groaned. He had to give up his hunt or go back to Old Town.

It was too risky to go near the library, but at the same time, he couldn't risk his coven finding the Hounds before him. They'd get someone else to take over his search now that he'd abandoned them. He couldn't give up. He had to stop his father from gaining any more power. But he couldn't do that if he got caught.

Harper went back and forth for two days.

He couldn't justify returning to the plaza in front of the library. It was too risky. His coven would be silly not to have someone watching the area. However, there could still be an alternative to abandoning his hunt.

He needed old stone, and there was more than one place to get it. He'd originally chosen the library because that plaza had once been the center of Shearwater Landing, so it was extremely likely that any demons who'd once lived here had passed through that area, if not regularly, then at least more frequently than more random parts of the city.

Now that Harper had screwed up, he had to settle for stone from a different source. Picking a random old section of the city outside of Old Town decreased his chances of finding anything, but it was the best he could do.

According to his coven's research and the anomalies they'd uncovered, the demons seemed to have a connection to the sooty shearwaters. Harper figured the waterfront would be a decent place to try and source new stone chippings. Parts of the seawall were old, and he'd just have to hope the demons had spent more than a few random days at the beach a century ago.

After Ollie went to work, Harper left the apartment with his chisel, knife, and enchanted satchel, all stowed in his shoulder bag. He'd walk along the river. That way, he could stay near the Banks and the Docks as long as possible and avoid getting anywhere near Old Town or the other places he used to frequent on his way to the waterfront.

The feeling of being watched that plagued him in the apartment had died down since the cookie incident, but as Harper stepped onto the street, his skin crawled. He could have sworn someone was watching him, but as always, he found no sign of anyone lurking or any trace of magic in the air.

It was probably all in his head.

He walked through the neighborhood until he reached the concrete riverbank, where a walkway ran along the water. There weren't too many people out on a weekday morning so at least Harper was spared worrying about crowds hiding someone following him.

Shops and restaurants lined the opposite side of the street. It might have been nice if Harper were here for fun and not fighting to look over his shoulder every ten seconds.

The walkway ended part-way through the Docks, where the old cannery backed onto the river. Harper cut in, away from the water, and followed the street parallel until he came to the river mouth.

The area was industrial rather than scenic, matching the part of the city he'd just wandered through. There was a port at the mouth of the river and much more activity here than near the half-abandoned warehouses he'd just left behind in the Docks.

Getting around the port was a slog. The area behind the docked ships was fenced off for containers and lumber and was much larger than Harper had expected.

He walked along the chain link fence, the road beside him busy with traffic. Harper's skin prickled and sweat slicked his palms. No one he passed seemed to pay him any attention, but he wasn't far from the Business District and closer than he wanted to be to parts of the city he'd sworn he'd never return to.

He checked his phone, his heart sinking. He was still a mile from the waterfront.

As he waited at a stoplight, he scanned his surroundings, eyes darting around quickly. This part of the port had a large windowless building backing up onto the sidewalk. It towered over him.

The light turned green and Harper crossed the street. He

cast out his magic as he'd been doing every few minutes, but this time, a prickle of something pushed back.

There was at least one witch or vampire nearby.

Harper swallowed, his throat suddenly dry.

It could be totally innocuous. There were plenty of witches in the city, but Harper had to wonder what one might be doing working at the port, a very human job.

He picked up his pace, walking between the back of the port and a row of warehouses across the street. No other pedestrians were on the block with him, and the vehicles driving by passed swiftly, but the feeling of magic nearby didn't fade.

Harper looked over his shoulder and saw a man crossing the street, headed his way but too far for Harper to get a good look at his face. Harper turned his attention forward and kept moving.

Was this man the source of the magic? Was he following Harper, or was his presence a coincidence?

Shit.

Maybe avoiding the main parts of the city hadn't been smart. At least with people around, any attacker would have to be discreet. Here, amid all the windowless warehouses and high fences, all an attacker needed was a break in traffic, and no one would see anything.

Shit, shit, shit.

Harper hurried on, trying not to look over his shoulder. He gave in, neck straining, as he quickly glanced around.

The man was still behind him and getting closer. Oh, Satan, he *was* following him, wasn't he? The magic Harper sensed grew stronger. It had to be coming from the man behind him. He needed a new plan.

Harper wanted the witch's presence to be a coincidence but couldn't make himself believe it.

How had his coven found him? His heart rate climbed and his chest tightened.

He tried to focus on the facts. Harper doubted he'd missed anything suspicious in the Banks or Docks. He would have sensed the man sooner if he'd been following for a while. Did that mean his coven was watching the port? Was coming here Harper's mistake? He wouldn't have thought so, but the port was a potential escape route. Passenger boats were less common than cargo ships, but they did dock in Port Shearwater.

Harper needed to get back to a crowded area and lose the guy. He still couldn't be tracked magically, so all he needed to do was disappear into the city once more. All wasn't lost.

He could do this.

At the next intersection, Harper would cut over and head into the Business District. It was only a few blocks away.

He glanced over his shoulder and his heart skipped. The man was much closer. Harper finally got a good look at his face. Recognition hit him like a punch to the gut and a cold sweat broke out on Harper's skin.

He'd never forget that sneering smile.

Harper's mouth went dry and the sounds of the port cut off, his pulse pounding in his ears.

He turned and ran.

No, not him. Why did he have to be the one to find me?

Harper's shoes slapped the pavement. Finch, one of his father's advisers, was the man who'd assaulted Harper two years ago, and if he'd left the compound to bring Harper back to the coven, Harper couldn't even think what Finch might be planning.

Harper ran like he never had in his life. Finch would hurt him. He'd threatened to do worse next time. His sick smile filled Harper's vision, and he gagged, not letting it slow him down even as his vision blurred, his eyes stinging and throat burning.

Something crashed into Harper from the side. He stumbled and fell, his knees screaming in protest against the hard pavement. Before he could get up, hands were on him. Another man hauled Harper to his feet and dragged him down a deserted side street.

Harper yelled, but the sound was cut off as a firm hand slapped over his mouth. He struggled and called up his magic to blast the man off him, but his spell fizzled out as they always did when he tried to cast against his coven.

Harper's chest tightened. *No.* This wasn't happening. He had to get away. He twisted and tried to stomp his attacker's foot, but the other man was stronger and his grip didn't falter.

Finch entered the side street, his face twisted in a smirk at the sight of Harper struggling.

Harper tried to scream, but the man holding him shoved something chemical in his face. Harper choked, his vision clouding as his balance wavered. He thrashed, but his arms flopped uselessly and his knees went weak.

Fear drenched him like he'd been dowsed in hot oil, burning every last one of his nerve endings. Something bad was coming, and Harper didn't think he could face it.

And then his world went black.

15

———

ASH

Ash followed Harper from his apartment to Port Shearwater, flying along behind him. He'd never seen Harper go so far from home. What was he up to?

His curiosity vanished the moment a man began following Harper down a deserted industrial street.

Harper had been extra vigilant as he'd moved through the less frequented parts of the city, but he clearly became uncomfortable the moment the man turned up, his posture tensing and pace picking up.

What should Ash do? This must be who Harper was hiding from, but why was a witch stalking a human?

Harper turned and must have gotten a better look at the witch because he broke into a run. Ash's pulse skyrocketed.

The witch ran after Harper.

Ash growled and sped up, diving low so he could grab the witch off the street like a bird of prey might snatch a mouse. His demon fire sparked inside him. He wasn't letting this guy get anywhere near Harper. Maybe he'd interrogate the witch and figure out what in damnation was going on.

As he closed in, about to snatch the witch, another appeared, attacking Harper and dragging him down a side street. Ash's blood boiled and he tasted smoke. These men were dead. He didn't need to know their aims. It no longer mattered why they were after Harper. No one laid their hands on his flower.

Abandoning the first witch, Ash landed in the side street in time to see the second witch smother Harper with a rag. The foul stench of potion hit Ash's nose as Harper went limp.

Ash dropped his illusion of invisibility and charged forward, ripping the man away from Harper. He held his sweet flower against his chest and closed his other fist around the attacker's throat. Ash sent demon fire burning through his veins and into the man as he choked him before dropping the limp body to the ground, smoke rising from his charred skin.

The other witch hesitated at the end of the street, mouth gaping as he took in Ash's full demon form. He didn't give the witch time to cast a spell. Nothing would save him. Ash released a bolt of lightning, hitting the man in the center of his chest and sending him to his damned afterlife.

Ash heaved a breath, his heart beating like it was trying to break free from his chest, putting up more of a fight than it had in at least two hundred years.

He checked Harper, brushing his disheveled hair from his brow. With his demon sense, Ash inspected the residual potion lingering around Harper's nose and mouth. It was meant to incapacitate, not kill, but that was a small comfort. Harper was uncommonly pale, his eyes closed and face slack. Ash's chest ached at the sight of his flower like this. Moisture prickled at the corners of his eyes.

He had to protect this young man. He had to keep him.

He had to make this right. Harper belonged in Ash's arms and deserved better than Ash denying it.

Ash forced his demon features away and his wings melded into his back, his horns and tail following suit. "Flower," he murmured, holding Harper closer.

Harper blinked, his eyes glassy. He parted his lips like he was going to say something, but his head lolled and his eyes fell shut. He'd be okay once the potion wore off. Ash could read the spell well enough to be sure, but Ash wanted Harper alert now. They had to figure out what came next.

The only way to undo the potion's effects would be to suck the toxin from Harper's blood, but Ash wouldn't do that without Harper's permission. He couldn't taste Harper for the first time like this, not when...

When Harper was his mate and a blood connection would mean so much more than it ever had before.

Ash glanced at the bodies strewn around the street. He'd killed two witches without hesitation for Harper, an extreme course of action and a complete overreaction, except in the case of protecting his mate. That was the only reasonable explanation for going this far.

His mate.

The man in his arms was the one he'd waited millennia for. He'd tried to deny it but couldn't let Harper go, no matter how hard he tried. He couldn't stay away. He'd do anything for Harper, anything to hold him like this, anything to make him smile.

Possibilities bloomed within Ash, filling him with a lightness like he'd never known, but it was quickly followed by a sour reality. Finding his mate, being this close, and having the opportunity to bond taken away terrified Ash. But he couldn't deny what was happening anymore.

He'd found his mate and needed to take care of him.

Asʜ sʜᴏᴠᴇᴅ the bodies behind a dumpster and cast an illusion over them, rendering them invisible. Fuck, he loved that specific demon trick. He'd deal with them later.

He flew an unconscious Harper back to his apartment and landed on the roof.

Ash lingered, a breeze ruffling his feathers as he cradled his flower. How would he explain being mates to Harper? He would have to reveal himself as a demon, but first, he needed to figure out how much Harper knew about the magic world.

Except, Harper hated Ash, and rightly so. Ash needed to clear that hurdle before revealing all or Harper might not want to hear it. He had to get this right.

Finding his fated mate didn't mean everything would work out smoothly. Lucifer was coming, and who knew what the Eternal Realm might do if they discovered one of the Fallen had finally found their mate. There were still so many unknowns. So many ways for this to go wrong.

Harper would choose Ash, wouldn't he? He'd want to cement their bond once he realized what it was, right? The possibility that he wouldn't made Ash feel small, like a breeze might blow him away as if he'd never been there at all.

But he was getting ahead of himself.

He carried Harper down the stairs to his apartment and shifted Harper in his arms so he could reach the doorknob. Human locks weren't a problem for demon magic.

Ash grabbed the knob and frowned. A protective spell had been cast on the lock and—a further inspection revealed—the whole dwelling.

The protection was strong, buzzing intrusively against Ash's senses. He examined it until he found a way to unweave it and let himself into the apartment.

He closed the door.

Harper must have had someone cast the protection for him, but Ash was surprised by how impressive the spell was. Most witches weren't that strong. He'd broken through it easily, but he was a demon. It would have taken a witch much longer...if they could have gotten through at all.

Interesting.

Ash didn't sense anyone else in the apartment, and he'd watched the building enough to be confident Harper's roommate was away at this time of day. He carried Harper down the hallway and through the living room to the bedroom facing the street.

He lay Harper on his bed and pulled a blanket over him.

The room was sparse, with no decoration or personal touches. Something Ash hadn't noticed when peering in from across the street. The lack of a homey feeling was unsettling. His flower deserved better than this. Why did Harper seem to have almost no possessions?

Ash set Harper's shoulder bag on the floor. He itched to snoop through it and the few things in the room but resisted. Harper wouldn't appreciate that, and Ash didn't need to dig himself a deeper hole.

With nowhere to sit other than the bed, Ash leaned against the wall and watched over Harper. He untied the T-shirt attached to his belt and pulled it over his head. No need to alarm Harper when he woke up by showing too much skin.

Eventually, Harper stirred, shifting in the sheets and making a soft little sound. He blinked awake and gasped, sitting bolt upright, and looked around in confusion.

His terrified gaze landed on Ash. "What's happening?"

Harper's eyes darted around the room again like he was trying to piece together what he'd missed.

"You're safe, Harper. You're home." Ash pushed off the wall but didn't get too close.

"What?" Harper stared at Ash, his eyes going wide. "Wait... You—you had fangs."

16

———

HARPER

ASH FROZE. "WHAT?"

"You had fangs." Harper pointed at Ash, his hand shaking. He'd seen it. He was sure. A brief flash, looking up at Ash with long, sharp canines.

Harper latched on to the absurd memory even though Ash couldn't be a vampire. Harper had never sensed any magic in him. But it was better than thinking about what happened before Ash turned up out of nowhere.

Where did Finch and the other man go?

"Are you working with them?" Harper's voice shook, his head throbbed, and nausea clawed at his insides.

What happened? Where had Ash come from?

"No, Harper. I'm not working with them." Ash stepped closer to the bed, reaching out a hand. "You're okay."

A sob tore from Harper's throat. He wasn't okay. Was Finch coming back? What was he planning to do?

"Harper," Ash said, softer this time. He sat on the edge of the bed and placed a hand on Harper's back.

Harper stiffened at the touch, and Ash immediately withdrew. Tears slid down Harper's cheeks. He wasn't safe anymore and didn't know what to do.

"Do you remember what happened?" Ash asked.

Harper tried to focus on Ash through his tears. Could he trust him?

"You were attacked," Ash went on when Harper didn't speak. "I was nearby and saw someone grab you."

"You were nearby?" Harper choked back his sobs in order to get the words out. "I—I didn't see you."

"No, but I was there. Right place at the right time. I'm not working with them."

"I don't believe you," Harper whispered. It was all too convenient.

Ash looked pained by Harper's distrust. He scrubbed a hand over his face. "Let me explain. First, you're right, Harper, you saw my fangs. I'm not human." Ash bared his teeth and let his fangs descend before retracting them. "I saw what happened, stopped those witches from attacking you, and brought you home. That's all there is to it."

Was that really how it had gone? Harper almost asked why he couldn't sense Ash's magic but stopped himself just in time. He didn't want to give away that he was a witch. His disguise should still be intact. A vampire wouldn't be able to see past the suppressing potion, so Ash would only know Harper was a witch if he was working with his coven.

"The witches attacking me just let you take me away?" Harper doubted it was that simple. Finch could have easily taken on a vampire with backup. Ash was huge and no doubt inhumanly strong, but witches had a wider range of magical abilities than vampires, and his father's advisers were formidable.

"No, they didn't let me take you away." Ash grimaced. "I killed them."

Harper's shaking hands stilled and all the air whooshed out of his lungs. It was the last thing he'd expected Ash to say. "R-really?"

"Yes." Ash held Harper's gaze, not faltering or sounding sorry about his actions. "They hurt you," he growled as if that were explanation enough for taking a life or two.

Harper's mouth fell open, but he shut it quickly.

Ash didn't break eye contact. There was something comforting in his hard stare that Harper didn't understand.

Satandamn him, Ash had killed two men, and Harper felt nothing but relief.

Harper had been so certain that the worst thing in his horrible life was about to happen, and Ash had come in out of nowhere and saved him. That sort of thing didn't happen in real life, but Harper believed Ash was telling the truth. He'd always felt safe with Ash. Inexplicably, sure, but now Ash had killed to protect him, and the feeling didn't seem so misplaced.

"You're safe, Harper. They aren't coming after you again," Ash said, tone firm but gentle. It was exactly what Harper wanted to hear.

Tears flooded Harper's eyes and he buried his head in his hands. It was too much. Someone's death shouldn't make him feel better. He shouldn't trust Ash or believe him, but he did.

"I'm sorry, Harper. Are you...? Did I do the wrong thing?"

Harper couldn't look at Ash, no matter how concerned he sounded. He shook his head. "No. They were bad people. They hurt..." He shook his head again. He wasn't getting into that now. "It's good they're gone. I can't believe you're a vampire and you killed them. Why would you do something like that when you don't even care about me?"

Maybe he should feel bad about his lack of remorse, but the world was better off, and Harper was glad he'd never have to be afraid of Finch again.

"I do care about you, Harper," Ash said so delicately that Harper looked up.

He frowned. "No, you don't. You literally ran away from me. You left me humiliated."

Ash's brow furrowed and his mouth pinched. It looked almost painful, like he was vastly more regretful for upsetting Harper than killing his attackers. "I can explain."

"Can you?" Harper sat up straighter, pushing the last of his tears away. "Then why didn't you explain in the coffee shop when I asked you to?"

"I wasn't..." Ash faltered, then pushed on. "I wasn't ready to reveal myself. I, um, didn't realize you know about magic. But you obviously do since witches attacked you..."

"What does magic have to do with it?"

Ash looked down at his hands, then like he'd decided something, he fixed his full attention on Harper. "That night after the club, I was overcome with the urge to bite you. Sharing orgasms with you in my arms overwhelmed me, and I almost... I couldn't control it. I ran before you saw what I was."

Harper opened his mouth, but no sound came out.

That actually made a lot of sense.

Now that Harper reconsidered, Ash had been fixated on his neck as they'd come, and he'd noticed Ash getting more and more keyed up. Ash must be a relatively new vampire if he didn't have control over his urges.

"So you didn't want to leave?" Harper was unable to quell the hopeful note in his voice.

"No." Ash reached for Harper's hand, and he let Ash take it. "I regret running away like that, but I had to make sure I didn't bite you, and by the time I calmed down, there was no way to explain without revealing myself... You're human, but you saw my fangs, so there's no reason to pretend anymore. I don't want to pretend anymore."

He didn't want to pretend anymore? What did he want?

Harper understood why a vampire wouldn't reveal himself just to clear up a one-night stand. Had something changed since then or was it really just that Harper had seen Ash's fangs?

Harper's gaze fell to their joined hands. "You wanted my blood that night." He wasn't sure how he felt about that. "Was that the only reason you ran? It wasn't because you were done with me and didn't care?"

"No." Ash squeezed Harper's hand. "I care, and I'm so sorry I hurt you. I hate that I hurt you. I couldn't risk giving myself away, but now I wish I had."

Ash cared.

Harper's heart rate picked up. "Do you want to bite me now?" He ached to lean closer and feel Ash against him, but the idea of anyone coveting his blood made him sick. He'd been tortured for his blood all his life. He couldn't stand it if that was all Ash wanted from him.

"I don't want to bite you, Harper," Ash assured him. "I was so attracted to you that I lost control that night, but it won't happen again. I'm under control. Your blood isn't why I'm here."

"Okay." Harper gave in and leaned against Ash, satisfied he wasn't in danger of being bitten. Ash draped an arm around Harper, giving him the secure feeling his touch always seemed to bring. "Thank you," Harper whispered. "For explaining and for helping me today."

Ash hauled him closer, nuzzling the top of Harper's head. "I only wish I'd explained myself sooner."

Harper did too, but he understood why Ash hadn't.

He snuggled into Ash's warm body, inhaling his spiced cologne. It shouldn't feel this good to be in his arms, but knowing what actually happened between them gave Harper hope.

Their hookup wasn't just another bad memory, tainted and confusing. Ash hadn't discarded him, and he wanted to bask in that and feel good, especially when he'd been doomed such a short time ago.

Ash wasn't working with his coven. Ash had saved him and couldn't have an ulterior motive if he was ignorant of Harper's connection to the magic world.

Maybe it was naïve to take Ash at his word, but Harper wasn't trusting Ash with everything. He wasn't admitting he had power in his blood, which might be what Ash craved. Ash thought he was human and that made Harper feel safer than anything.

Though Ash's touch helped too.

Harper slipped an arm around Ash, the scent of spiced smoke filling his nostrils. It was as if Harper had been aching for this hug his whole life. Ash was solid against him, and Harper didn't want to let go.

Ash laid them on the bed, keeping Harper tucked into his side. "You should rest. They drugged you with a sedative potion. It might not be completely out of your system."

Harper remembered being smothered by a chemical smell. The toxin was likely out of his system since he was a witch and the magic in his blood healed him faster than a human. Not as fast as a vampire, who wouldn't have been knocked out by a potion-soaked rag, but even Harper's headache was fading.

He settled into Ash anyway, soaking up his warmth. Harper could almost believe there was nothing complicated about the two of them together. He wanted this, at least for a little while.

HARPER GASPED AND CHOKED. A horrible chemical smell

surrounded him as Finch's face loomed over him. He thrashed as his world closed in.

Strong arms wrapped around him. "Harper, you're okay."

He yelped and opened his eyes. Hadn't they been open before? They mustn't have been. He was in bed. In his room. Ash was holding him.

It was just a dream.

Harper was sticky with sweat. He forced his tense muscles to relax, but the chest-tightening fear from his dream wouldn't go away. He hadn't felt like this in so long. He'd moved past what had happened with Finch. He didn't want it to fuck him up all over again. It wasn't fair.

Ash loosened his hold on Harper. "Can I get you anything?" His words came in warm puffs, hitting Harper's ear.

"Water," Harper croaked, throat scratchy. As comforting as Ash was, Harper was relieved when he got up and left the room.

How had he fallen asleep? Was he really that relaxed with Ash, or was he emotionally exhausted? He couldn't have been out long, but he needed to get Ash out before Ollie came home.

Ash reappeared with a glass of water and handed it to Harper. He leaned against the wall rather than returning to the bed. At least Harper didn't have to spell out his need for space.

"Why were those witches after you?" Ash asked.

Harper took a sip of water. What kind of lie would work here? He wasn't telling Ash the truth.

Ash's brow furrowed. "I don't mean to pry. I'm only trying to help you, Harper. If you're in trouble, I can protect you."

Damn, the offer was tempting. Harper wished he could turn to Ash, but that would be beyond reckless.

"I don't really know you," Harper reminded him.

Ash frowned like he'd forgotten that mattered. "You can get to know me. I'd like to get to know you." He flashed a small way-too-handsome smile.

Yes. Harper wanted to say yes. He could hook up with Ash again, date him, and see where they went. But Ash wasn't human, and that made everything so complicated.

No one in the magic community could know who Harper really was. Ash saving him didn't make him an exception to that rule, and Harper still couldn't detect any magic in Ash, which was suspicious. He had to be wary of his feelings and not get caught up in attraction.

He had to be careful.

Ash must be suppressing his magic like Harper, but why? There was no way to ask without giving himself away.

Harper set his empty glass aside. He couldn't trust Ash, but that didn't mean he had to push him away completely. The safe feeling Ash gave him had to mean something, and Harper didn't want to ignore it. He just had to be smart and not let it override his better judgment.

He fiddled with the bedspread. "We can get to know each other."

Maybe Ash would explain what was happening with his magic without Harper needing to ask. Maybe Harper was being paranoid and Ash wasn't hiding anything big.

"Perfect, I'm glad you agree." That handsome smile was back, melting Harper's heart.

Damnation. Why couldn't he throw caution to the wind, tell Ash all his secrets, and let Ash take some of the weight off his shoulders? The thought of Ash caring for him, protecting him, created a hollowness in his chest. He ached for it.

But longing for a man he didn't know was silly. None of these feelings should be this strong. Maybe he was just tired of facing everything alone.

Ash's smile disappeared into a serious line. "Even if you don't want to explain what happened with the witches today, will you tell me if you're safe now that they're gone?"

Harper chewed his lip. How much could he say without putting himself at risk?

17

—

ASH

"They aren't the only ones looking for me," Harper said at last.

Ash clenched his jaw. "I see."

The problem was worse than he thought.

If only Harper would explain, but he clearly had trust issues. Could Ash really blame him? It wasn't as if Ash was being honest. He could have revealed his true nature and laid all his cards on the table rather than let Harper think he was a vampire. But he wasn't ready.

At least they'd cleared up what happened the night of their hookup. He'd been able to tell Harper the most essential truth, and now Harper didn't seem to hate him.

He should earn Harper's trust before revealing the whole demon's mate thing anyway. And Ash really couldn't expose himself without talking to Dante and Onyx. Even if Harper was his mate, Ash needed to be sure Harper would keep his demon nature to himself. Harper needed to trust Ash and understand why being a demon was a secret to be kept at all costs, especially now that Lucifer was in the Human Realm.

Ash would have to protect Harper from Luc as well as whatever witches Harper was in trouble with. Shit, this was a mess. The worst timing to find his mate.

Harper could be ripped away from him before they had a chance to bond. Ash's muscles seized and his fire flared hot. He absently rubbed at the center of his chest.

He had to concentrate. Keep Harper safe. Win him over. Find Lucifer. Deal with him. Break the mate-news to Dante and Onyx. Simple. Except he was almost dreading that last one more than dealing with Luc.

Harper eyed Ash wearily, clutching the bedspread.

"I'm not going to interrogate you," Ash said. Harper visibly relaxed. "Let me give you my number. You can call me if you need help. Anytime. No questions asked."

Harper blinked at him, his glasses giving him an owlish appearance. "Thank you," he whispered.

"I'm happy to help." Ash let his growing affection for the young man break through his usually hard facial expression.

He pulled out his phone and they exchanged details.

Ash wanted to offer more. He planned to watch over Harper as much as possible, and as soon as he left, he would protect the whole building with his strongest shield.

Not that he could tell Harper this.

Harper wouldn't want Ash spending all his time hovering around—that behavior only made sense in the context of mates —and vampires didn't have the ability to cast protective spells. Almost all of a vampire's magic was caught up in maintaining their immortality, with the exception of the hypnosis-like illusions they could cast on anyone they made eye contact with.

Ash had to assume Harper was up to speed on the realities of vampires and not give himself away until he was ready to tell Harper the whole truth. Having a fated mate was a lot for a human to get their head around, even one aware of the magic world.

Harper might not know demons were real, given so few were in the Human Realm. Just because a human was aware of magic didn't mean they were familiar with magical history and demons having given birth to the original witches. Knowledge of the existence of mates was even rarer.

Ash needed time for all the pieces to fall into place. There was a lot to unpack and rushing wouldn't serve him.

He wanted to ask Harper out on a date and make it clear he was serious about getting to know him, but now wasn't the time. Harper had been through a lot and still seemed shaken.

"Would you like me to stick around?" Ash couldn't help asking, even though he suspected Harper needed space. He didn't want to go. It was much nicer watching over Harper from in here, where they could talk, than outside.

Harper averted his eyes. "No, I'm okay, and it's probably best if you aren't here when Ollie gets home."

"Who's Ollie?"

"My roommate. He was at the club with me that night..." Harper's cheeks bloomed with color. "Anyway. He doesn't know about magic at all."

"Right." That was good to know. "I'll leave you to it, but if you need anything, please call."

Harper's pink cheeks flushed a darker red. "Thanks."

Ash let himself out, locking Harper's front door behind him. There was no one in the hall, so he took a moment to reconstruct the protections he'd broken to get inside, only repairing what was there before rather than enhancing the spells, just in case any of Harper's enemies inspected the dwelling.

That done, Ash headed up to the roof. The place was starting to look a little too familiar.

He rendered himself invisible and got to work protecting the building with everything his demon magic had to offer, then he masked all his spells in a web of illusion. He couldn't have his extra protection giving his presence away, and the spells he cast were much stronger than anything a witch could produce.

This way, any witch walking by would think the building was normal and completely exposed, similar to what Dante had done to his house in Old Town and his new one on the hill.

Dante.

Ash wasn't looking forward to talking to him. What would giving Dante more hope do? Just because Ash found his mate didn't mean Dante would. Ash hated that he'd found what Dante had never stopped believing in. Ash didn't deserve it compared to his brother.

Fate was cruel that way.

Though he didn't want to leave Harper, Ash stripped his shirt off, leaped from the roof, and spread his wings. He soared high over the city, heading to Dante's house.

Harper would be fine on his own for a few hours. Ash doubted he'd be going out again today. He didn't seem to leave his apartment much as a rule.

Ash growled and beat his wings faster. He hated that Harper was in serious trouble and uncomfortable leaving home, but Ash couldn't fix it if he didn't know what was happening.

At least Harper would be safe in the apartment. Ash would get back to him as soon as possible, but he needed to check in with Dante and Onyx. The lack of any sign of Lucifer was more worrying by the day.

"Anything?" Dante asked as Ash flew in through the wide open doorway, landing in the living room. He obviously assumed Ash had been out trying to get a read on Lucifer's location.

Ash didn't correct him. He shook out his wings. "No, nothing."

"Are you *sure* Luc left the Realm of the Damned?" Onyx called from where he lay on one of the large sofas.

"Yes." Ash bristled. "I know what the confinement magic feels like. No demon has breached it since we left."

"Hm." Onyx's tone made his doubts clear.

"I don't think you were mistaken." Dante got up from his armchair and paced in front of the open doorway. "I noticed something strange with my flock this morning."

Ash narrowed his eyes. "Strange how?"

Dante stopped pacing. "Several birds died."

"Died?" There had to be more to it than that.

"Yes, but I'm not sure how." Dante frowned. "I couldn't see anything in the collective memory, but it was too many at once for the deaths to be natural."

Onyx twisted to his side, propping up his head with a hand. "You think it was Luc?"

Dante rubbed his eyes. "Possibly, but I don't see how Luc could have killed them without the others recognizing his magic and telling me."

A few dead birds wasn't exactly a shocking development. If it were Luc, why not kill the whole flock and take out one of their advantages?

"If he were here picking off birds, I'd sense him," Ash insisted.

"Maybe he just doesn't care about us." Onyx glared at the fingernails on his other hand. "He could have left the Realm for some other reason. Maybe the birds ate poison or something."

"I doubt Luc's gotten over our escape and decided to forgive us and leave us be," Dante snapped, losing his patience with Onyx.

What had they been discussing before Ash arrived? Dante didn't usually get short with Onyx.

"Well, I'm going out." Onyx got up from the couch and straightened his clothes. "You two are boring, and talking about birds isn't getting us anywhere."

Neither Ash nor Dante gave him the satisfaction of responding. Onyx walked out without another word.

Dante returned to his armchair. "It could be nothing, but my gut is telling me those birds didn't die naturally or by any human poison."

"You searched the area where they died?"

"Yes. There was no trace of magic."

Ash glanced out the window. "Where were they?"

"Near the waterfront, on the rocks out at the point."

That wasn't far from their nests on the cliff near Dante's house. There was no way Luc could have been that close without Ash sensing his magic, even as distracted by Harper as he'd been. Besides, Dante or Onyx would have detected him that close.

Ash settled on the vacant couch. "We've chosen to sit and wait. So that's what we'll have to do. Maybe Luc is biding his time, trying to lull us into a false sense of security, hoping we'll get careless the longer he stays away."

"Maybe." Dante scratched one of his horns. His were taller than Ash's, curving up and out rather than back along his head. "I'd still rather take a stand here than run and hide. At least this way, we'll only be looking over our shoulders for so long."

Ash agreed, even if he wouldn't have a week ago. He'd rather deal with Lucifer and put this firmly behind them. Now that he had his mate to consider, running from Luc was too unpredictable and carried too much risk.

Ash hoped they could wrap up this conflict with Lucifer for good, then he could claim his mate and focus on giving him the life he deserved.

"Why are you so sure your mate will be in Shearwater Landing?"

Dante quirked a brow in surprise. "It's just a feeling. I'm certain this is the place. I can't explain it beyond that. Why?"

"Just curious." Ash tried to ignore the twist in his gut.

He couldn't bring himself to tell Dante he'd found his mate. What if Dante's sure feeling had been about Harper and not Dante's mate?

"You aren't going to tell me I'm being delusional?" Dante gave Ash a playful smile.

Ash's chest tightened and he cleared his throat, trying to dislodge the discomfort. He shouldn't have given Dante such a hard time for hoping all these years. "No, I'm not. Who knows how fate works. We can't ignore our gut feelings."

"No, we can't." Dante frowned. "And I think the dead birds are a bad sign."

18

———

HARPER

HARPER STARED AT HIS PHONE, still in bed, curled under his blankets. He hadn't slept well. He'd lain awake most of the night and had nightmares when he'd finally fallen asleep.

Was it weird that Ash texted? It was sweet but a bit much, right? The kind of thing a boyfriend would send, not a guy he barely knew.

Harper smiled anyway.

He might not know Ash, but there was something between them, something that went deeper than a hookup or merely looking for a repeat. Harper still couldn't believe Ash had saved him. Not that he doubted Ash's story. He just felt strangely lucky.

He replied:

Harper was drawn to Ash like he never had been to anyone

else. He wanted to see him again, be in his arms, and feel that warm, content feeling. In comparison, Harper was cold in his bed and more aware of his loneliness than he'd been in a while.

Everything in his new life was falling apart. He hadn't gotten any more stone and didn't think he could bring himself to try again. He didn't even want to leave the apartment to go to The Herb Emporium.

Just getting out of bed seemed like too much. What was the point? The apartment was empty, and getting up would mean he had to do things, figure out how to fix this mess.

He wished Ash were here.

Which was silly. He couldn't lean on Ash. He couldn't lean on anyone. He was stronger than this and needed to pull himself together.

Harper tugged the blanket over his head and pressed his face into his pillow.

His phone buzzed and his heart skipped.

Was this overattachment because Ash was Harper's first crush in a long time or because Ash was the first man to touch him with any real affection?

The vampire side of Ash had to be subconsciously drawn to the magic in Harper's blood, whether Ash realized it or not, so Harper couldn't even be sure all that affection was really for him.

He still smiled at the new message, doubts fading away.

ASH:

Got any exciting breakfast plans?

Was Ash going to ask him to breakfast? A zing tingled down Harper's spine.

HARPER:

No, I haven't even gotten out of bed yet.

ASH:

> I hope I didn't wake you.

HARPER:

> You didn't. I'm just being lazy.

ASH:

> Nothing wrong with that. Especially if you didn't sleep well.

Harper paused. How did Ash know? Had Ash guessed when he'd ignored that part of Ash's initial message?

ASH:

> What's your favorite breakfast food?

HARPER:

> Pancakes.

> What's yours?

Did Ash eat breakfast? Vampires didn't need human food.

ASH:

> Scrambled eggs. I had some this morning.

He wouldn't ask Harper to breakfast if he'd eaten. Which was okay. Ash's messages chased away the remnants of Harper's nightmares, filling his chest with butterflies instead of dread.

OTHER THAN TEXTING Ash about random little events and answering all of Ash's questions about his favorite things, Harper's day didn't improve.

The prospect of leaving his apartment made his stomach cramp. He didn't do anything except shower and have some toast all day. If he hadn't had Ash to talk to, he might not have gotten out of bed.

What should his next move be? Going back to The Herb Emporium, where Nico surely knew something was up, was a risk Harper didn't want to take after yesterday.

It wasn't likely anyone followed him and Ash home without the vampire realizing, but Harper's coven was closer than ever, and he couldn't be certain a third witch hadn't been lurking near the port, waiting to see what happened.

It might not be safe to go out.

At the same time, Harper couldn't stop selling potions to Nico altogether. If he did, he'd run out of money and, much sooner than later, be unable to pay rent.

The uncertainty paralyzed him. He should have been able to come up with a new plan, but fear settled in his bones, and he couldn't shake it off, no matter how much Ash asked about pancake toppings or how Harper liked to take his coffee.

Ash had said he wanted to help, but Harper couldn't make himself ask. It went against everything he had in place to keep himself safe.

The next few days were no better. Harper was unable to do anything except sit around and worry. But Ash texted every morning. He really seemed to want to get to know Harper.

Harper's phone buzzed on his nightstand and he snatched it before it had even stopped.

ASH:

Can I take you out for coffee?

Harper clutched the phone. He should say yes. It sounded like a date, and even as horrible as he'd felt all week, his feelings for Ash hadn't dimmed.

He had to be sure. Who cared if it wasn't cool to ask or if he should automatically know whether Ash was being casual or asking him out. He couldn't handle mixed signals.

Harper chewed his lip. Going out for coffee was a stupid risk. What if his coven was searching the neighborhoods closest to the port after two of their men disappeared? There was always the possibility that someone had followed him and Ash home, even if it was unlikely for a vampire—with enhanced senses—to miss a tail.

He might feel safe enough to leave if he wasn't alone. They could walk to Seaside Coffee together.

Harper should be stronger than this and face things on his own. He was powerful and smart. He wasn't weak. Finch was gone and couldn't hurt him again. But it wasn't weak to need people. He just didn't have any people he could turn to. He'd always managed by himself.

But that had never been a choice. Maybe Ash could be his person.

ASH:

> Sure thing, sweet. I'll be there in an hour if that
> works for you?

Harper's cheeks heated as memories of Ash calling him sweet the night after the club filled his mind.

HARPER:

> Perfect. See you soon.

AN HOUR LATER—ALMOST exactly—Ash buzzed to be let into Harper's building.

Harper buzzed Ash in and hurried to grab his keys and phone. He ran a hand through his hair.

A knock sounded on his door, and he jumped. Great, he was skittish before getting a foot out the door. Harper checked the peephole, confirmed it was Ash, and opened the door.

"Hi." Had that sounded breathy? Desperate? If only Harper could relax.

Ash's lips curved in the most radiant smile, wrinkles appearing at the corners of his eyes. "Hey, sweet thing. Good to see you."

Butterflies exploded in Harper's chest.

Ash held up a paper bag in one hand and a coffee carrier with two cups in the other. "I've got treats."

"Oh." Harper stepped back from the door, allowing Ash to enter. "I thought you wanted to go out."

Ash shrugged. "I wanted to see you. We can have coffee here if you'd rather stay in."

Harper closed the front door, his shoulders sagging. This

was better than going out. He wouldn't be distracted scanning for witches or worried something bad might happen. He could focus on Ash.

"How'd you know I'd rather stay in?" He'd only said to meet at the apartment, not that he didn't want to leave.

Ash bumped his shoulder against Harper's. "You've had a rough week, Harper. I understand wanting to stick close to home."

He seemed to have a knack for picking up on things without Harper having to spell them out. He appreciated it, along with Ash's apparent lack of judgment.

Harper ducked his head and led Ash to the living room. What would Ash think if he knew he hadn't left the house in days? Would he still want to have coffee together? Hopefully.

Ash set the drinks and paper bag on the coffee table and sat, spreading his legs wide as he got comfortable.

"I'll get plates." Harper hurried to the kitchen, trying not to think about the last time he'd been on the couch with Ash. This was much more intimate than going out for coffee. Harper didn't even have his shoes on, just socks.

He brought plates and cutlery to the living room and sat down. Was he sitting too close? Not close enough? It felt silly to be bashful after Ash had seen him practically naked.

Ash handed him a coffee and opened the bag. He pulled out scones and pastries, then cut them all in half so they could share.

Harper glanced at the logo on his cup. "You went to Seaside Coffee?"

"Yeah." Ash nudged him playfully with his elbow. "I figured you must like it since I ran into you there."

Harper sipped his drink. Ash had remembered he liked hazelnut almond lattes, or maybe he'd looked back at their text conversation. "Thanks. This is perfect."

"You're most welcome." Ash sipped his coffee and shifted, half turning toward Harper and casually placing an arm along the back of the couch. "How are you doing?"

"Okay." Harper squirmed. Ash might not have judged him yet, but he wasn't admitting he'd hidden inside all week.

Ash nodded, a serious furrow appearing on his brow. "You haven't had any trouble since I last saw you?"

Wait. Was that why Ash was here? Harper didn't want this to be about his witch problems. At least he'd already asked and Ash had said this was a date. Maybe he was just showing concern, which was fine. More than fine. Harper wanted Ash to care so badly it made the coffee churn in his stomach.

"No problems. I haven't gone out much." Harper broke eye contact, inspecting his coffee lid.

"I didn't imagine you'd be rushing to go out," Ash said like he really did understand. "But we don't have to talk about that unless you want to. What pastries look good?"

Harper considered the food, more than relieved to move on. "All of them. But I think I want that berry one first." Icing clung to the pastry and the berry filling in the center. Harper hadn't had a treat like it in ages.

Ash handed him half, taking the other for himself. They each had a bite. "Good choice," Ash rumbled, his deep voice giving Harper chills.

The pastry was really good. Harper smiled as he ate, sinking back into the couch cushions. Ash's arm brushed his shoulders and he sighed, relaxing as if the small touch had relieved what was left of his tension.

Ash sipped his coffee and grabbed another pastry. "Have you lived in Shearwater Landing long?"

Harper licked some icing off his finger. "Not really. I've only just moved in with Ollie."

Ash nodded. "He's a close friend?"

"No. We only met when I signed the lease. But I hope he'll become a close friend. I like living with him. How about you? Have you lived here long?"

Ash frowned at his coffee. "No. I lived here a while ago but only just came back. My brother lives here. Well, my brothers, but the second one wasn't as happy to see me."

They chatted and ate their way through the treats. Just like in their text conversations, Harper found Ash easy to talk to.

The longer they were on the couch, the closer Harper shifted to Ash, drawn like a magnet. Ash responded to the shrinking distance, brushing his fingers along Harper's shoulder and bumping their knees together.

It was so different from their hookup. Soft and sweet, yet Harper's heart was still in his throat. Talking was just as good as kissing, and his confidence rose as he realized Ash must be enjoying this too.

Harper might not have been on other dates to compare, but Ash's interest was evident. He looked at Harper like he was trying to soak up every detail in front of him.

It made Harper want to kiss him. Not because Ash was hot or because Harper was horny, but to connect. It had been so good that night, and this was even better.

Ash brushed some sugar from Harper's lower lip, and the touch sparked. Harper held back a groan.

"Thank you for giving me another shot," Ash murmured.

Harper bit his lip, worrying the spot Ash had touched. "You certainly didn't waste it."

Ash chuckled. "Glad to hear you don't think so."

Harper shifted closer, and Ash leaned in. The arm he had on the back of the couch slid down, embracing Harper, and Harper angled his face, tilting his mouth up ever so slightly.

Ash closed the distance and brushed his lips gently against Harper's. Harper caught the spiced, smoky scent of Ash's cologne and sighed into the kiss, his body melting into Ash like it belonged there.

Ash rumbled against Harper's lips, almost purring, a sound so content that Harper shivered. It was as if Ash had been waiting for this and was relieved to finally kiss Harper again. Could Ash really feel that strongly?

Harper kissed Ash back. He wrapped his arms around Ash's neck and pressed closer. Damn, it felt good to be back in Ash's arms. Why couldn't everything feel this good? It was like nothing could touch him when they were together.

Ash kissed along Harper's jaw and tugged lightly on his earlobe.

Harper whimpered. "Want to go to my room?"

Ash pulled back, fixing a smoldering stare on Harper. "Sure."

Harper stood from the couch. He hesitated to take things too far in the living room, even though Ollie wouldn't return for hours. He wasn't nervous like when he'd first taken Ash home, but there was something delicate about this time. Whatever it was, Harper wanted it to happen behind closed doors, where he felt safest.

Ash followed him into his room, toed off his shoes, and shut the door. Harper hovered near his bed, but he was saved from having to decide what to do next as Ash pulled him close.

He pressed his lips to Harper's ear. "What do you want, sweet? Would you like to call the shots? Tell me how you want me, and you can have it."

Harper's breath hitched. Ash lingered, kissing his ear. "I'm not sure what I want." The honest words slipped out before Harper could stop them.

Ash pulled back, cupping Harper's cheek. "We don't have to do anything like we did the other night. That's not why I came over."

Harper appreciated the lack of pressure. It made it easier to open up. "I want to. I just don't really know what I like." His cheeks burned. He wanted Ash to see him, to know him, even if it was kind of embarrassing. "I don't have a lot of experience. This is my first real date."

Ash's thumb stroked Harper's cheek. "I'm honored to be your first real date, flower."

Fuck, Ash was intense. Harper loved it. Most guys would never say anything like that, but it wasn't cheesy or fake when Ash did. It seemed genuine and made Harper feel safe being himself. "Maybe I can find out what I like with you?"

Ash hummed. "I'd love nothing more. We can take our time exploring anything you want."

Yes, that sounded perfect.

Harper pulled Ash onto the bed. He laid back and Ash settled beside him, propped on his side. He placed a hand on Harper's stomach.

Ash ran his hand up to Harper's pecs, brushing his nipples lightly through his T-shirt. "You liked it when I touched you here last time, right?" Harper nodded, and Ash pinched one of his nipples, making him gasp. Ash grinned. "May I explore the rest of you?"

"Okay," Harper breathed.

Ash's hand trailed back down his body. "Is there anywhere you don't like being touched?"

"I don't think so." Harper squirmed as Ash's hand neared his groin. "No one's ever touched me like this." His gaze shot to Ash's face. Was that too much to admit?

Ash seemed thoughtful. "Your past lovers didn't touch you?"

Harper bit his lip. "I've only had one. It wasn't like this."

"I love touching you, watching your reactions, and seeing

what brings you pleasure. Nothing feels as good as your body against mine." Ash hauled Harper against him in a tight hug.

Harper's heart swelled almost painfully. "It feels so good when you hold me," he whispered.

Ash nuzzled Harper's neck as he stroked his back. "I'll hold you whenever you like. If you ever need a hug, call me. I'll be there." He kissed Harper's cheek.

"You'd really do that?" Harper gripped Ash's broad shoulders. "Not even to get off or anything? You'd come to see me just to hug me?"

"Yes," Ash murmured in his ear.

Harper's throat constricted. He wanted someone to be there for him whenever he needed. To hug and comfort him and listen to his ramblings. He wanted it more than sex. And Ash wanted that too? With him?

Ash squeezed Harper tighter. "I loved your mouth around my cock, Harper, but that's not all I'm after. I want you any and every way you'll have me."

Harper had never felt so loved. It was ridiculous and way too soon to feel that way. He didn't even know if he could deal with a boyfriend—let alone love—with all his secrets. He still hardly knew Ash.

Maybe it would be better if they stopped talking, no matter how much Harper liked hearing all these things. "Kiss me," he begged, his hands on either side of Ash's face.

Ash flattened Harper onto the mattress and kissed him, working Harper's mouth open. Harper's heart thudded and his cock ached. He pulled Ash on top of him and gasped as Ash's weight pressed into him.

Harper was secure and protected. Nothing could touch him. It was silly how fiercely he believed it.

Harper hauled Ash's T-shirt over his head. He wanted to be closer, to feel Ash's warmth against his skin.

Ash sat back and pulled Harper's shirt off, and Harper went for the button on Ash's jeans. Ash stripped them off, along with his underwear, and knelt naked, looming over Harper. He had a tattoo of what looked like a rope wrapped around his hips. How strange.

"Mine too," Harper requested, hands trembling on his jeans button.

Ash helped him, pulling off Harper's pants and socks. Ash reached for the waistband of Harper's boxer briefs. "You're so pretty." He pealed the underwear away and drank in Harper's naked body.

"Now hold me?" Harper reached for Ash, not caring how needy he sounded. "Please?"

Ash wrapped himself around Harper, holding him close.

Harper spread his legs so Ash could settle between them, and their cocks rubbed together, nothing but skin on skin everywhere.

Ash covered Harper's mouth with his and kissed him deeply, his tongue exploring slowly like he was savoring it. He didn't roll his hips or make any move to seek out friction on his very hard cock. Ash seemed solely focused on kissing and holding Harper, and Harper liked it so much his head spun.

The kiss went on and on, Harper's need building. Ash kissed him like he'd never get tired of it.

Harper rolled his hips. He loved the sweetness of doing nothing but kissing and the acknowledgment that they didn't need to get off just because they were naked together, but he wanted it all. Harper couldn't resist rubbing against Ash, a moan catching in his throat.

"Please, Ash."

Ash ground their hips together. "Is this what you need?"

"Yes." Harper moved with him, their thrusts meeting until they found a rhythm.

"You feel so good," Ash said against Harper's lips.

Harper whined, and Ash thrust into him, his breaths coming faster. Ash pressed his forehead against Harper's, their noses rubbing. Harper got lost in it.

He wanted more and fisted his hands in Ash's hair, arching his back as Ash ground him into the mattress. "Ash, please."

Ash gasped, his rhythm faltering. He gazed down at Harper, his eyes flickering with a golden glow as he let out a chest-vibrating moan. The hot wetness of Ash's release flooded Harper's stomach, smearing all over his cock and belly as they rolled their hips.

Damnation, Ash had come just from Harper writhing and moaning beneath him. Harper rode out Ash's orgasm, rubbing against him with everything he had, ringing all the pleasure he could from Ash.

Eventually, Ash stilled and rested his head on Harper's chest. "Fuck, Harper, sweetheart, you make me lose my mind." He sat back on his knees and surveyed Harper with a hungry look.

Harper glanced down at the mess smeared across his skin. Ash had marked him. Harper's whole body flashed hot.

"I want to get on my knees for you."

Harper's gaze shot back to Ash. "Yeah?"

Ash licked his lips, his expression ravenous. "Oh, yes. Will you let me suck your cock?"

Harper nodded. Not like it was a hard decision.

Ash grabbed a T-shirt and wiped Harper clean, then pulled him to the edge of the bed. Ash sunk to the floor, kneeling between Harper's spread legs.

Harper caught sight of the edge of a tattoo on each of Ash's shoulders, like he had something inked on his back.

Ash placed his hands on Harper's inner thighs and spread his legs wide. Harper's cock bobbed between them. Ash seemed to be drinking the sight in, making circles with his thumbs on Harper's sensitive flesh.

Ash bent and kissed Harper's inner thigh. "Has anyone ever done this for you?"

Harper's legs trembled. "No."

Ash kissed him again, swiping his tongue along Harper's skin. His fingers flexed, holding Harper tight. "I'll take care of you, sweet. Make you feel so good."

Harper bit back a strangled sound.

Ash moved his mouth to Harper's other thigh, kissing and licking, his hands kneading Harper's muscles. Harper placed a tentative hand on Ash's head, letting Ash's hair run between his fingers. He could see Ash's tattoo better now that he was bent farther forward. It was a design of intricate feathers, like folded wings.

Harper trembled as Ash kissed up his inner thigh, getting closer to his cock. He took his time, and Harper would have been impatient, except it was so clear Ash was enjoying this, almost worshipful in the way he caressed Harper, that Harper couldn't possibly rush him.

Ash hummed as his face came to the crease between Harper's thigh and groin. He licked and buried his nose in Harper's skin, smelling him.

Harper's breathing shallowed, his cheeks impossibly hot. His hips twitched. Ash groaned and turned his attention to Harper's balls, licking and sucking them as a hand finally wrapped around Harper's cock.

Ash gave him a few strokes before running his tongue up and down his shaft. Harper whimpered, trembling all over, his hand tightening in Ash's hair.

"You taste so good," Ash murmured against his cock. "I can smell myself on you."

"Fuck," Harper hissed and almost went over the edge. "Ash…"

"I've got you, sweet." Ash's gaze found Harper's as he wrapped his lips around Harper's cock.

"Oh…fuck." Harper's head dropped back as Ash's hot, wet mouth encased him.

Ash took him down, sucking and teasing Harper with his tongue, and Harper's whole world narrowed to Ash's mouth.

So good.

He watched Ash take him, lips stretched, gazing up at Harper like he was unable to tear his eyes away. Harper panted, letting out little whimpers as his pleasure built. Ash groaned around him, making that almost purring sound.

"Ash," Harper gasped. He was close. He wanted it to last longer but couldn't hold back.

Ash took him deep, humming again, and Harper came, his eyes falling shut as he clung to Ash's hair. Harper's hips twitched and his muscles clenched. He shook and cried out as his release filled Ash's mouth. Ash swallowed, working him through each aftershock before pulling off his spent cock, a satisfied smile tugging on his full, spit-slick lips.

In one fluid motion, Ash stood and picked Harper up, lying him back on the bed. Ash wrapped his arms around Harper and held him close.

It felt even better than the blowjob.

19

ASH

Ash ran his fingers through Harper's hair as he slept, head resting on Ash's chest. Ash's fire simmered low and content. At least he'd given his mate one of the things he needed.

After watching Harper's apartment over the past several days, Ash was almost certain Harper hadn't left the building since the attack. He'd hoped coffee would help him feel comfortable getting out. Perhaps they could work up to it if Harper accepted his help.

Would Harper ever open up?

It was hard to be patient with Harper in his arms. The mate connection tugged at Ash's heart, growing stronger, urging him to soothe and protect.

Harper stirred, shifting and nuzzling into Ash. "Oh no," he groaned. "I fell asleep."

Ash stroked Harper's hair. He was adorable. "Don't worry, sweet. Nap all day if you want."

Harper propped himself on Ash's chest and pouted. "I don't want to nap all day."

Ash quirked a brow. "No?"

Harper shook his head. He adjusted his glasses.

Ash trailed his fingers down Harper's spine. "What would you like to do?"

Harper flashed an evil grin and climbed on top of Ash, straddling his hips, their soft cocks brushing as he braced his hands on Ash's chest. "I want to keep exploring." He rolled his hips and his cock stiffened against Ash's.

"Is that so?" Ash teased, gripping Harper's hips. He sat up and toppled Harper backward, pressing him into the mattress.

Harper let out a surprised laugh, his legs flailing.

Ash grabbed his ankles and brought them over his shoulders, leaning down and bending Harper in half. The position had a delicious intimacy to it. Ash thrust his hips, caressing Harper's ankles as he held them in place.

A leather band caught on Ash's thumb. He paused, catching a hint of magic.

Harper went completely still beneath him, his playful expression blanking.

"Harper?" Ash let go of his ankles and lowered his legs.

Harper's eyes widened, his breathing shallow. He seemed frozen and increasingly afraid.

Ash's pulse spiked. "What's wrong?" He shifted off Harper and knelt beside him. Harper didn't move. "Harper, what is it? Did you not like the way I handled you?"

Harper averted his gaze and didn't respond.

Ash's fire went cold, his gut twisting. He'd hurt his mate.

But wait. Harper never shied away from telling Ash his limits. He was open about sex. He was only this avoidant regarding his situation with the witches.

Ash glanced at the leather bracelet tied around Harper's ankle. He'd missed it when he'd undressed him. Now that it had his attention, the spell trapped in the leather was obvious.

Ash quickly analyzed the magic.

The bracelet would disguise a witch's magic from casual inspection, but not from Ash. If Harper were a witch, he'd have to be doing a lot more than wearing this to fool him. But if Harper wasn't a witch, why wear the bracelet? There was absolutely no reason for a human to wear something with this particular spell cast on it.

Was Harper a witch? How had he missed something like this?

"Harper." Ash paused, hating the tension. "Are you suppressing your magic?"

Harper's breathing shallowed, his chest rising and falling too fast. "I forgot... I forgot I was wearing that. It's...it's nothing." He shook his head.

Why was he scared? "It's okay, Harper. It's fine if you're a witch." And it was fine. Ash might grumble about witches, but this was Harper. His flower. There wasn't anything he could learn about Harper that he wouldn't accept.

Harper made a small, strangled sound, and Ash's heart clenched.

His mate needed him.

"It'll be all right." Ash grabbed Harper's boxer briefs and passed them to him. Harper's shirt was the one Ash had used to wipe him up, so he passed Harper his own as he pulled on his underwear.

Harper seemed grateful for the clothes, adjusting them with trembling hands.

As he dressed, Ash discreetly inspected him with his demon sense, searching carefully for any trace of magic, just as he'd done with Dante's old house. Eventually, he detected something hidden. A powerful spell ran through Harper's blood, suppressing any evidence of his magic. If Ash wasn't a demon, he wouldn't have seen through it.

Harper's gaze darted around the room, looking anywhere

but at Ash, like he didn't know what to do. Why was he so worried about this?

Ash settled against the headboard, giving Harper space even though he longed to hold him close. "You can talk to me, Harper."

He stood at the foot of the bed and shot Ash a suspicious glance. "Can I? You aren't telling *me* everything. Why can't I detect *your* magic? Are *you* suppressing it?"

Harper had him there. He must have been shocked to find out Ash was a vampire if he'd magically assessed Ash and determined him to be human.

Ash rubbed the spot where his horns were hidden. They weren't going to get anywhere like this. He couldn't expect Harper to trust him if he didn't do the same. Harper was scared. He wasn't going to make the first move. Ash needed to show Harper he was safe. He had to put himself out there.

And there was only one way to do that. He had to reveal his true self.

How would Harper react when he realized a demon was in his bedroom? Some witches hated demons, and others worshipped them to a sickening degree. Then there were the witches hunting them. But Harper was Ash's mate, and whatever Harper's initial reaction, they would figure this out.

They had to.

Dante and Onyx were going to be furious. Ash still hadn't told them about Harper, but revealing himself wouldn't put his brothers in danger. Not in this case. Harper was kindhearted, and Ash would do whatever he had to for Harper to accept him as a demon and agree to keep his secret.

"I am suppressing my magic," Ash began. Harper went completely still, shock on his face like he hadn't expected Ash to admit it. "I always suppress it."

"Are you hiding?" Harper asked so quietly Ash might have missed it if he had human hearing.

"Yes." Ash's tattooed wings and tail tingled. "I'm hiding, just like you."

"Who makes your potion?" Harper's eyes raked over him. "Vampires can't brew."

Ash's heart pounded, swallowing a few times before he could get the words out. "I'm not a vampire, Harper. I never said I was, but I didn't correct you when you made the assumption."

Harper shrank back. "What? But your fangs?"

Ash stood from the bed, momentarily lightheaded, moving slowly so Harper wouldn't take it as a threat. "I'm a demon." An unexpected lightness filled Ash, urging him on. "I can suppress my magic without a potion. I've been doing it since I entered the Human Realm."

Harper's mouth dropped open, more shocked than afraid.

Ash's heart beat rapidly as something like excitement stirred in him. He turned away, showing the tattoos on his back before facing Harper again. There was a kaleidoscope of butterflies in Ash's chest. His hands shook and he clenched his fists to steady them.

With a smile, Ash brought his demon features forth. His tail unwrapped from around his hips, his horns sprang from his hair, and his wings rose from his back, folded tight in the small room.

All traces of fear fled Harper's expression. Awe shone in his eyes, and Ash stood straighter, the last of his discomfort gone.

His mate was impressed with him.

The pull between them seemed to hum in satisfaction, like showing his true form had strengthened their connection. Ash's blood heated with the desire to connect further.

"I don't know how much you know about demons," Ash continued before he got distracted, showing Harper just how impressive he could be. "But we keep our existence in this

Realm a heavily guarded secret. I've never revealed myself to anyone." Harper had to know what this moment meant, what he was risking to gain Harper's trust. "I'm sorry I deceived you. I was never trying to trick you. But now you know. This is who I am, and I promise you can talk to me. I'll listen. I'll help you."

Harper gave his head a tiny shake. "You're one of the Hounds."

Ash smiled despite hating the nickname. "You know your history then."

Harper raised one shoulder in a half-shrug. "You and the other Hounds escaped the Realm of the Damned hundreds of years ago and have been hiding in our Realm. No one ever called the demons by their names. At least not that I ever heard. Ash..." He trailed off like he was trying the name out.

This was good. Harper knowing about the Hounds meant he would understand what a big deal it was for Ash to reveal himself.

Ash sat on the edge of the bed, his wings shifting and in the way. "Now that you know why I'm hiding my magic, will you share what's happening with you?"

Harper trapped his bottom lip between his teeth, his eyes narrowing slightly. "I'm hiding from my coven," he said at last.

Ash nodded, hoping Harper would go on, but he didn't. "You've done a good job. Are you brewing the potion yourself?"

Harper's cheeks pinkened. "Yes. I have a knack for potions." He averted his eyes, fiddling with the hem of Ash's shirt. "I'm not doing a good job if they found me," he whispered.

Before Ash could disagree, Harper stiffened, fixing Ash with a calculating stare. "Wait. If you aren't a vampire, why did you run away from me that night? You couldn't have been overwhelmed with the urge to bite me. You're not new to immortality and the need for blood. You're ancient."

"Ouch." A gruff laugh escaped Ash. "Ancient. Really, Harper, that stings."

Harper's lips twitched. "Sorry, but I mean, it's technically true. The fall was thousands of years ago."

"It was." What did Harper know about the fall? The quest for mates had been lost in retellings over the centuries and the story was often told as a rebellion against general oppression in the Eternal Realm. "I may be *ancient*, but I wasn't lying about being overcome with the urge to bite you. I almost revealed myself by accident, wings and all. I wasn't expecting my reaction to you."

Harper seemed to mull this over, skepticism remaining in his slightly narrowed eyes.

Ash wished Harper would open up rather than ask questions. He couldn't reveal that they were mates. He wasn't ready to be that vulnerable. But the more Harper asked, the harder it would be to avoid the topic without lying, and he didn't want to lie to Harper.

"Is it the magic in my blood?" Harper fisted the end of the shirt, knuckles turning white as he spoke. "Is that why you had the urge to bite me? Is that what's...what's happening between us?"

There was fear in Harper's words, which was surprising given witches were well aware that feeding on blood was normal for other magical beings. "No, Harper. I had no idea you had magic in your blood until I unmasked your suppression just now."

"But subconsciously," Harper argued. "It could explain your strong reaction to me and why you didn't expect it and were caught off guard."

"It's not that. Demons need blood to survive, but feeding isn't about magic. When we first arrived in the Human Realm, there were no witches. The blood we drank was purely human. We don't crave magic. We're the source of it."

"Right." Harper seemed to accept this, his tense posture relaxing. "You wouldn't need more magic, would you?"

"No." Ash longed to shift closer but didn't want to push his luck. "I wasn't overwhelmed by your blood but by my own feelings." Ash's stomach twisted. "I've spent a lot of time alone over the past century, especially the last few decades. I don't do feelings and wasn't ready for them to sneak up on me."

Harper unsuccessfully bit back a grin, the corners of his mouth curving upward. "Feelings, huh?"

"Yes, Harper. I have lots of feelings for you." He'd been so lonely before Harper and unable to acknowledge it until the mating connection tugged at his jaded heart, reminding him he'd always wanted more.

Harper slowly inched closer until he stood next to Ash. "Feelings make demons lose control?"

"Yes," Ash hummed, a self-deprecating grin tugging on his lips. "Surprising, I know."

Harper let out a shaky laugh and sat on the bed, leaning his head against Ash's shoulder, almost like he couldn't help it.

The contact sparked.

"Your wings are beautiful," Harper murmured.

"Thank you, flower." Ash's tail twitched. "I'll have to show you my full wingspan sometime. It's hard to get a good look while we're inside."

"I'd like that." Harper nuzzled Ash's shoulder. "Did you really mean it when you said this was a date?"

"Yes." Ash's brow furrowed. Where had that come from?

"One of the legendary Hounds of Hell wants to date *me*? I never thought demons would be interested in dating."

Ash cocked his head. "What did you imagine we were interested in?"

"I don't know. I guess I never thought about it."

Ash chuckled. "You're taking me being a demon rather well."

"Finding a demon is a shock, but not... I mean, I know enough about demons. Your identity is a huge secret. I can't imagine hiding from Lucifer." Harper shuddered. "I get why you let me think you were a vampire, and I know you wouldn't reveal yourself to me for no reason."

"No. I wouldn't." Ash took Harper's hand and squeezed. "You're important to me, Harper."

Harper squirmed. "That's hard to believe."

Ash tilted Harper's chin up so he couldn't keep hiding his expression. "Why?"

Harper seemed tired, eyes creased with sadness. "We don't know each other well, and even if we did, I've never been important. No one has ever cared about me as a person."

Ash's fingers tightened on Harper's chin. "I'm so sorry, sweet."

Harper pulled away. "It's not your fault."

"I know, but I'm still sorry anyone treated you that way. I promise you're important to me. I'll make sure you know it."

20

HARPER

Could Harper believe Ash? He was saying everything Harper wanted to hear, but it was too perfect. What were the chances such a powerful being would be so taken with *him*? Why did Ash care?

Feelings couldn't make a demon lose control. Ash's feelings couldn't be strong enough, especially when they first met.

It didn't add up.

Ash must have some sort of angle, but what could it possibly be? A demon trying to trick him to gain his trust made no sense. Harper was nobody compared to Ash.

He may have planned to tell the Hounds about his hunt and his coven's aims, fantasizing that they would help him in return, but being offered that and so much more out of nowhere was suspicious.

Wanting everything Ash said to be true didn't mean it was, and until Harper figured out what was going on—the full story —he'd keep his cards close to his chest. Most people weren't good, and so many magical beings had a sinister side. Harper wouldn't disregard all the lessons he'd learned in life just because a demon said he had *feelings* for him.

Ash ran his fingers through Harper's hair. Fuck, it felt good. Harper leaned into the touch, unable to stop soaking up the affection, even with his doubts.

Harper had a lot of his own damn feelings.

Why not indulge them? Ash revealing himself meant something, and until Harper figured it out, he could enjoy this. He was on a date, and Ash touching him felt better than anything he'd ever experienced.

He needed something good. He needed to feel safe and okay. He needed Ash. He just wouldn't give Ash everything.

Harper straddled Ash's lap, and the demon smiled, his hands finding Harper's hips. Fuck, Harper could get lost in Ash's eyes. They'd shifted when he'd let his demon features out, a gold-orange glow warming the deep brown of his irises.

How was this real? He was sitting on a demon's lap. A demon who wanted to date him.

"What's that look for, sweet?" Ash purred, hands flexing on his hips.

Harper blinked, not sure what he'd given away with his expression. "You're beautiful," he said because it was true.

"Not scary?" Ash teased, ducking his head and bumping a curved horn against Harper's cheek. They poked out of his dark hair and curled back across his head, as inky black as the darkest feathers of his wings.

Harper laughed. "No, but I'm sure you could be if you wanted."

Demons were pure magic, the closest things to gods in their world. Harper was sure Ash could be terrifying, but the adoring look in his glowing eyes was worlds away.

"Yes, I can be when I want." Ash's smile twisted mischievously. "But only for your enemies. I'd never hurt you."

The air whooshed out of Harper's lungs. He believed Ash, even though he shouldn't. He trusted no one. But sitting on the lap of the most powerful being he'd ever encountered, someone who could end or entrap him with magic so easily it wasn't even funny, Harper had never felt safer.

He didn't understand it. Maybe he was losing his mind after the stress of running and trying so hard to find freedom.

"I'd never hurt you either," Harper whispered as he wrapped his arms around Ash's neck, burying his fingers in the hair at his nape.

Ash grinned. "Glad to hear it." He probably found the promise funny when the power imbalance was so far in Ash's favor. But Ash only hauled Harper closer, fingers digging into his hips. "You don't mind dating a demon?"

Harper shook his head. It was wild, but he didn't mind. "Not at all. I love seeing your wings."

Ash's eyes flashed. "You can touch them. Touch me anywhere you like."

Harper ran his fingers along the black feathers towering over Ash's shoulders. They were soft and surprisingly warm. All of Ash seemed to burn like a furnace.

As Harper stroked the beautiful feathers, Ash's cock hardened between them, pressing needily into Harper's groin. Ash dipped his fingers down the back of Harper's boxer briefs, teasing his ass, and Harper's cock hardened in turn.

Ash's eyes sparked, flame flickering in the depths of his dark irises. "I like being with you in my full form. It feels so much better than before, and I didn't think that was possible."

Harper's cheeks heated. "I like being with you in this form too." He ran a delicate finger along one of Ash's horns. The skin was callused and leathery, unlike anything Harper had ever felt.

Something tickled Harper's lower back, and he gasped. Both Ash's hands were still on his ass. He tore his gaze away from Ash's face to find his tail snaking around him.

"You can touch my tail too," Ash purred, twitching it against Harper's back. "The base is very sensitive."

Harper wrapped a hand around the section of Ash's tail pressing against his thigh. It was thick, the skin black like his horns but much softer. Harper stroked, and Ash let out a contented sigh. The tip of his tail wound from its place along Harper's spine to his chest and flicked one of his nipples.

"Fuck." Harper squeezed Ash's tail and moved his hand toward the base. It got thicker closer to Ash's body. The base was even girthier than Ash's cock, but the tip teasing his nipple was more like a large finger.

Harper rolled his hips, wishing they hadn't gotten half-dressed. He let go of Ash's tail and tore off his shirt. The sight of Ash's tail wrapped around his chest made his dick throb. "I love you touching me like this."

Ash's tail teased his other nipple. "Music to my ears, flower." He shoved Harper's underwear down, exposing the tops of his ass cheeks. Harper's erection strained against the scrunched fabric until Ash freed it. "I love that you're turned on by my true form. I hate having to hide it."

Harper gasped as Ash pushed his own underwear out of the way and brought their cocks together. He wrapped his arms around Ash, buried his fingers in the feathers of his wings, and thrust. "Oh fuck, Ash. Yes."

They both leaked precum, Ash's fist perfectly tight on their cocks as he stroked. Harper crashed their lips together and kissed Ash hard. Ash's body heat enveloped him like smoldering fire, his smoky scent filling Harper's lungs. The tip of Ash's tail continued teasing Harper's nipples, one hand kneading Harper's ass while the other jerked their cocks.

Harper couldn't get enough.

Ash's tail disappeared from Harper's chest, and he whimpered at the loss.

"Patience, sweet," Ash murmured against his lips. "I want to explore you. Is that still okay?"

"Yes," Harper panted. "Touch me anywhere." He sealed their mouths together once more.

Ash pushed his tongue into Harper's mouth as he jerked their aligned cocks. His tail found its way to Harper's inner thigh, winding toward his groin. The tip caressed Harper's balls before nudging behind and pressing against his taint.

Harper moaned into Ash's mouth. His tail slid farther back, between Harper's ass cheeks. Harper's heart thudded and his body flamed. "*Please.*"

Ash hummed against his lips and jerked them harder with his hand. The other pulled Harper's ass cheek, spreading him as his tail brushed against Harper's hole.

"Oh fuck." Harper jolted, his nerve endings lighting with pleasure. "Don't stop."

The tip of Ash's tail circled his rim, skin silky soft against Harper's most sensitive place.

"You feel divine, flower." Ash withdrew from their kisses, fixing glowing eyes on Harper's hot face. "Everywhere we touch." He ruffled his wings where Harper's hands were buried in his feathers, squeezed his hands, and rolled his hips, flicking his tail.

Harper moaned, head falling back. Everything tingled and sparked like his body was made for pleasure. "Yes, more," he groaned, no shame for how greedy he was.

The tips of Ash's fangs showed as he smiled. His tail pressed against Harper's hole, and Harper thrust back into it.

"Do you want me inside you?"

Harper whimpered and slammed his eyes shut, nodding frantically. "Yes."

Ash's tail disappeared from Harper's hole and his eyes popped open.

Ash's fangs descended fully, a look of pure hunger on his face. Harper's heart stuttered and lust curled inside him.

Abandoning their cocks, Ash ripped Harper's underwear in two and tossed the destroyed fabric aside before doing the same to his own. He picked Harper up and tossed him on the bed, looming over him, his wings spreading just enough to encase them, blocking out the rest of the room.

"Harper, sweet, I'm going to make this so good for you."

Harper spread his legs wide, gaze falling to Ash's erect cock. Precum beaded at his slit and dripped down his plump cockhead. Harper wanted that cock inside him. He wanted Ash to touch him everywhere, even his deepest places. He squirmed. Could he take it?

"Not yet," Ash rumbled, stroking Harper's cheek. "I need to get you ready for my cock, sweet. I won't rush this."

Ash read him like a book. It was almost as if he had a sixth sense for what Harper needed.

"I liked your tail," Harper murmured, reaching for it.

In this position, Harper could cup Ash's ass. He let one hand rest on the tight muscle as his other encircled the thick base of Ash's tail, skin so soft he couldn't help stroking.

"Fuck," Ash grunted, his feathers ruffling. "Careful, flower. You'll make me come."

Harper squeezed, mesmerized by the pleasure twisting Ash's face, his mouth open, fangs down, glowing eyes half-lidded.

Harper expected to be uneasy with Ash's fangs, but he wasn't. Ash wouldn't do anything without asking, and if Harper said he didn't want to be bitten, Ash wouldn't push. Ash didn't desire his blood. He desired Harper.

He looked hot with his fangs down. There was something heart-poundingly primal in seeing Ash like this, lost in pleasure. Lost in Harper. It made Harper's core go molten.

Harper stroked the underside of Ash's tail where it met his body. The muscle quivered in his palm and Ash's cock leaked.

"Harper, flower," he groaned. "You're killing me."

The tip of Ash's tail wound between Harper's legs, delving into his crack. It flicked against Harper's hole, and Harper's rhythmic stroking faltered.

"Do you have lube?" Ash asked in a breathless huff.

"In the side table." Harper released Ash and twisted to get it, only to be met with a large wing.

"Let me." Ash shifted and retrieved the lube before blanketing Harper with his body and re-encasing them with his folded wings.

He kissed Harper gently on the lips, not so much as brushing him with his fangs. "Ready, flower?"

"Now you're killing me. Yes, I'm ready."

Ash chuckled, kissed him one more time, then sat back on his haunches. He spread Harper's legs and turned his attention to his hole. Harper clenched in response, but Ash's tail was there to massage his tension away.

Opening the lube, Ash squeezed a generous amount onto Harper's hole and his tail's tip. He reached between Harper's legs, his thumb rubbing and circling Harper's rim in tandem with his tail.

Chills coursed through Harper's body as he adjusted to the new, pleasurable sensation. Ash was truly stunning, his large, muscled frame looming over Harper, intense stare heated with lust. Ash's fangs were a promise to eat Harper alive in the best way. And his wings. Harper couldn't get over the wings.

He ran delicate fingers over the warm feathers.

Ash caught his eye, gaze so hot Harper could almost feel it. "How's this?"

"Good." Harper pressed into Ash's touch and his hole twitched.

Ash purred, his tail applying more pressure as his hand moved to stroke Harper's cock. Ash didn't seem to be trying to penetrate him yet. The pressure didn't last long before Ash went back to massaging the entire sensitive area.

A flash of insecurity hit Harper in the chest. "Am I too tight?"

"Not at all, sweet. You're perfect." Ash's lust-laden stare turned affectionate. "I want to take my time. I like seeing how you respond to me."

"What if I can't relax?"

"Then we can keep doing this. I'm not forcing myself inside you. I want to make you feel good." Ash demonstrated by swirling his tail and twisting his fist over the tip of Harper's cock.

Harper keened, body rolling into Ash's touches. "I haven't done anything like this before," he whispered, the heat from his face spreading down his neck. "But I want to."

Ash cupped his cheek. "I'll give you whatever you want. However you want it, sweetheart."

Harper whimpered, knowing Ash would take good care of him.

Ash leaned forward and realigned their cocks, dribbling lube over them. He fisted their lengths and stroked, rolling his hips as he played with Harper's hole.

Harper's eyelids fluttered shut. He almost couldn't cope with all the good feelings, his orgasm building. Ash was everywhere, their bodies so in sync it was like they were meant to be together.

The tip of Ash's tail breached Harper, and he gasped, clenching around it. "Fuck, Ash."

"Feel good?" His rumbling voice washed over Harper like a caress.

"Yes." Harper thrust into Ash's hand, and Ash's slick tail

pushed farther inside, stretching him the perfect amount, not much more than a finger's worth.

Ash groaned and the deep sound vibrated around them. "You're so hot, flower. You feel so good around my tail. I want to bury it inside you."

Harper nodded. "Yes, more."

Ash pushed his tail farther inside. The stretching sensation increased. Not enough to hurt, but enough to give Harper the foreign feeling of opening for Ash.

"How's this?" Ash pumped the tip of his tail in and out, fucking Harper in time with the strokes of his hand on their cocks.

"*Ugh*, good." Harper thrust into it.

Damn, it felt perfect. It might not be Ash's cock, but Harper loved the feeling of being fucked. Of Ash pushing in, filling him, touching him in such an intimate place.

Ash thrust another inch of his tail inside Harper, not stretching him open much more but still giving him what he needed. Harper clenched, and Ash made a guttural sound.

His tail brushed a spot inside Harper, and he lit up from within. "Oh, Ash!" Harper shouted, digging his fingers into Ash's firm shoulders. "Fuck."

"That's it, sweet," Ash cooed, stroking the spot inside him.

Harper bucked, fucking into Ash's fist as Ash teased his prostate with targeted strokes of his tail. A mix of moans and swears fell from Harper's lips as pleasure built inside him.

Ash crashed their mouths together, kissing him, fangs pressing into Harper's lips, and Harper came like an explosion. His hole spasmed. He clenched around Ash's tail as his cum flooded Ash's hand. Harper shouted Ash's name, everything in him screaming with pleasure. It raced down his spine and burst from within.

"Oh, sweet, yes, that's it," Ash rumbled against Harper's

lips. Harper shook, his orgasm going on and on as Ash worked his tail inside. "Come for me, beautiful. Just like that."

"*Ash.*" Harper gripped the demon's hair, locking eyes with his mesmerizing glowing irises.

Ash shuddered, flames flaring behind his eyes, and hot cum flooded Harper's stomach. Ash's spiced, smoky scent filled the air and Harper breathed deep, filling his lungs.

He'd be happy to smell nothing but Ash for the rest of his life.

Ash buried his head against Harper's neck and let out a deep, growling moan.

"My sweet flower." Ash kissed Harper's neck, then brushed Harper's lips with his. "I can't wait to make you mine."

21

ASH

Asн тucкеd his demon features away despite Harper's protests. The bed wasn't big enough otherwise, and he needed to hold Harper, skin to skin.

Ash closed his eyes. What felt like seconds later, he blinked, but he must have fallen asleep because the light had changed outside.

Harper's head rested on his chest, soft breaths ghosting over his skin. The arm thrown over Ash's stomach tightened its hold as Harper snuggled closer.

Ash smiled at the ceiling.

Sex with Harper in his true form had unlocked something deep within him. He hadn't claimed Harper, but he felt closer to his mate than ever. They'd connected as their purest selves, a witch and a demon.

He wanted to bask in the afterglow, get lost in exploring each other, and show Harper all the ways they could worship each other's bodies. He'd like to keep his mate in bed for a week, maybe a month, and spoil him until they were ready to bond.

But Ash needed more than sex to win Harper over. Harper was comfortable sharing his body with Ash, and Ash loved that, but it wasn't all Ash wanted. Harper still hadn't opened up in any other way.

Ash glanced around the bare room. Harper was hiding from his coven and had said he'd only recently moved in with Ollie. He must have taken almost nothing with him when he'd run and not had time to settle in permanently. But that was all Ash knew about the situation.

Which coven was he running from? Why would a coven turn against one of their own? A coven's group loyalty was supposed to come above all else. Families of witches were usually tight-knit and ruthless toward outsiders who tried to harm them.

Harper stirred on Ash's chest and Ash's hand went automatically to his hair.

"What time is it?" Harper murmured.

"Not sure, sweet." Ash glanced out the window. "Looks like early evening. Are you hungry?" They must have slept a while. Ash should have set an alarm. He didn't like his mate missing meals.

A door closed somewhere else in the apartment.

Harper sat bold upright. "Oh no, that's Ollie."

Ash rubbed Harper's back, smiling at the slight squeak in Harper's voice. "Why is that an *oh no?*"

Harper twisted to meet Ash's gaze. His cheeks bloomed with color, and he seemed to lose his train of thought.

Ash brushed Harper's red cheeks with the back of his hand. "What are you thinking, sweet?"

The flush spread down Harper's neck. "Just thinking about what we did earlier..." He bit his lip. "With your tail." The tips of his ears turned red and his fresh floral scent rolled off him in waves.

Ash purred, his cock thickening. "I'd love to do it again, but not if your human roommate is here. Next time, we can go to my place. That way, I can show you my demon form without restrictions."

Harper let out a soft, panting breath. "Yeah. I'd like that." Another noise from the apartment caught his attention, and he glanced at the bedroom door. "But you're right. Let's not, you know, while Ollie is here."

Ash poked Harper in the side, and he squirmed. "I'm not sure I do know. What are you saying?" He furrowed his brow in feigned confusion.

"Ugh." Harper rolled his eyes. "I mean...have sex." The last word came out in an adorable whisper.

Ash sat up and pulled Harper into a kiss. "I like hearing you say what you mean. There's no need to be embarrassed."

A shudder rolled through Harper's body. "So if I ask you to...to fuck me with your tail again, you won't think that's weird?"

"No." Ash brushed his nose against Harper's. "Your desires could never be weird."

Harper grinned. "Good to know."

They got up and dressed, Harper glancing at the door so often you'd think it was about to burst open. Was he hesitant to have Ash around Ollie because he was human and unaware of magic, or was it something more?

He followed Harper into the living room. Ollie was on the couch, legs folded beneath him as he scrolled on his phone.

"Hey." Ollie shot a glance Harper's way, then did a double take, staring at Ash. He sat up straighter. "Who's this?"

"Ollie, meet Ash." Harper shifted restlessly. "From the club, remember? I had his number, and, um, we got coffee."

Ollie smiled. "Coffee. Nice. Good to see you again, Ash."

"Likewise." Ash slid an arm around Harper. "I'll leave you be, sweet. Have a good evening."

Harper's cheeks flamed. "You too."

"Text you later." Ash kissed him on the cheek and released him. With a nod to Ollie, who watched them gleefully, phone forgotten, Ash exited the living room and walked down the hall, slipping out the front door.

He went to the roof. Even though he wanted to stay and watch over his mate, Ash flew home.

His talk with Dante and Onyx was overdue.

"Where have you been?" Onyx asked when Ash entered the kitchen.

"Out in the city." Ash opened the fridge and pulled out a bag of blood.

He longed to taste Harper's blood like he longed to kiss or bury himself inside him, but biting Harper should be special. What was a little more waiting when the mate bond was his prize?

Onyx slunk closer, leaning against the counter beside Ash. "You're out an awful lot."

"So?" Ash cocked a brow. "You understand not wanting to be cooped up."

Onyx frowned, ignoring him. "More of Dante's precious birds died. You see anything that might explain that while you were *out in the city*?"

"No." Not that he had been looking. "Where's Dante?"

Onyx shrugged. "He should be back soon. I'm sure his flock saw you come in and told him."

Ash drank his blood, unsettled by the dead birds. He tried not to feel guilty for spending the whole day with Harper.

"We've missed something," Onyx went on. "For all we know, Luc could be in the city taking out Dante's flock."

"How?" Ash set his mug down. Onyx hadn't thought that the other day.

"I don't know how. That's the whole problem. How are we supposed to know what we're missing?"

"If Luc were here undetected, why wouldn't he come for us? Why spend his time killing birds? That would be wasting a huge advantage. Surely, he'd realize every passing day gave us more time to find him."

Onyx crossed his arms. "Who's killing the birds then? If it's not Luc, then it has to be someone else who's on to us. You know there've been rumors in the magic world about the demon flock."

Ash's brow furrowed, and he scowled at the remaining blood in his cup. "You think it's the hunters?"

Onyx wrinkled his nose. "Maybe."

"What about the hunters?" Dante asked, coming in from the deck, folding his wings against his back.

Onyx turned to face him, a hand on his hip. "Think they could be the ones after your birds?"

Dante slumped onto one of the barstools on the opposite side of the kitchen island. "If they're trying to find us and know about my connection to the birds, killing them doesn't make sense. Why not try to use the birds to track me down?"

"Maybe they're trying to draw you out by killing them," Onyx countered.

Dante didn't look convinced. He cut a sidelong glance at Ash. "Where've you been?"

Ash swallowed the urge to deflect. He had to tell them about Harper. "I've been seeing someone." There, that sounded off-hand. He turned to wash his mug in the sink.

"Wow." Ash could practically hear Onyx's eyes roll. "And I thought I was the irresponsible one. Luc is knocking at our door, and you're out getting laid."

Ash clenched his teeth. "It's not about getting laid." He turned and faced his brothers.

"So you haven't been out fucking around?" Onyx raised a

brow. "Wait. Is that what you've been doing all this time? Have you even tried to track Lucifer?"

"Yes, of course, I've tried to track him," Ash growled. He wasn't irresponsible. "I can handle more than one thing on my plate, you know."

"Didn't think you were sharp enough for that," Onyx sneered.

"Stop it." Dante slapped the counter. He looked tired, the lines around his eyes more noticeable than usual. "Who have you been seeing, Ash? It's not like you to get involved."

Ash held Dante's stare, his stomach twisting as he hesitated, a strange emptiness in his chest that felt a lot like dread. "You're right. I don't usually get involved. But this man isn't just anyone. He's... He's my mate."

Onyx laughed. "You've got to be kidding me."

Ash ignored him, his gaze fixed on Dante.

"Your mate?" Dante whispered, cocking his head. "But you don't believe we'll ever find our mates. You haven't believed in over fifteen hundred years."

Ash's tail twitched. "No, I didn't, but I was wrong. I know it's him. I can't explain what's happening between us in any other way."

"Wait." Onyx grabbed Ash's shoulder and pulled him around. "Are you serious?"

"Yes, I'm serious." Ash confessed what happened the night Harper took him home from the club and how he'd been following Harper around for two weeks.

As Ash explained, Onyx's face hardened. He shook his head in tiny, jerky movements like he was trying to dislodge something from his brain. Dante, on the other hand, was uncharacteristically devoid of emotion.

Onyx threw up his hands. "How would you even know he's your mate? How do you know you're not wrong?"

"I just know." Ash shrugged, warmth filling him as he pictured Harper in his arms. "It's instinct. Being with him is right in a way nothing has ever been. I'd do anything for him. I want to spend all my time with him." Ash ran a hand through his hair and over his horns. "My future feels so much brighter now that I can see him in it. The connection is already growing, and I want nothing more than to feed it, bond us together, and spend the rest of eternity learning my mate inside and out, sharing everything with him."

Onyx blinked, his mouth slack.

Ash turned to Dante. "Do you believe me?"

"Of course." Dante smiled, but his eyes betrayed a hint of melancholy. "Ash, I'm so happy for you. I *knew* it wasn't impossible. I *knew* we'd find them. I told you this place was special."

"You were right." Ash's heart warmed, and he hoped, more than anything, that Dante was right about finding his mate here. "I'm sorry I didn't believe you."

Dante waved him away, joy sparking in his dark eyes, pushing the sadness away. "So, can we meet him?"

"Wait. What does your *mate* think is going on between you two?" Onyx cut in. "It's not like he knows mates or demons exist. Dante won't be able to meet him without getting all sappy, making it weird, and giving something away."

Dante glared at Onyx. "I won't make it weird. I know how to talk to humans."

"Harper isn't human," Ash said before the two could get lost bickering. "He's a witch."

Both demons fixed looks of surprise on Ash.

"You went home from the club with a witch?" Onyx's brows disappeared beneath his blue bangs. "What happened to not trusting witches?"

Ash didn't appreciate the sharpness in Onyx's gaze. "It's not about trusting or not trusting witches. Harper is my mate. I trust *him.* And I didn't go home with a witch. I couldn't tell he had magic when we were at the club."

There was a beat of silence.

"Explain," Dante said a little too calmly.

Ash told them how Harper seemed to be in some kind of trouble and how he'd saved Harper at the port. "Today, I discovered he's suppressing his magic. When we were in bed, I found a charmed bracelet that only a witch would wear, and after inspecting him more closely, I saw through the strong magic he'd used to mask himself."

Onyx looked at Dante. "I don't like this."

Dante frowned, tapping the counter. "Do you think it could be one of Lucifer's tricks?"

"What?" Ash growled. "No, of course this isn't Luc."

"Harper lied to you, Ash," Dante said gently. "Don't you think Luc might exploit our longing for our mates to distract us?"

Onyx pointed at Ash. "And you've been very distracted."

"It isn't Lucifer. Onyx, Dante, I'm telling you, he's my mate. There's no faking the connection. Harper is hiding from his coven. His magic suppression and lies aren't about me."

Onyx gave him a withering look. "You sound so naïve right now."

Ash ignored him in favor of Dante. "I've been distracted, but not completely. I've been trying my best to track Luc. A few more hours a day searching wouldn't change anything. Harper isn't getting in the way of that. And besides, if he were part of some distraction plot, why would he push me away when I approached him after our night together?"

"That's a good point." Dante's shoulders sagged like he was relieved to agree. "If he had an agenda, he'd have jumped at the chance to pull you back in."

"Harper has been wary of me." Ash averted his eyes,

inspecting the countertop. "He has trust issues and seems reluctant to let me in at all. That isn't how he'd act if he were trying to trick me into thinking we were mates."

"No," Dante agreed more firmly. "And it's hard to imagine Luc enchanting a fake mate to trick you if the witch was completely clueless about what was happening. Luc wouldn't leave that much to chance. He's always preferred controlling every aspect of a situation. Involving a witch at all would be surprising, actually."

"Oh, come *on*." Onyx glared at them both. "The timing is sus as fuck."

Dante shrugged, his wings ruffling. "I've known Shearwater Landing was significant for a century. It's not suspicious at all when taken in that light. It might not be ideal timing, but fate doesn't play by our whims."

Ash wasn't sure what he'd expected of this conversation but he needed to get to the most pressing point before it completely derailed. "I told Harper I'm a demon," he said in a rush. "It was the only way to show him he could trust me. I had to be the first to take the leap of faith."

Onyx took a step back, eyes flaring. "We've never revealed ourselves."

"But he's my mate." Ash tried to suppress the growl creeping into his tone. "I can't explain how the mate connection works, but I knew it would be all right to tell him. It's fate for us to be together. Harper isn't the kind of witch who hates or worships us. He reacted well. He understood what me revealing myself meant."

Dante nodded. "And he opened up to you?"

"Not completely." Ash couldn't help picturing how Harper had trusted him with his body. As much as he liked that, it wasn't a complete comfort. "He needs time to get there."

Onyx snorted.

Ash's insides twisted, and he glared at Onyx.

"It's a complicated situation," Dante admitted. "Honestly, the only way I can imagine you revealing yourself is to your mate, Ash. I don't doubt your judgment in trusting Harper. Maybe if we meet him, it'll be easier for us to feel the same trust."

Onyx threw up his hands, shooting daggers between them, and stormed out of the kitchen.

Ash hadn't revealed himself in the right way, but of course, Onyx would latch onto his failure rather than try to understand what pushed Ash to go against their pact.

He averted his eyes. "I'm sorry."

Dante stood and moved around the counter, placing a hand on Ash's shoulder. "He'll forgive you for revealing yourself."

Ash snorted. "And you?"

"Already forgiven." Dante squeezed Ash's shoulder. "Your mate, Ash. This is wonderful. I'm so glad. After all this time."

"It's terrifying." Ash met Dante's steady gaze. "What if he doesn't accept? I trust him not to betray us, but that doesn't mean he'll ever trust me enough to share himself and bond with me. What if something happens. There are too many unknowns."

Dante rubbed his shoulder soothingly. "You'll find a way. I know you will. And I'll help in any way I can."

Ash covered Dante's hand with his. "Thank you, Dante. I don't deserve you."

"No, Ash. You deserve so much more."

22

ASH

Ash left Seaside Coffee carrying two drinks and a berry Danish and headed toward Harper's apartment. Hopefully, his flower had a good night. Ash hadn't come to watch over him after everything with Dante and Onyx, who he hadn't seen since he stormed out.

He tried not to dwell on Onyx's reaction as he walked through Harper's neighborhood. He'd just have to smooth things over. Show Onyx there was no risk in opening their small circle to Harper.

Ash arrived at the apartment building and texted his mate.

ASH:

Fancy another coffee?

HARPER:

I'd love one.

ASH:

Perfect. I'm downstairs.

Harper buzzed Ash into the building, and he headed to the top floor and knocked on Harper's door.

"You really didn't have to," Harper said as he opened the door, grinning wide.

Ash handed him the hazelnut almond latte. "When it makes you this happy, I couldn't possibly do anything else."

Harper let out a short laugh, eyes widening a fraction. "Thanks."

Ash followed Harper to the living room and handed him the pastry before sitting on the couch. Harper sat beside him, and Ash dragged him onto his lap, humming at Harper's nearness.

Harper leaned into Ash and sipped his coffee. "How was your evening?"

"Fine." Ash didn't want to broach the subject of meeting the other demons yet. "And yours?"

"Ollie and I cooked dinner and watched a movie. It was fun." Harper opened the bag and pulled out the pastry. "He had lots of questions about you."

"Did he?" Ash smiled and buried his nose in Harper's hair.

"He wants to know if we're dating, like a couple."

Ash chuckled, pulling back. "*Ollie* wants to know if we're a couple?"

Harper's cheeks flushed. "Okay, I want to know too. Is this casual dating, or what? I don't know how demons date, and I like having this stuff clear so I don't get the wrong idea." He averted his eyes, inspecting the pastry.

"Being clear is a good place to start. There's no reason to keep you guessing, sweet." Ash wrapped an arm around his mate. Harper should know how much he cared. It was vital after the way others had treated him. "I'd like for us to be a couple, making this more than casual dating, and if it's not too soon to be exclusive, I'd like that too."

"It's not too soon," Harper murmured, his soft voice carrying a hint of surprise. "Exclusive sounds good. I don't think casual is for me."

"Me either," Ash agreed.

Harper's brows pinched in momentary confusion. "Cool, we've got that in common then."

Ash purred softly as they drank their coffees, his hand slipping under Harper's T-shirt to rest on his belly. Harper let out a soft little sigh and squirmed in Ash's lap.

Connecting with his mate wasn't all about physical touch, but it heightened their interactions. Was it too much to always be touching Harper? Probably.

"Is there anywhere you'd like to go today?" Ash asked as Harper set his empty cup on the coffee table.

"Anywhere I'd like to go? What do you mean?"

Ash wasn't admitting to how much time he'd spent watching Harper—not until he revealed what being mates meant—but he couldn't ignore Harper's fear of leaving home.

"I'd understand if what happened at the port has been bothering you, Harper. You're hiding from your coven, and such a close call would make anyone think twice about walking around the city. So, if there's anywhere you need to go or things you need to do, I'm happy to accompany you."

Harper turned to stare at him, chewing his lower lip, studying Ash like he was trying to read his mind. Eventually, he muttered, "I haven't left the house since I was attacked."

Ash tightened his arm around Harper, his other hand resting on Harper's knee. "Would it help if I was with you? We could go out together."

Harper looked away. "I shouldn't be scared. I'm not helpless, so I don't know why I'm acting like this."

"Of course you're not helpless." Ash rubbed his hand up and down Harper's thigh. "You're brewing a powerful potion and dealing with something incredibly difficult. You can have whatever feelings you want, and none of them make you any less capable."

Harper shot Ash a contemplative look. "Maybe not, but I can't let them find me again. I can't risk it."

"I won't let them get to you, Harper." Ash fixed a flame-flecked stare on his mate, letting his fire burn, showing how much he meant it. "You know what I am and what position demons hold in the magic world. No one will get through me."

A shiver ran through Harper. He squirmed. "Is getting all protective of your brand-new boyfriend a demon-dating thing?"

Ash chuckled and Harper's lips twitched. "It is. We aren't the most casual creatures."

Harper barked a laugh. "I'm starting to get that."

"So, would you like to go out, or is it too soon?"

Harper sagged, his shoulders drooping. "I need to go out. I... um...I sell potions to make money and need to deliver my latest batch."

"Perfect." Ash shifted Harper off his lap and stood.

Harper hesitated.

"Is there something else?"

Harper collected the empty coffee cups and paper bag and took them to the kitchen. "I think the shop owner can tell I'm lying to him. I've told him I'm selling the potions for my boss and that I'm human. He can't detect my magic, but the last time I was there, he kept hinting like he didn't think my boss was real."

Ash paused as Harper tidied away the remnants of their coffee date. "You're worried about him?"

"Yeah." Harper fiddled with a dishtowel, eyes glued to it.

"Does the shop owner have any connections to the coven you're hiding from?"

Harper shook his head, hand tight on the towel. "No, but it would still be smarter to get another job. I can't have anything giving me away to people in the magic world."

Ash frowned, hating to see his mate agonize over everything he did. "Do you think this witch will sell you out?"

Harper's head snapped up, eyes wide. "No, I don't think so. It's not like that, but he could give me away by accident. He could mention something to the wrong person, and they could tell someone else. It could get back to my coven that way. Not that he really knows who I am. I've tried to change my appearance so descriptions don't give me away. But it's not foolproof."

"I see." Harper was being extremely cautious, maybe even too cautious in this particular case. "If you don't think this man is dangerous or about to sell you out, then it's probably safe to keep selling potions to him. But if it makes you uncomfortable, you don't have to. You're not under any obligation to him, are you?"

Harper stepped closer to Ash. "No, there's no obligation. But I don't exactly have any other way to make money."

Ash longed to pull Harper against him and tell Harper he didn't have to worry. Ash would take care of him—pay his rent, give him a place to live, anything. But he couldn't. Offering would be too much, and he didn't want to attract Harper's suspicion about why he was so committed or hurt Harper's pride by implying he couldn't take care of himself.

"If this guy turns out to be untrustworthy, I'll protect you, Harper. On the other hand, if he isn't a problem, maybe this job will be good, and you'll get to know the shop owner better. I assume you don't plan to be isolated forever, hiding from your coven and all other witches?"

"No, I don't want to hide forever." Harper ran a hand through his hair. "I was going to leave the city when I could afford it, but I'd rather stay. Though now that they've found me, I'm not sure."

"I can make them go away," Ash said softly like he was whispering sweet nothings, not offering to release his demon wrath on a group of witches. "If you tell me what's going on, I can do more than keep you safe day-to-day."

Harper stepped back, giving Ash an awkward smile. "Let's start with Nico and The Herb Emporium." He turned and walked out of the kitchen.

"Sounds good." Ash tried to mean it, even though his stomach sank. Harper still didn't trust him. He must be dealing with so much fear. Ash wanted nothing more than to take it all away.

Patience. He had to be patient. In time, Harper would learn that he could always turn to him. Ash just had to be here waiting when Harper was ready.

Harper retrieved a shoulder bag from his room and headed for the front door, Ash following in his wake. Harper hesitated at the door.

"All good?" Ash asked.

"Yeah." Harper opened the door and stepped into the hall.

"We can walk or fly." Ash closed the door behind him. "No one will see us if we do the latter."

"Fly?" Harper whirled around. "Really? That would be so cool."

Ash grinned. "Then I'll definitely take you flying. Shall we go up to the roof?"

Some of the joy in Harper's eyes dimmed. "No. Let's save that for something strictly fun. I need to get used to walking around again."

See, he was strong, facing what made him uncomfortable.

"I like the idea of flying being fun," Ash said. "I'm so used to it. I haven't thought about it that way in years."

Harper laughed. "Well, I can't imagine it ever being anything else."

With Harper, flying could be something special. Everything had the potential to change when they were together.

They left the building and walked through the Banks along the familiar route Ash had seen Harper take to the apothecary. Harper checked over his shoulder constantly, no less vigilant because Ash was with him.

"I don't see anyone or sense any witches," Ash murmured, hoping to provide reassurance.

"Me either," Harper agreed, glancing over his shoulder again.

Harper's fear ran deep. What had his coven done to him? Whatever it was, Ash would make them pay. No one should be this afraid to walk down the street.

Once they reached the apothecary, Harper turned to Ash. "Is it okay if you wait out here for me?"

"Of course."

Harper reached out and squeezed Ash's hand. "Thanks." He disappeared inside the shop.

Ash kept watch over the street while he waited, periodically glancing through The Herb Emporium window. When Harper exited the shop, his eyes immediately darted around the street, but his posture seemed less tense than before.

"How did it go?" Ash asked.

"It was good." Harper made an exasperated sound. "Nico didn't say anything weird or hint at anything. It made me feel like I was stressing over nothing."

Ash had suspected that might be the case but didn't say so. "I'm glad he put you at ease. Are you going to continue selling potions to him?"

"I think so." Harper glanced back at the shop. "There's a position open for an in-house brewer, but I can't take it while pretending I'm human."

Ash tried to get a look at Nico through the window, but there was too much clutter in the shop. "Do you think Nico would understand and still be interested in offering you the position if you explained why you're hiding your identity?"

Harper grimaced. "I don't know. Maybe. He seems like a good guy. But I can't trust him enough to tell him I'm hiding. It won't work."

"All right." Ash clasped Harper on the shoulder. He wasn't here to be pushy. He might not be able to solve all of Harper's problems, but he could still bring his flower joy and care for him in other ways. "Want to do something fun?"

23

HARPER

"Like flying?" Harper perked up.

He'd had more than enough sorting out his life for the day. Everything he did felt like a monumental decision. Any wrong move bound to be his last. Fun and a little distraction would help keep him going so he could face whatever agonizing choice came next.

Ash's eyes flashed. "Yes. Exactly like flying."

Harper melted, his muscles going lax and core burning to match the heat in Ash's gaze.

Why was Ash so into him? Maybe it was a demon thing to go from zero to a hundred in the relationship department. But did that mean Ash would get tired of him quickly too? Was all his intensity and apparent adoration just how he was in all relationships?

"Let's do it." Harper pushed his doubts aside. He wanted to see Ash's wings when he wasn't cooped up in a small apartment.

Ash took his hand and led him down the street. "You're not afraid of heights, are you?"

"Nope, never have been."

"Good." Ash pulled him down an alley. "Here. Let me cast an illusion over us so no one will see."

Magic tingled along Harper's skin as Ash wove his magic. "Demons can be completely invisible?"

"Yes." Ash seemed surprised Harper didn't know. "We have a few unique tricks."

Harper would kill for a detailed list but wasn't going to ask. It wasn't fair to expect Ash to answer a bunch of questions when he wouldn't do the same. He couldn't let Ash in, no matter how much he ached to.

Why would a powerful demon care about solving his problems?

Letting Ash help him today tempted Harper to open up. He wanted whatever was happening between them to be special. He wanted Ash to be his person—his demon—but didn't see how that kind of devotion could be real this early on.

He'd get to know Ash. Then, if it all worked out, he'd open up. And hopefully, he'd figure out what to do about his life and job in the meantime.

Once the illusion was cast, Ash took off his shirt and tied it to his belt. His brown skin gleamed in the sun and his eyes flashed deep orange.

Ash released his wings and horns, and Harper's heart thudded. Ash grinned at him and spread his wings, black feathers fading to a snowy white along the edges. The span had to be more than ten feet across.

"You're so beautiful, Ash."

Harper swore the demon puffed out his chest. "Thank you, flower." He readjusted the waistband of his jeans to free his tail, unwrapping it from his hips.

Harper's gaze traced the sleek appendage, his face heating. "It won't be hard to carry me?" he asked so he didn't say anything embarrassing. He didn't know if he'd ever be able to look at Ash's tail without remembering how it filled him.

"Not at all. Carrying you will be easy." Ash ruffled his feathers. "Come here."

Harper obeyed, situating his shoulder bag between them.

Ash brushed a gentle kiss against his lips and pulled him close. "Wrap your arms around my neck, and I'll lift you so you can wrap your legs around my hips."

They got into the position, Ash lifting Harper effortlessly.

Harper held on tight. "You sure it won't be hard to hold me while we fly?"

"Yes, I'm sure." Ash secured one hand under Harper's ass and the other around his lower back. "I won't get tired, and there's no way I'll drop you." Ash met Harper's gaze. "You'll be perfectly safe. I'd like to take you over the city to where I'm staying, at my brother's house. Is that okay?"

"Yeah." Butterflies made a racket in Harper's chest. "Will your brother be there?"

Harper still needed to tell Ash about his failed hunt and his coven's plans, but he'd worry about that later.

"He's out at the moment. They both are, so we'll have the place to ourselves, but they want to meet you."

"They do?" Harper was surprised Ash had even mentioned him to his brothers. Why would the other Hounds of Hell want to meet him?

Maybe Ash really was serious about him. Ash had been serious enough to reveal himself. Was Harper being too suspicious? His worry over Nico seemed to have amounted to nothing.

Ash tightened his hold on Harper. "They'd love to meet you, but you don't have to see them today. We can leave before they get back."

Harper nodded. "Okay. Can we go flying now?"

Ash chuckled. "Sure thing, sweet. Hold on tight." He squeezed Harper against him and launched into the air.

Harper gasped and clung on.

Ash's leap cleared the surrounding buildings. He pumped his wings and soared higher, catching the wind, and flew up and over the river. A flock of birds parted, making way for them. Ash dove, dipping just above the water, then shot back into the sky.

He cut toward the center of the city. Harper couldn't believe they were flying, the wind whipping his hair and buildings getting smaller beneath them. It was like being on a roller-coaster.

Harper let out a laugh, catching Ash's eye.

The demon grinned, climbing higher, then dove.

Harper shrieked, joy bubbling out of him as he laughed harder. "Damn, this is amazing!"

Ash chuckled. "Yeah? How about this?" He rolled, spinning them around like a corkscrew, and Harper screamed with delight. Ash straightened out. "Haven't pulled that move in a while. It's like being young again."

Harper nuzzled his cheek. "I take back calling you ancient. Do it again?"

Ash obliged and Harper swore he could feel Ash's excitement echoing his.

They flew across town toward the ocean. Salt tinged the air, filling Harper's nose. He buried his face against Ash's neck and breathed in his smoky scent. Ash's arms tightened around him. Here, high above the city, with nothing securing him but two strong arms, Harper had never felt safer.

He should tell Ash about his hunt and his coven. He didn't have to accept Ash's help or risk everything by relying on him, but he felt so secure with this man, this demon. Maybe he could take a little risk.

What was the worst that could happen? Surely Ash

wouldn't hand him over to his coven after killing to protect him. Maybe there wasn't too much risk in sharing his life with Ash, even if he didn't understand Ash's interest.

He trusted Ash not to drop him. Couldn't he trust Ash with the truth of who he was and what his life had been?

Harper watched waves crash on the beach as Ash flew along the waterfront, heading for the cliffs north of the city where a private nature reserve prevented development and kept the clifftop green and free of people.

Was that where the demons lived? Harper never would have figured that out through the city's stone memory.

Ash flew over a flock of sooty shearwaters nesting on the cliff face. A magical spark skittered across Harper's skin, and a house appeared where a second before, there'd been nothing but wild shrubbery and tall trees.

Ash smoothly landed on a large deck and lowered Harper to his feet. "Did you enjoy that?"

Harper's pulse pounded. He still felt like he was soaring. "It was incredible. Ten out of ten, best thing ever."

Ash flexed his wings, looking at Harper like he was every-thing he wanted, his smile so warm Harper could almost feel it.

Harper wanted to be Ash's everything. He wanted all the feelings inside him to grow until they fell in love, which was a lot to want from someone he hardly knew. But what if he leaned in and followed his feelings, even if they didn't make sense? Where would they take him?

Ash was one of the best things to happen to him. Harper seemed to be stumbling into all kinds of good people. What if he embraced Ash instead of letting fear rule every aspect of his life?

Harper pulled Ash into a kiss. His fangs remained retracted, even with his other demon features out, so Harper was free to devour his lips. Ash opened for him and Harper let his tongue explore Ash's mouth, only pulling back when he struggled to breathe.

Ash smiled slyly. "You really like flying."

"Mm-hmm." Harper continued kissing him. What he really liked was Ash. The flying was a bonus.

Humming against Harper's lips, Ash picked him up, Harper's limbs automatically wrapping around Ash's strong body.

Ash carried Harper from the deck, entering a large open doorway into the house. Everything seemed built to accommodate a demon's wings.

They entered a room with a view of the nature reserve rather than the ocean and city the other side of the house overlooked. Ash closed the door and tossed Harper onto the bed, taking his shoulder bag and setting it on the floor.

Harper's heart did summersaults.

Ash spread his wings as he climbed onto the bed, the large room easily accommodating him. His chest heaved and his golden-brown eyes burned bright.

Faced with the intensity of Ash's desire, Harper's breath caught and his core liquefied, desire coiling deep inside him as his cock hardened. He pulled off his shirt and pants like he was in a race to get naked.

Ash grinned and his fangs descended. "My sweet flower, so eager for me."

"Yes." Harper laid back and spread his legs, his erection pushing against the soft fabric of his thong.

Ash ran a hand up his thigh and brushed Harper's covered bulge. "Will you turn over for me? Let me see that round ass?"

Pleasure pooled between Harper's legs, his cock leaking. He turned onto his stomach and then up on his knees with his legs spread. He arched his back, sticking his ass up.

"Fuck, you're beautiful. Look at you presenting yourself to me." Ash's hands trailed up Harper's thighs to his ass, and

Harper moaned. Ash spread Harper's ass cheeks and something —Ash's tail—teased along Harper's G-string. "Do you want my tail inside you, hitting your sweet spot?"

"Yes." Harper fisted the bedspread. He wanted more than that. *Damnation.* He wanted all of Ash.

There was a rustle of cloth. Harper peered over his shoulder to see Ash discarding his jeans and boxer briefs. He grabbed a bottle of lube from his nightstand and settled behind Harper.

"Are you enjoying this position?" Ash asked as he massaged Harper's backside.

"Mm-hmm," Harper moaned, wiggling his ass. "It's hot."

He felt powerful spread so wantonly for Ash. He never imagined he could stick his ass in the air without embarrassment or uncertainty, but all that filled him was heat and a deep craving to be close to Ash. To give his body to Ash in every way.

Ash's tail tickled his hole and Harper sucked in a breath.

"So hot, flower." Ash's touch ran along Harper's G-string. "Can I leave your thong on? It might be covering your hole, but I can't bring myself to take it off completely."

"Okay." Harper clenched in anticipation, his face and neck burning.

Ash pulled the G-string to one side, the tug of the fabric making Harper feel naughty, like he was too horny to get undressed, so desperate to be filled that Ash had to satisfy him just like this.

Lube trickled down his crack as Ash's tail circled his rim.

Ash pressed his tail inside Harper, the feeling familiar. Harper relaxed more easily than before, thrusting back and taking what he wanted. Ash fucked in and out of Harper, massaging his ass cheek as his other hand held Harper's thong out of the way.

When Ash's tail brushed Harper's prostate, Harper groaned

into the mattress. He rocked back into Ash, trying to take more of his tail. "I need you, Ash. More, please."

Ash pegged his prostate. "Like this?"

Harper shouted. "Yes. Oh fuck. Ash, more. Fuck me, please. I need your cock."

Ash growled, fingers flexing on Harper's ass. "You want me to stretch you open and fill you up?"

"*Yes.*" Harper moaned as Ash's tail did something mind-blowing inside him. "No one's ever fucked me. I need it to be you. Please."

"Anything you want, sweetheart," Ash rumbled. "My cock was made for you."

24

———

ASH

Ash's chest tightened with longing. His flower wanted and trusted him enough to give him his body in new ways. Ash glowed, his internal fire radiating happiness.

He pulled Harper's thong down around his thighs, exposing him completely and freeing his cock. Ash ran his finger around his tail, where it penetrated his mate, adding more lube. "You still like this position, sweet?"

"Yes." Harper pressed back into his touch, and Ash slipped his finger in alongside the tip of his tail. Harper moaned and clenched, rocking his hips and trying to fuck himself.

The sight made Ash dizzy. "How does that feel?"

Harper groaned. "Good. More."

"Patience. I'm going to take my time with you." Ash withdrew his tail. Harper whimpered in protest but quieted when Ash's tail moved to tease his balls. Ash replaced it with another finger, filling Harper's hole with two.

"Yes, touch me, Ash." Harper tightened around his fingers, and Ash's demon fire flared in his chest.

His mate was so passionate. He might hold back in other

areas, but not here. Harper's openness deserved to be rewarded, and that Ash could do. He'd make this the best it could be.

He pumped his fingers, scissoring them and stretching Harper bit by bit. "Do you want me to use a condom?"

Harper glanced over his shoulder. His cheeks and neck flushed deep red. "We don't have to, right?" His eyes fluttered closed, and he groaned as Ash added more lube.

"No, we don't have to." Ash fucked the lube into his mate. Harper needed to be dripping with it by the time Ash's cock got anywhere near his hole. "I'm immortal and can't carry or catch human ailments, but it's about what you're comfortable with. Not everyone likes the mess of taking a load."

"No condom," Harper said in a rush. His hole fluttered around Ash's fingers. "I want you in me."

"Fuck." Ash could come just seeing Harper like this. He squeezed his dick to keep his pleasure at bay. "You want me to fill you with my cum, flower?"

"Yes." Harper thrust back.

Ash purred so deeply that it sounded more like a growl. Their desires aligned. His mate wanted his seed.

Harper wanted to be mated.

Ash squeezed Harper's ass and drove his fingers in deeper. "Good. I want nothing more than to claim you."

Harper's mouth fell open on a whimper, his wide-eyed gaze locked on Ash.

He clamped his mouth shut and focused on touching Harper. It was too soon to speak of claiming and mating, even if he longed to call Harper his mate aloud.

One day. Today, he'd mark Harper with his cum. Fuck Harper's virgin hole and show Harper what an eternity of pleasure would be like. They'd get to mating eventually.

Ash pressed a third finger into Harper, going slow and

adding more lube. Harper hissed a stuttered breath, and Ash stopped. "Are you okay?"

"Yeah, just give me a second."

Ash waited, stroking Harper's leaking cock with his hand as his tail teased his inner thighs.

A few moments later, Harper pushed back. "I'm ready."

Ash sank his fingers in slowly, fucking in and out, going deeper each time until he was buried as far as he could go. He found Harper's prostate, and Harper let out a shout of pleasure. Ash fucked Harper with his fingers until he moved easily.

He slicked his cock. "I can't wait to bury my dick inside you, Harper." His voice came out in a growl. "Are you ready for it?"

"Yes, fuck me, Ash. I want your cock, please. I need to feel you."

Ash withdrew his fingers and lined himself up, pressing against Harper's hole. "I've got what you need, Harper." He pressed forward, rumbling as Harper opened for him, enveloping his cockhead beautifully, so tight and perfect. "There you go, sweet. Take my cock."

"Oh fuck, Ash," Harper moaned. "You're splitting me open."

Ash paused with just his tip inside his mate. "Is it too much?"

"No." Harper shot a look over his shoulder. "Not too much. I like feeling you taking over my body. I like you so much, Ash."

"I adore you, Harper." Ash caressed his hips with his hands and tail. "This cock is yours now. Whenever you want it, I'll give it to you."

Harper whimpered, his eyes glassy. "Ash…"

He hummed, squeezing Harper's ass. "You're mine, Harper. And I'm yours."

Harper closed his eyes. "*Please.*"

Ash pushed forward, filling Harper another inch. He

paused and pulled back before filling him again, his movements slow and reverent. "Do you feel it? This is what it's like to be cherished, sweet. To have someone who belongs to you, giving you everything you need. I want to be that for you. Give you my cock, my soul, whatever you want."

"Ash," Harper sobbed. "No, you can't. Don't. It feels too good."

Ash stilled his rocking hips, his heart skipping a beat. "Sweetheart, are you crying?"

Harper rubbed his eyes, pulling off his glasses and blinking wet lashes as a choked sound passed his lips. "Don't say stuff like that if you don't mean it."

Ash pulled out of Harper and blanketed him with his body, folding his wings around them in a cocoon. He nuzzled Harper's ear. "I'd never say something I don't mean. I adore you, and making love to you is shaking all my mushy thoughts loose. If it's too much, we don't have to do this."

Ash could have cursed himself for overwhelming Harper. But he didn't know how to be this intimate with his mate and not spew his feelings. Ash wanted this moment to be everything to Harper, but it was everything to him too.

"I want this," Harper whispered. "I just need to know it's real. That you like me and aren't just saying sex things that you'll take back later."

Ash kissed his cheek. "I like you more than anything, Harper. You're a sweet, brave man, and you've captured my heart. I want to get to know everything about you. Your body and pleasure, your history and dreams. I want to be yours. If it isn't too much to ask?"

"It isn't. Not at all." Harper rubbed his cheek against Ash. "I want all that too. So much it scares me."

"Then I'll protect your heart." Ash tipped Harper's head back until their lips met. "I promise. You're safe with me."

Harper's lips trembled as they pressed against Ash's, the tremor flowing down his body. "Then fuck me like I'm yours."

Ash purred, his heart swelling. "I'd be honored, flower."

He pulled back enough to align his cock with Harper's slick hole and push in. Harper let out a sweet, breathy moan as he pulled Ash back inside him. Ash kept his chest flush against Harper's back and wrapped his tail around Harper's waist. He rocked his hips, kissing the back of Harper's neck and nibbling his ear. With one hand bracing himself, Ash used his other to toy with Harper's nipples. Harper trembled, beautiful groans falling from his sweet lips.

Harper's fresh bluebell scent filled the room, and Ash swore he could feel mountain air caressing his feathers. Pure bliss washed over him. He was meant for this moment more than anything in his long life.

Ash pressed his hips forward until he slid all the way into Harper, filling him completely.

"Ash," Harper gasped.

"I've got you." Ash tilted Harper's chin and captured his mouth in a kiss. "My sweet flower, I've got you."

He worked Harper's lips with small, sweet movements, immersing himself in his mate. Harper thrust back, and Ash took the hint. He rolled his hips, savoring Harper's tight heat. He was home, connecting with his flower, and nothing had ever felt so right.

"Ash, you feel so good. I'm so full. I've never..." Harper's words broke off with a moan. "I never thought it could be like this."

"Me either, sweet. You're tight and perfect, and you let me stretch you so wonderfully, but it's more than that. I feel so close to you. You feel so right in my arms."

"Yes!" Harper cried, squirming beneath him. "Fuck me, Ash. It feels so right. Please don't stop."

Ash snapped his hips and Harper lurched forward, letting out a cry of pleasure. He met Ash's next thrust with one of his own. Ash growled and pushed to his knees, gripping Harper's hips. He pulled out and thrust back in.

"More," Harper begged, and Ash did it again. He adjusted his angle, and on his next stroke, he hit Harper's prostate, setting him screaming and burying his head in the sheets.

Ash's fangs descended. He flexed his wings and thrust, watching his cock disappear into Harper's sweet hole.

Harper met every hard stroke and their moans bled together. Pleasure tightened inside Ash. He needed to fill his mate, claim him with his cum, and give him everything. He reached for Harper's hard cock and stroked him in time with his fucking.

Harper pressed back, bucking against Ash. "Fill me, Ash. Make me yours."

"*Mine,*" Ash growled, tail tightening around Harper's waist. "You're mine, Harper. Mine to love and cherish and please."

Harper came crying Ash's name, his hole squeezing and pulsing around Ash's aching cock. Ash thrust deep, pressing his groin hard into Harper's ass, and pumped Harper full, wings beating like he was trying to take off as his orgasm rattled his soul.

Harper whimpered, his movements stuttering to a stop, and Ash stroked his back. He seemed to melt, going boneless under Ash's touch.

Ash slowly pulled out and massaged Harper's ass cheeks. Harper's hole was pink and looked thoroughly used. A rumble rolled through Ash as his cum leaked out, dripping down Harper's inner thighs and balls.

Ash traced Harper's rim delicately. "So pretty."

Harper's breathing picked up. He squirmed.

"Never seen anything lovelier." Ash gripped Harper's hips

and rolled him onto his back, removing the thong from around his thighs and tossing it away before pulling Harper into a tight hug. "Thank you, sweetheart. That was wonderful, best sex of my life."

Harper's eyes widened. After a long moment, he said softly, "Same. Well, I mean, not that I can compare, exactly." His cheeks flushed a deep crimson. "I used to be so nervous, but I wasn't. With you. It was even better than I dreamed, and I thought my fantasies were pretty good. You know?"

Ash grinned, and Harper's smile broke free.

"That makes me very happy," Ash murmured before covering Harper's mouth with his.

ASH CLEANED them in the adjoining bathroom and brought Harper back to bed, where they curled up under the covers, Harper's head resting on Ash's chest. He'd returned his wings to tattoo form to make it more comfortable to lie on his back, but he'd left his horns, fangs, and tail in their natural state.

Ash was boneless. He could lie like this for a week and not get bored.

Harper's fingers trailed over Ash's left pec and down his side. Ash's tail twitched. He brought it over his lap and laid it across Harper's hips.

"Will you really help me with my coven?" Harper whispered.

Ash peered down but couldn't see Harper's face in this position. "Yes, I'll help any way I can. If you tell me what's going on, we can choose the best approach together. We can handle them however you want."

Harper's arm tightened around Ash. "They worship Lucifer. Does that change anything?"

"It won't change me helping you if that's what you mean. But I can't say more than that without knowing the details. It may change how we tackle this."

Harper peeked up at him, uncertainty in his eyes.

Ash waited. What was Harper thinking? He didn't want to push and risk Harper shutting down again.

Harper's gaze strayed to his glasses on the side table.

Ash reached for them. "Do you need these back?"

Harper shook his head. "They're fake. I only started wearing them to change my appearance. My hair used to be brown too."

Ash smiled. "I noticed the hair at your groin was lighter."

Harper blushed. "I actually like how I look in the disguise. I never got to dress or style my hair how I wanted. My coven was controlling..." His words petered out, sounding defeated.

Ash ran a hand through Harper's hair, hating that anyone had squashed his flower's spirit. "I'm sorry you couldn't express yourself around your coven, but I'm glad you've taken the chance to do it now and that you like how you look."

"Me too." Harper's lips twitched in a tiny smile that lit Ash's world. "My coven is awful. My dad's the leader, and I couldn't use magic against him or anyone. He kept me at the lowest rank."

Ash frowned. "Your coven uses blood loyalty?"

"Yes." Harper seemed confused. "Isn't blood loyalty automatic within families? I know not all covens make members swear blood oaths to join, but families already share blood, so isn't rank inherent?"

"No. Sharing blood isn't enough to enforce blood loyalty. Not all families use blood to control their relatives. The practice is very old and has become less and less popular over the centuries."

"Makes sense we'd still be doing it. It fits with everything else." Harper let out a long sigh, drawing circles on Ash's chest. "I'm powerful. My father would drain my blood to access my magic. I could never fight back enough to get away. When I got older and stopped cooperating, he would tie me down."

Pain seared through Ash. "I'm so sorry, Harper. No father should abuse their child like that. You did so well, escaping him even with everything set against you. You made it through something most people couldn't even imagine."

Harper squeezed Ash tight, whispering, "I can't let him find me. I'll never escape if he gets his hands on me again. He used to lock me away, leave me weak and helpless. No one in the coven helped me."

"Fuck, sweetheart, that's awful. But don't worry." Ash tilted Harper's head so their eyes met. "I promise I'll protect you. Your father will *never* hurt you again. You won't have to live in fear of him or anyone ever again."

Ash meant it with every cell in his being. He'd use all his considerable power to ensure Harper was never hurt again.

"Even a demon like you couldn't take on a whole coven," Harper whispered, showing how deep his fear ran. Not even Ash's presence could banish it. But that was understandable. Harper had been alone and abused and had never had another person to lean on.

No wonder he was so afraid and guarded. Ash would have to show him what love and family were supposed to be like.

"You're right. Going against a whole coven doesn't leave me with great odds." Ash wouldn't treat Harper with kid gloves or sugarcoat things. Harper could handle anything, especially if he had support. "I'm not invincible. But I have my brothers. We don't have to take on everyone at once. We can target your father or the coven members searching for you in the city. If you want to go after them rather than wait to see what they do next, just say the word. You can take control of the situation, Harper. I'm here to help you do that."

Harper gave him a startled look. "You really think we can take control?"

"Yes." Control over what happened would be important to Harper after everything. "You're in charge of your own life. No one, especially not your father, can take that from you again."

"But how can we be sure?" Harper's face filled with conflicted emotion. "I can't ask you to kill him, but I don't know if he'll stop otherwise."

"Of course you wouldn't ask for your father's death, sweet. You're a kind person, and that isn't something I'd expect you to want, even if the man deserves it. But I don't think I need to kill him to ensure he leaves you alone."

"No?"

Ash smiled. Putting Harper's father in his place would calm the anger building inside him. "He'll be surprised to find one demon at your side, let alone three. Surely, threatening him would be enough to make him run and hide."

Harper bit his lip. "He might not be that surprised."

"Why not? Even if he's well-educated in magical history, we're more legend than real to most witches."

"True." Harper shifted so he was facing Ash, bracing against his chest. "But not to my coven." He averted his eyes. "Supposedly, the Nightingales are descended from Lucifer, and my father is pretty serious about serving him. He made it his mission to find you and your brothers. He suspected you lived in Shearwater Landing a long time ago and sent me to search the city's stone memory."

Ash's whole body tensed.

Harper's gaze darted to Ash's and caught his rigid posture. "I was never going to tell him if I found you. I was failing at my search anyway, and being sent here was the only reason I was finally able to escape."

"Your coven is the one hunting us?" Ash was having trouble processing. What were the odds of that?

"Yes. I'm sorry I didn't tell you sooner." Harper's hands flexed on Ash's chest. "My plan was to warn you and the other demons if I found you and ensure my coven never found out anything about you. I wasn't letting them get any more power. I promise."

Ash relaxed, his shock dissolving. Harper's fear kept him guarded, and Ash would never hold that against him.

"I can see why you didn't tell me right away. I'm only beginning to understand what you were running from, and I wouldn't expect someone in your position to trust blindly. But what do you mean by letting your coven get more power? How would finding us help them achieve that?"

If Harper's coven had been planning to slay Ash and his brothers for the magic in their demon blood, Ash didn't think he could stop Onyx and Dante from killing the Nightingales.

"My father planned to hand you over to Lucifer and hoped to gain favor and power for being such a good servant." Harper wrinkled his nose. "I'd never have let that happen. I was only ever looking for you to warn you. I swear."

Ash ran a hand through Harper's hair. "Of course you wanted to warn us. You're kind, Harper. You'd do nothing less. You've been fighting against your father your whole life. You'd never choose to serve him."

"Thank you for believing me," Harper murmured. "I wish I'd trusted you sooner."

"Don't worry about it. You were being smart." Ash cupped Harper's cheek. "I'm just happy I've finally won you over. It feels like quite an accomplishment."

Harper tried to bite back a smile but didn't quite manage.

Ash rubbed his hands up and down Harper's back. "How'd you escape? You said your coven isn't in Shearwater Landing?"

Harper rested his chin on his hands and told Ash how he grew up on a remote compound in the Colorado mountains. His upbringing made Ash's demon fire burn with rage, but it also showed him how strong and resilient his flower was. Harper told Ash how he planned his escape for months. He'd been more careful and patient than Ash ever could have been.

Ash couldn't imagine facing his future with anyone else. Harper would be a rock by Ash's side.

"You've accomplished so much on your own, Harper, but you aren't alone anymore. When you need to face something, I'll be right there with you. You only have to ask."

"Thank you." Harper's hands clenched, then relaxed. The rest of his muscles seemed to follow, a small shiver coursing through him.

"How did your coven plan on handing us over?" It was almost harder to capture a demon alive than to kill one. Not much on Earth could hold them.

Harper frowned. "I don't know. It's one of the holes in my father's plan. He liked to imply he had a connection to Lucifer, but I think he was lying. I don't know how he planned to relay your location. I doubt Lucifer responds to séances."

A sharp laugh escaped Ash. "No, he definitely doesn't." At least that was good news. The Nightingales didn't seem like a strong threat, except to Harper.

"What happened?" Harper hesitated, curiosity shaping his face. "I mean, I know demons fell to Earth in a rebellion, but how did Lucifer become someone you needed to escape? Weren't you all on the same side? Why are all the demons in Hell and not on Earth like they used to be?"

Ash hated what had happened to his relationship with Luc. What if it had all turned out differently? Could it have, or was betrayal always part of his and Luc's story? "That's a long story, sweet."

"I don't have anywhere else I want or need to be," Harper said softly. "But if you don't want to tell me, that's okay."

Ash hauled Harper closer and kissed him. "There's nothing I don't want to tell you. I want you to know me."

Harper's eyes shone. "I want that too."

Ash cradled Harper against him, Harper's head tucked into Ash's neck, and Ash told him about Luc. How they'd known each other from childhood and were the closest friends. Ash ached for the love he once had for his first chosen brother and resented the pain that had replaced it, but he shared it all with Harper.

He explained how the Eternal Realm had damned them for creating witches and how Luc had twisted over the years, seeking power until he betrayed them all and imprisoned them.

Ash didn't mention mates. He wanted to. They were so close to the topic. Would Harper want to hear it now? They'd become so much closer today. Maybe it wasn't too soon.

"How could he betray you like that?" Harper asked.

"I'm not sure," Ash admitted. "I've always wondered what I missed. When did he go from my brother to someone as controlling as your father? No one has ever hurt me like Luc did. I trusted him with everything, and he used that for his own benefit, making the most of the bad situation he created but not trying to improve it for anyone but himself."

There was never supposed to be a new ruler after the fall. They were escaping the council and finding their mates, not founding a new controlling society, but when that failed, Ash still hadn't seen Luc's quest for power over others coming.

"Can I admit something?" Harper asked.

Ash dragged his mind out of the deep past. "Of course."

Harper gave him a sheepish smile. "I never really understood why it was such a big deal that witches were damned. Hell isn't what humans make it out to be. It isn't eternal torture or a place for morally corrupt people to be punished, so why does it matter which afterlife we go to?"

"It's not a place of torture, but it's not peaceful. There's something not right about the Realm of the Damned. It feels wrong and unsettling. You know in your gut you aren't supposed to be there. It's not how things are supposed to be. Even beings who never knew the Eternal Realm feel it, almost as if witches know in their souls they were meant for mortality and reincarnation. It's subtle, but eternity is a long time."

Harper ran a hand through Ash's hair and along one of his horns. "I'm glad you got out."

"Me too, sweet." If he hadn't escaped, would he have found Harper in their damned afterlife? He preferred being here, but at least he might not have been alone forever.

"Was the rebellion worth it?" Harper asked, clearly still curious.

Ash paused. This was it. He either had to lie or tell Harper the rebellion wasn't what he'd been led to believe.

Harper waited patiently, his soft brown eyes eager. He'd given Ash so much today. How could Ash hold back after that?

Ash kissed Harper on the forehead, and his stomach swooped. "It wasn't a rebellion as such. We left the Eternal Realm to find our mates."

Harper's brows rose. "Mates?"

"Yes, our fated loves. Our other halves. The souls we were destined to be with for eternity. Mates must be granted in the Eternal Realm, but Luc and many others like me believed that was false. Fated connections existed regardless of approval, so we came to Earth to find our mates and live freely, only they weren't here, and after centuries of searching, I gave up."

"You gave up?" Harper breathed, eyes wide.

"I did. I was sure we'd never find our mates. The Eternal Realm punished us for falling by keeping our mates in the afterlife. We'd never be able to earn forgiveness and get them back." Ash's throat clogged. "I lost hope a millennia and a half ago, and everything that's happened since only aggravated me. The world became such a mess, and with no hope left, I just glared at it all, telling myself being alone was what I deserved."

Ash cleared his throat. He sat up and pulled Harper onto his lap, cradling his face. "But I was wrong, sweet flower. All hope wasn't lost. I finally found you."

25

HARPER

"Found me?" The question fell from Harper's lips in a barely audible puff.

"Yes, Harper." Ash's eyes burned with golden flame, heat and his smoky scent swelling around them. "You're my mate. Can't you feel it?"

Harper's head spun, stomach dropping like he was falling even though he hadn't moved. Something tight pinched his chest. "Feel it how? What do you mean?"

Ash brushed the hair from Harper's forehead. "I'm drawn to you. Nothing feels as good as being near you or seeing you happy. The night after the club, before I realized who you were, my instincts took over. My magic recognized you even though I'd stopped believing. I was overcome by you and have felt our connection growing since."

Harper gripped Ash's waist, trying to steady himself. All his inexplicable longing for Ash—the feelings he'd tried and failed to fight—churned inside him, giving way to something secure. "Is that why I feel safe with you? My reactions never made sense. I was drawn to you too. I figured I was just overly attached. But it's magic?"

"It's the mate connection," Ash corrected with a soft smile. "It's magic, but it's not a spell influencing you. The magic comes from within us. Fate brought us together. That feeling is the divine alignment between our souls."

"Oh." The truth of Ash's words vibrated through Harper, feeling as right as everything else between them. He'd never have believed in fated mates if he hadn't felt it. "So we're mated?" An excited shiver wound through him.

"Not quite." Ash gave him that devastatingly handsome smile. "Fate may have connected us, but only the beginning of the bond exists. We have to choose to accept it, and if we do, the mating ritual will cement it, giving you an eternal life to match mine so we can be together without end."

Together forever.

Harper laughed, then clamped his mouth shut. "Sorry. This is all so far from anything I ever imagined. How can I be your mate? Me? I'm no one, and you're you."

"You aren't no one, Harper. You are the most special person in my world. We're equally matched. Maybe not in magical power, but that isn't what being mates is about. Please don't speak badly about yourself."

Harper looked at his lap. "Sorry. I'm not used to being special."

"Get used to it, Harper, and don't apologize." There was a smile in Ash's tone, and Harper met his gaze. "I'm going to treasure you for the rest of time. You gave me hope again, and I can never repay you for that, but I'm going to try."

Harper's chest burst. His future opened before him into this bright, unfathomable thing, and the possibility undid him. All he'd wanted was a simple life, free of pain and other's control, but what he'd found was so much more.

He crashed his mouth into Ash's.

"You're mine, sweet flower," Ash murmured against his lips. "And if you'll have me, I'll be yours forever."

"Yes." Harper kissed him, licking carefully around his fangs. "Yes, Ash. I want to be yours."

Ash rumbled, pulling Harper closer, the deep sound turning to a purr as Harper's cock hardened against Ash's stomach.

"How do we mate?" Harper asked in a desperate pant. "How do we cement the bond?"

Ash let out a deep whine. He pulled back from their kiss, revealing a raw expression. "There's a ritual. A spell to complete the connection. It involves sex and an exchange of blood, but we aren't doing it right now."

"We aren't?" Harper fought with disappointment, even as the reality of blood exchange gave him pause.

"No." Ash stroked Harper's cheek. "Don't get me wrong, I want to, but you need time to absorb all this. We don't have to rush. Just knowing you want to accept the bond is more than enough. I'm so happy, Harper. I can't wait to begin our life together, but I want to do it right."

"Okay." Harper could see what a big deal this was to Ash and had to admit, time to get his head around everything wouldn't hurt. He wanted to appreciate this as much as he could and pledge himself to Ash with as much emotion as Ash clearly had for the situation. "We'll wait until we're ready."

"Perfect." Ash beamed before covering Harper's mouth with his.

They belonged together. They'd been meant for each other since before Harper was born, since the beginning of time. This was better than Harper's wildest fantasy. He'd wanted a partner, someone to be his person, but he'd never imagined a connection like the one he could have with Ash.

All of Ash's affection was real, and now that Harper knew where it came from, he could feel their connection buzzing between them stronger than ever. He wasn't just safe with Ash. He was home.

Pounding on the bedroom door sent a shock through Harper. He broke their kiss and glanced over his shoulder.

"You better not hide in there all day, Ash," a voice called, laced with annoyance.

Ash pursed his lips. "Go away."

There was a huff, but the intruder said nothing more.

Harper looked between the door and Ash. "Who was that?"

"Onyx." Ash ran his hands down Harper's bare back. "Would you like to meet the other demons?"

He'd rather stay in bed, ideally so Ash could fuck him again.

His ass ached, and he clenched at the thought. Maybe round two should wait. Not that Harper was complaining about the slight discomfort. He'd never wish away the reminder of what they'd done. Being fucked by Ash had changed Harper's world, and he liked this version so much better than the one he'd left behind.

Ash was his demon. His.

Harper kissed Ash's neck, feeling his warm skin everywhere. He yearned to get lost in Ash's body, but there would be plenty of time for that.

"I'd like to meet your brothers." Harper paused. Would the other demons like him? "Do they know I'm your mate?"

"Yes." Ash cut an apprehensive glance toward the door. "Dante is thrilled I found you. He never gave up on finding his mate. But Onyx is more complicated. He and I don't usually get along."

Hopefully, the other demons wouldn't be mad about his hunt. Ash understood because they were mates. But Harper couldn't expect that of the others.

"You don't have to meet them now," Ash added, seeming to sense Harper's hesitation.

"No, I want to." Harper didn't want to hide from the other demons. Besides, he had Ash in his corner.

"They'll love you, Harper." Ash rubbed circles over his hips with his thumbs. "Just don't take anything Onyx says to heart. He wasn't pleased I revealed myself to you without telling them first."

"Were you supposed to tell them?"

Ash nodded. "It was a strict rule among us, and Onyx's anger is justified. We've been very careful since returning to the Human Realm and have stayed out of the magic world as much as possible."

"I'd never give you away. I'll make sure Onyx knows that."

"I know, sweet. He'll come around. Don't worry." Ash patted Harper's hip, and he got off Ash's lap. "Come on."

They got out of bed and Ash picked up Harper's lube-soaked thong, lips twisting in a satisfied smile. "I'll wash this for you and return it next time I see you."

Harper's whole body heated. "Okay." He ducked his head and pulled on his jeans.

Ash set the thong aside. "Would it be all right if I bought you some things?"

Harper tugged his shirt over his head. "Like what?"

Ash rubbed his jaw. "It'd be good for you to keep some clothes here. I could get you the essentials. That way, I don't have to worry about ruining anything, and you can still be dressed properly after I'm through with you."

Harper laughed. "Sure." Having things at Ash's place gave him a warm fuzzy feeling.

Ash moved closer, putting an arm around Harper. "I'd also like to buy you some more pretty underwear. If you're comfortable with that."

Harper stifled a groan. Ash dressing him up and fucking him? "Yeah, I'm very comfortable with that."

Ash kissed him chastely, eyes glowing. "Perfect."

Harper pressed his palms against his hot cheeks. "You can't make me meet your brothers now. I'm all red."

Ash chuckled. "Sorry. Would you like me to go out and see what they're doing and give you a minute?"

Harper nodded.

Ash left the room, and Harper sat on the edge of the bed. He picked up his glasses and put them on. He was about to meet the other Hounds. How wild was that?

Not as wild as one of them being his mate, but still. Harper might start laughing uncontrollably. It was all so outrageous.

Once he'd collected himself, he exited the room and walked down the hall, catching the sound of voices as he neared the end.

"Just be civil, Onyx," Ash grumbled.

The response was too low for Harper to catch.

His stomach tightened.

If only Ash hadn't felt the need to reveal himself before talking to the others. Harper didn't want to start off on the wrong foot. But if Ash hadn't been truthful about who he was, Harper might not be here now. He'd have pushed Ash away.

He entered the living room, determined to win the other demons over. They were important to Ash, and gaining the Hounds' favor had been his plan all along. Hadn't it?

Ash's wings were out, folded against his back. His tail twitched as he loomed over a blue-haired man sitting in an armchair. Beside them was another demon, looking out the large windows, his dark-gray wings and tail snagging Harper's attention.

The second demon was almost as tall as Ash, though less bulky. He turned slowly, his gaze finding Harper's like he'd felt him staring.

The demon had black irises so mesmerizing Harper couldn't

help taking a step toward him. "Hello." The demon smiled, showing no fangs. "Welcome to my home. I'm Dante."

"Hi." Harper waved like a dork.

Dante stepped forward and offered his hand. Harper shook it. "It's an honor to meet you, Harper."

He laughed nervously. "Thanks."

Dante seemed as intense as Ash. Which made sense if they'd been searching for their mates for thousands of years.

Harper's gaze shot to Ash, only to find Ash beaming at him.

The guy in the armchair glared. He must be Onyx, but with his wings, tail, and horns hidden, it wasn't obvious he was a demon. He was smaller than the other two in height and build, his skin pale and eyes an icy blue.

He stood and stalked over to Harper, sweeping his gaze up and down like he was inspecting something suspicious. "So you're Ash's mate?"

"Um, yes?" Harper couldn't help it sounding like a question. Why did Onyx sound skeptical?

Ash pushed past Onyx and slipped an arm around Harper, staring down the smaller demon. "Are you ready to accept that Harper isn't one of Lucifer's tricks?"

Onyx frowned, still inspecting Harper. "Do you feel the connection?"

Harper nodded. "Yeah, especially now that I know what it means."

"Hm. Why should we believe you? You've been lying to Ash," Onyx challenged.

Ash growled.

Harper frowned at the blue-haired demon. "I'm not lying about my feelings. I've been hiding from my coven, and it's not like I'm foolish enough to trust random guys the second I meet them, so I didn't tell Ash my problems at first. But I've told him everything now."

"Not trusting blindly is a good trait to have," Dante said diplomatically.

Onyx rolled his eyes. "Yeah, well, if you meet a taller, more handsome version of me, don't trust him."

Harper glanced at Ash, not sure what Onyx meant.

"Lucifer has returned to the Human Realm," Ash explained. "We've been unable to track him and aren't sure what he's up to other than coming for us. But don't worry, I'll keep you safe."

"We'll imprison Luc before long, and he won't be a problem anymore," Dante added.

"Do you think he's in the city?" Harper's heart rate picked up. The idea that the Satan his coven worshipped was in their world made his skin crawl.

Ash's arm tightened around him. "Probably not, but we can't say for sure."

Dante hummed thoughtfully. "I wonder, if he is here, perhaps he's made contact with the witches hunting us. He might have realized what they were up to like I did."

"He wouldn't work with witches." Onyx waved a dismissive hand. "Luc doesn't bother with beings of lesser power."

It was the same attitude Harper's father had.

"That's not what you said before. When you were sure Harper was one of Luc's tricks." Ash turned from Onyx to Dante. "Luc hasn't contacted the hunter. Harper's coven is looking for us, but Harper was the only one searching."

"What?" Onyx's face bloomed with color.

"Relax." Ash sounded exhausted with Onyx. "Let me explain." He relayed how horrible Harper's coven was while keeping most of Harper's personal hurt out of it. "Harper escaped and was only trying to find us to warn us."

"I was never going to share anything I learned about you with my coven," Harper promised.

Onyx ground his teeth. "And we're supposed to believe him just because he's your mate?"

"Yes," Ash said, tone firm. "He's one of us. He's meant to be on our side."

"I thought you weren't worried about witches, Onyx," Dante cut in.

"And I thought you didn't trust witches," Onyx spat at Ash, jabbing at him with a pale finger.

Harper flinched. Ash wasn't kidding when he said they didn't get along, but Harper wondered if something deeper was happening here. Was there more to Onyx not accepting him than suspicion? He seemed different from the other demons, and only partly because he was hiding his demonic features.

"In general, no, I don't trust witches, vampires, or humans," Ash growled. "I don't trust demons either, outside of the two of you."

"Onyx, think about it." Dante laid a hand on the small demon's shoulder and was promptly shaken off. "Harper being the hunter makes sense. He was destined to find Ash. They're mates. Of course his fate was to look for us."

Onyx stared at Dante with an unreadable expression. "You've always been so sure about our mates. I don't get it. Why would Ash find his after so long? Why him and not you? How can you accept this so easily?" Onyx ran a hand through his hair. "I'm done. I don't need to stick around and watch *Ash,* of all people, get lovey-dovey." He turned and stormed out of the room.

Ash let out a deep sigh. "Don't worry, Harper. He'll get over himself eventually. He always does. He just likes to throw his toys first."

Dante stared after Onyx, concern lining his face. "I don't think he likes being caught off guard."

"Come." Ash tugged Harper toward the adjoining kitchen. "Let me make you something to eat."

Harper pushed away guilty feelings about upsetting Onyx. It would take time for Onyx to realize Harper wouldn't betray them, and Harper got that. The demons had been hiding for hundreds of years.

Onyx was probably just scared of things changing, especially with Lucifer closer than ever, but hopefully, change would be good for all of them.

26

HARPER

Ash pulled out a stool at the kitchen island. "Would you like anything to drink?"

Harper settled on the seat. "Just some water, thanks."

Ash brought him a glass and began pulling things out of the fridge.

Dante sat beside Harper, bracing his forearms on the counter. "I'm sorry meeting us wasn't more pleasant."

"That's okay. I get it. It's not like I trusted Ash at first."

Dante grinned, studying Harper in a much friendlier way than Onyx had. "How long have you been in Shearwater Landing?"

Harper's usual lie was on the tip of his tongue, but why lie to Dante? "About a year. How about you?"

Dante waved a dismissive hand. "I've been hanging around since the city was built."

"Oh, right." Harper should have seen that coming. His coven suspected the demons had been here a hundred years ago. Harper surveyed the room around them. There was no way Dante lived here back then. "Your home is beautiful."

"Thank you." Dante seemed pleased Harper liked it, feathers ruffling. "Has Ash told you about his place?"

"No?" Harper turned to Ash. "You said you were living here."

"I am." Ash measured flour into a stand mixer. "But until recently, I was off in the Rocky Mountains, near the Canadian border."

Dante leaned in and whispered to Harper. "He lives in a hut."

"It's a hunting lodge, which you very well know," Ash muttered.

"I grew up in the Rocky Mountains, only in Colorado." Harper looked between the demons. "Do you think that's a coincidence?"

Ash paused as he spooned dried yeast into a small bowl of water. "Probably not. Before, I'd have said there was no particular reason I settled where I did. I chose the mountains because they appealed to me. But maybe I was being drawn to you and didn't realize."

"So you weren't just avoiding us over the last few decades?" Dante teased.

Ash scowled. "I was multitasking."

Dante snorted.

Harper eyed Ash, trying to imagine him alone in the mountains. What would it be like to live together in an isolated hunting lodge? Even if it wasn't near where Harper had grown up, the idea chased away all his warm feelings. "Do you want to go back to your lodge?"

"No, not really." Ash opened a container of mushrooms. "Being by myself isn't as appealing as it once was. Now that I'm back, I've realized I missed being around others." He cut Dante a sheepish glance.

"Wow." Dante leaned back in his seat. "Never thought I'd hear you admit that. I like Harper's effect on you already."

Harper grinned, warmth flooding him again. "I'd like to stay in Shearwater Landing. I get along with my roommate pretty well and want to have friends and build a real life like I couldn't have before."

"Then we'll stay." Ash sounded happy with the decision. "I'll make sure your coven doesn't bother you, and once we deal with Luc, we can do anything you like."

Harper drew a deep breath like it was his first taste of fresh air.

With Ash's help, he could escape his coven permanently. True freedom was possible, and for the first time, Harper wasn't scared of what the future had in store.

"You aren't worried about Luc?" he asked. It was weird referring to Lucifer so informally.

"Yes and no." Ash abandoned the mushrooms and began mixing what looked like dough in the stand mixer. "He's a serious threat, but we know how to handle him."

"He isn't acting as we'd expected now that he's in the Human Realm, which is worrying, but we have an advantage in the city," Dante explained.

Ash rested his hand on Harper's. "I've already protected your apartment building, and I can give you personal protection until we cement the mating bond."

Harper's heart skipped at the mention of mating. "Why do I only need protection until we bond?"

"When we mate, you'll be granted all my immortal abilities, like rapid healing and complete disease immunity. You'll be almost as hard to kill as a demon. The bond also gives us an extra connection, so I'll always be able to find you. Before then, I'd like to cast some spells on you to help me track you quickly if anything happens."

"You mean you won't be with me twenty-four-seven," Harper joked.

"No." Ash's cheeks reddened. "But I'll watch over you if that makes you feel safe."

Harper squirmed. It would make him feel safe, but he kept it to himself. There was no need to get mushy in front of Dante.

Watching Ash cook was a treat. At first, it seemed odd for a demon with huge wings and horns to be in the kitchen, but the longer Harper watched, the more it seemed Ash was genuinely enjoying himself. He looked at home and happy, and it made Harper all gooey inside.

"What are you making?" he asked.

"Mushroom pizza." Ash set a ball of dough aside. "You said the other day that it was your favorite."

Butterflies filled Harper. He might actually float away.

AFTER PIZZA, Ash flew Harper home.

Ash opened the service door for Harper, pausing outside. "I'll track down the members of your coven who're in the city and let you know what they're doing. Then, we can decide how to approach them."

Harper nodded. He'd given Ash a description of the witches that had been following him—the ones he'd seen anyway—as well as his father and his advisers and told Ash where he used to live.

Ash said being familiar with Harper's magic would help him track his coven due to the blood loyalty binding its members. All the Nightingales' magic would feel similar to Harper's, at least enough to get Ash started on his tracking. Apparently, Ash had been getting a sense of Harper's magic ever since he'd unmasked Harper's suppression.

Ash leaned in and kissed Harper's forehead. "Text me if you need anything."

"I will," Harper promised, but with Ash's tracking spell cast over him, there wasn't much to worry about. "I can't wait to have everything with my coven behind me."

"Me too." Ash squeezed Harper's shoulder and flew off.

Harper headed down the stairs to his apartment.

Too bad he couldn't tell Ollie about Ash. The whole situation was like a dream, especially now that Ash was out of sight. But Harper wasn't sure about telling Ollie magic was real, at least not yet. If they became close, like true best friends, then Harper would tell him.

"Hey," Ollie called from the couch when Harper got inside. "What's that smile for?"

Harper tried to get his grin under control. "I was with Ash."

Ollie waggled his eyebrows. "I'm glad that's working out."

"Me too." Harper held back a laugh. Imagine explaining being a demon's mate to Ollie... "How was your day?"

Ollie dropped his head back on the couch. "Good. Work was busy, and I'm tired. My neck is killing me. I'm going to order in if you want to split something?"

"I can cook dinner," Harper offered.

Ollie gave him a sweet smile. "You're the best. I'll do tomorrow night. Promise."

Harper wasn't all that hungry but didn't mind cooking if Ollie was exhausted from work. It was a good use of the extra energy buzzing around inside him.

They ate and watched a movie afterward. As they finished up, Ollie scowled at his phone.

"Is everything all right?"

"Yeah." Ollie tossed his phone aside. "Just this guy I was talking to. He asked if I wanted to meet up tonight and was kind of a dick when I said I was busy. Like I owe him my time just because he messaged me a few times."

"Sorry, that sucks." Harper hated the guy instantly. "Have you met up with him before?"

"No." Ollie grabbed a pillow and hugged it to himself, making a face. "I've blocked him. At least I didn't sleep with him."

"Yeah, someone like that doesn't deserve you."

"I hate hookup apps." Ollie shot a sideways look at Harper. "But at the same time, I don't want to get zero action while taking a break from relationships, you know?"

"I don't exactly know from personal experience, but I get what you mean."

Ollie smiled, brow raising. "You've never used a hookup app?"

"No." Harper cringed, cheeks heating.

Ollie shook his head good-naturedly, like he thought Harper was cute. "Are you happy your one-night stand turned into a thing?"

"Yeah." Harper didn't even hesitate. "I really like Ash. We should all hang out sometime so you can meet him properly."

"Sure." Ollie grinned, leaning closer to Harper. "So, is he your boyfriend?"

Harper nodded.

"You look so happy right now, it's ridiculous." Ollie swatted Harper with a pillow.

He covered his face. "Sorry. I had a really good afternoon."

Ollie snorted. "I bet you did. And hey, if Ash has any hot friends, send them my way. But only if they're down for just a hookup. I don't need my one-night stands turning into more."

Were the other demons any more casual than Ash? Surely not if they were looking for their mates. "I don't know Ash's friends very well."

"I don't have to know them well, if you know what I mean." Ollie gave Harper a sly look, then cracked up at Harper's panicked expression. "Don't worry. I'm just teasing. I'll leave Ash's friends out of it."

Harper swatted Ollie with the pillow. Hopefully, he found what he was looking for.

HARPER SMILED AS SOON as he opened his eyes the next day.

Was it too soon to ask Ash for round two?

He grabbed his phone off the nightstand and found a message waiting.

ASH:

> Morning, sweet. Hope you slept well. I wanted to let you know I haven't sensed anyone with magic similar to yours in the Banks, and I've tracked almost all of your coven's advisers. They're out of state. I haven't located your father yet, so I can't say if he's in the city or not, but that's what Dante and I will be doing today.

Harper set down the phone, relief running through him. Not even wondering where his father was dampened his spirits.

Arthur probably had an anti-tracking spell cast on himself that Ash would have to get through before he could find him, but it was unlikely Arthur was using a suppressing potion. They'd find him eventually. If none of the other coven members were in the Banks, his father wouldn't be either. He never went anywhere alone.

Harper was safe.

Maybe they'd have this whole thing wrapped up by next

week, and Harper would be free of them. He picked up his phone and replied.

HARPER:

Thank you! Knowing for sure no one's in my neighborhood makes me feel so much better.

ASH:

Happy to hear it.

We're keeping an eye on the apartment complex where you used to live and the few coven members lurking near the port and library while we track down your father. I'll let you know if any of them head your way.

HARPER:

Why would they think I'd return to the port after last time?

ASH:

They might be trying to figure out what happened to the missing witches rather than looking for you.

True. His coven didn't know what had happened at the port. They didn't even know Finch had found him. At least not for sure.

ASH:

Don't worry. There's no evidence of what I did to the witches who attacked you. They won't discover anything, no matter how much they poke around.

HARPER:

Thank you, Ash.

Having Ash on his side changed everything. Possibilities opened like flowers in the sun, and for once, Harper didn't hesitate to seize them.

HARPER:

I think I've decided what to do about Nico.

ASH:

Oh?

HARPER:

If things with my coven are coming to an end, there's no reason for me to hide from Nico. I want to see if he'll offer me the in-house brewing job.

ASH:

That's great. It's the perfect opportunity for you. I think you're making the right choice.

HARPER:

Me too. Next time you're free, we can go over and tell him.

Harper could go on his own, but with the end of his coven problems in sight, what was the harm in hiding for a few more days? The apartment building was protected, and Ash could track him. He was the safest he'd ever been in his life, but he wasn't taking any unnecessary risks. Just in case.

ASH:

Sounds like a plan, flower. Have a good morning.

Harper smiled and pressed the phone to his chest.

Ideally, he'd walk over to Seaside Coffee and enjoy his good mood with a sweet treat. Once his coven was gone, he'd definitely do that, but for now, he'd compromise. Harper made a cup of coffee topped off with hazelnut creamer and took it to the roof.

A light wind tickled his skin as he stepped out of the stairwell. The late morning sun bathed the rooftop, city sounds drifting up from the street. It reminded him of flying with Ash. His heart fluttered and the sun warmed his face.

What a gorgeous morning.

Harper sipped his coffee and glanced around. He stopped short, the hair at the back of his neck prickling. He wasn't the only one up here.

A man stood close to the roof's edge, smoking and gazing into the distance. He must have sensed Harper's stare because he turned, showing no surprise at finding someone there.

"Good morning. You've found my secret smoking spot." He flashed a perfect smile.

It was the human from Seaside Coffee who Harper had run into on the sidewalk and seen around a few times. He must live in the building. No wonder they kept bumping into each other.

Relaxing now he knew who it was, Harper stepped farther onto the roof. "Sorry. Didn't mean to disturb you."

The man waved him off and smiled charmingly, putting Harper at ease. "You aren't. I always enjoy the company of a handsome young man."

Harper froze. "Oh, um, thanks, but I have a boyfriend."

The man's lips twitched, pulling down briefly. "Pity. I never seem to have any luck in the romance department." He turned toward the street and buildings beyond, a breeze ruffling his jet-back hair. "I love the view up here. You can just see the ocean."

"Really?" Harper stepped closer. He hadn't noticed when he'd been up here with Ash.

The man pointed to the right. "Just off that way. See?"

Harper strained and just caught a hint of dark blue in the distance. "Oh wow, you're right."

The man chuckled, shifting closer. "I don't know why people are always so surprised when I tell the truth. It's not like I lie very often."

Harper glanced at him, awkwardness creeping up on him. The man was a little too close.

"I mean," he went on, something changing in his smile. "I don't always set out to deceive, but I still seem to have that reputation."

"Um." Harper took a step back.

The man grabbed Harper's wrist, yanking him closer. "In this case, though, I'd be guilty as charged." His nails dug painfully into Harper's skin.

"Hey, let go." Harper pulled his arm away, trying to shake him off and spilling his coffee, but the man's grip tightened. Harper's heart raced. What the fuck?

The man was strong. Too strong.

He swung Harper around and yanked him closer to the roof's edge. Shit. Harper stumbled, and the man let go. Hands collided with Harper's back, and he lurched forward, losing his balance.

The floor dropped out from beneath him, a scream tearing from his lips as he fell over the edge.

27

———

HARPER

HARPER SCREAMED, the wind whipping against his face and terror scrambling his senses. He was going to die.

Strong arms wrapped around him and the consuming sensation of falling stopped. He jerked upward, his stomach heaving as he was hauled against a firm chest.

"Ash," Harper choked, his throat so dry the word barely came out.

"Not quite." The body behind him shook with laughter, and Harper's blood went cold.

Slowly, he turned and looked at his rescuer's face. It was the man from the rooftop. But how? He was human...

Not according to the large red wings flapping at his back.

Harper's pulse pounded in his ears. The only other demon in the Human Realm was Lucifer. This was bad. So bad. They weren't heading back to the roof either. Harper's building disappeared as they soared away.

"W-where are we going?" Harper's voice shook. He'd be okay. He would be. Ash could track him. He just had to realize something was wrong and start looking. Fuck, if only Harper could reach his phone, but his arms were trapped by the demon's tight embrace.

Lucifer didn't respond. He crushed Harper against his chest, nails digging into his skin, and flew on.

Fuck, fuck, fuck. Harper called on his magic, but where his power usually hummed inside him, he felt nothing. It was like a wall had been erected in his mind. He couldn't see past it. Was his power gone? It couldn't be.

"Stop that," Lucifer snapped, shaking Harper. Harper's stomach dropped. "You aren't accessing your magic. Not that it would do anything against me."

Was Lucifer blocking Harper's power? How was that possible? What the hell was going on? Ash hadn't even been sure if Lucifer was in the city, but he'd been lurking around Harper for weeks.

"What do you want?" Harper asked, desperately trying to find a way around the wall cutting off his magic.

Lucifer shook him again, arms loosening like he was about to let Harper fall. Harper screamed and grabbed onto the demon as best he could.

"Be quiet." Lucifer picked up his pace, sweeping low and cutting between two buildings. He must have cast an illusion of invisibility because the people around took no notice.

Harper screamed for help, but no one reacted.

"They can't hear you," Lucifer growled, tone tight. "Now, shut up."

The demon landed in a fenced-in lot full of old junk. He strode to a nearby building and kicked the door in, carrying Harper inside.

Fuck. This was bad. Nothing good ever happened in a deserted secondary location.

Harper struggled. He had to run. He had to let Ash know he

was in trouble. But Lucifer's grip was vice-like, and he couldn't get free.

"What are we doing here?" Harper pushed against Lucifer's chest, a sob of frustration sticking in his throat. He couldn't be this helpless. Not again. Not after escaping his father and getting so close to kicking him out of his life for good.

Lucifer sighed and dropped him. Harper hit the cement floor, gasping as pain shot from his hip up his side.

Run. Harper struggled to his feet, refusing to let his aching hip slow him down, and lunged for the door.

Flames erupted in front of him, the heat knocking him back.

"Don't try to leave." Lucifer sounded amused.

Harper whirled around to face him. The Devil leered, baring his fangs. His horns curled on either side of his head like a ram's, wine-red, matching his tail. His shirt hung in tatters around his shoulders, destroyed, no doubt from when he'd freed his wings before diving off the roof.

"Why am I here?" Harper straightened his spine. He could do this. He could figure this out and walk out alive. "What do you want?"

"I want to talk to you." The fire at Harper's back spread along the bare floor, encasing him and Lucifer in a large circle.

Sweat trickled down Harper's spine.

"Okay, fine. What do you want to know?" Talking couldn't be all Lucifer wanted, but buying time was good. It gave Ash a chance to figure out something was wrong and come find him.

"You're agreeing to talk to me after I pushed you off a roof?" Lucifer cocked his head, handsome features twitching as if he were trying not to laugh.

Harper clenched his jaw. "Yes, now ask me something."

Lucifer snorted. "Getting dicked down by a demon is giving you some seriously misplaced confidence."

Harper's face flamed. "W-what?"

"Oh, yes. I know Ash has been railing you. You didn't think I was following *you* around, did you?" Lucifer's amusement twisted into something meaner. "I don't care about you, witch. But Ash, on the other hand, I'm fascinated by."

"Ash hasn't been railing me." He shouldn't bother defending himself. Who cared what the Devil thought? But he couldn't stand referring to what he and Ash had done so crudely.

"No?" Lucifer smiled like he knew all of Harper's secrets. "You're not aching for his big demon cock?"

"Stop it," Harper snapped, his gut twisting. "Are you seriously here to ask about my sex life?"

"No, it's Ash's sex life I'm interested in. Why is he so obsessed with you? I don't get it." Lucifer's eyes raked over Harper as if he were mentally undressing him and found him lacking.

Harper crossed his arms over his chest. "Ash isn't obsessed with me."

"He's fucked you more than once. That's an obsession by Ash's standards. Plus, he's been following you around."

"He has?" A day ago, Harper would have freaked out about Ash stalking him, but he was Ash's mate. Everything between them felt right, even this. No wonder Ash was at the port that day, exactly when Harper needed him.

"Yes, he has." Lucifer frowned like he couldn't make sense of the behavior. "I don't know what's wrong with him."

Surely the possibility Harper was Ash's mate had crossed Lucifer's mind, or had he given up on the idea of mates so absolutely that it hadn't? Should he tell Lucifer he was Ash's mate?

Harper needed to text Ash. Even a mash of characters would be something. He discreetly reached for his pocket. Lucifer's gaze caught the motion and his eyes flashed red in warning, the fire around them flaring.

Fuck.

Harper needed Lucifer distracted. Hell, he needed answers. This was all so fucking weird. "So, what? You've been following Ash around?"

Why hadn't Lucifer attacked Ash and the others if he'd found them? He'd tricked everyone into thinking he wasn't in the city. Wasn't he trying to drag the other demons back to Hell? Why bother with Harper when he could have caught the other demons completely off guard?

"Yes, I've been following him." Lucifer shrugged. "He's been more interesting than the others."

"Others?" Harper asked like he didn't know what Lucifer meant.

Lucifer curled his lip. "You've met Dante and Onyx, so don't play dumb. It's never as cute as men like you think it is."

Harper glared. "I don't play dumb."

"Whatever. I don't care." Lucifer took a step toward him. "Tell me why Ash is so obsessed with you, or I'll slit your throat."

Harper blanched, his stomach heaving.

"There you go," Lucifer sneered. "You finally remembered who you're talking to. So, explain. Now."

"Will you kill me after I tell you?" Fuck, why even ask? It wasn't like Lucifer was going to be honest. He'd only give the answer that suited him.

Lucifer stalked closer, wings outstretched so they curved around Harper, brushing his back in an unwelcome embrace, trapping him. "If the next thing out of your mouth isn't an explanation, I'll kill you, so it really doesn't matter what I'll do after you tell me, does it?"

Harper swallowed, his throat parched. He almost choked. Sweat broke out on his palms and forehead. He tried his magic again, hoping for any kind of shield, but came up empty.

Fuck this. Harper hadn't survived his miserable life for it to end this way.

"Ash will kill you if you hurt me," he said barely above a whisper, his tone harsh despite the low volume.

Lucifer snarled, grabbing Harper around the throat and squeezing. He raised his opposite hand, the nails lengthening into deadly points. "That wasn't an explanation."

Lucifer struck Harper, slicing his cheek. Harper cried out, his voice strangled, but the sound died as Lucifer placed his deadly claws at Harper's throat like a knife.

Harper's vision swam, his heart beating a desperate rhythm against his ribcage. "I'm his mate," he croaked as Lucifer's other hand squeezed him tight. "I'm Ash's mate. He's not obsessed with me. It's the mate connection."

Lucifer wouldn't kill him if he was Ash's mate. Right? Not when he'd once been as desperate to find his mate as Ash had been.

The Devil narrowed his eyes. "Bullshit." He loosened the hand crushing Harper's throat, but didn't retract his claws. "Ash is telling you fairytales to get you to bend over."

Harper shook his head as best he could. "He isn't. I've felt it. We have a connection. I didn't understand until he told me what was happening, but it's been there since I first saw him."

"*Liar*," Lucifer growled, spit flying from his mouth and landing on Harper's cheeks. "There are no mates for the Fallen." His eyes burned red. He shook Harper, his hand squeezing, crushing Harper's windpipe. "Liar," he hissed again, heat flaring around them like it was linked to his anger.

No. Fuck.

Harper clawed at Lucifer's hand, gulping in air that wouldn't come. Lucifer's grip was too tight, relentless, and as hard as stone. *Shit.* Harper kicked. His chest tightened, lungs burning. He clawed at Lucifer's face, going for his eyes, but the Devil didn't even flinch.

He needed air. No, no, no. It burned. His lungs, his head. His throat pulsed, blood fighting past Lucifer's deadly grip.

Harper's vision flickered, darkening around the edges. The tunnel closed in and Harper's hands slipped from Lucifer's face, falling limp. He tried to scream. This couldn't be the end.

Feeling like he was weighed down with sandbags, he clawed at Lucifer's hands but his fingers were weak, barely moving where he wanted them to.

He couldn't see.

Spots of white appeared in Harper's blacked-out vision. He screamed for Ash within his mind, but there was no answer.

It was over. His world went black and nothingness took over.

28

———

ASH

ASH PACED BACK and forth along Dante's balcony, taking a brief break from tracking Arthur Nightingale. He scowled. The witch proved elusive. Of course he'd be easier to track if Ash had a sense of his magic firsthand rather than through his similarity to Harper, but there wasn't anything Ash could do about that.

Nearby, Dante leaned against the railing, his eyes clouded a milky white as he connected with his flock. He blinked, his gaze clearing. "Everything at the complex is quiet and no one at the port or library is doing much."

"Good." Ash scrubbed his stubble-lined chin. "I'm grateful your birds can keep watch for us." Without the shearwaters, Ash wouldn't be able to keep tabs on every witch, especially while searching for Arthur.

"Wow, you're finally acknowledging their merit," Dante teased before saying more seriously, "Anytime you need my birds, let me know. I want Harper to be safe as much as you do."

"Thank you, Dante." Ash clasped his shoulder, their folded wings brushing. "We need to figure out what's been killing your shearwaters. I wonder—" Ash's throat tightened, and he choked on a cough.

Dante's brows knitted together. "Are you all right?"

Ash nodded—it was nothing—but he coughed again. He pulled in a deep lungful of air, and it burned all the way down. "What in damnation?"

Dante gripped Ash by the shoulders. "What's going on?"

"My throat. Fuck, it hurts." Ash gasped and coughed.

"Could it be Luc?" Dante's gaze turned assessing and his magic washed over Ash. "Could he be cursing you from afar?"

Ash's head spun, and he couldn't speak. His vision flickered. Fuck. He grasped the railing, doubling over, coughing.

"I can't detect anything." Dante hauled Ash up. "I'd sense a powerful spell if Luc were attacking you."

"Then w-what is t-this?" Ash sputtered.

Dante's face paled. "You haven't mated with Harper, right?"

Ash shook his head. "Not yet. He wanted to, but we d-decided to wait. I need him to understand—" He choked and couldn't continue.

Dante's eyes widened as they darted over Ash. "When we mate, we're completely connected. You'd feel his pain, but if you haven't mated..."

Ash's chest tightened, and he pressed his palm over his heart. "We haven't mated, but we intend to. Making the promise seemed to strengthen our connection. What if—" His words cut off as he took a wheezing breath.

Dante nodded in understanding. "What if the mating bond isn't all or nothing. The ritual completes it, but your bond has already started knitting you and Harper together."

"*Harper*," Ash gasped, ice racing through his veins.

The full bond would allow them to share subtle emotions as well as physical sensations like pain or pleasure, but at this stage, was it possible for serious pain to travel down the partially formed connection?

It was the only thing that made sense. Harper must be in grave danger.

Ash cast out for the tracking spell he'd placed on Harper, only to find it completely severed. "I can't find him. Someone broke my spell."

Ash's pulse raced. No. This couldn't be happening.

Dante's eyes clouded over. "No one from the coven has moved, and there's nothing around Harper's apartment." His white eyes darted back and forth, seeing through his birds. "I can't see Harper through his window, but I wasn't watching his building before."

Ash gripped Dante's forearms, sweat breaking out on his brow. "I fucked up. Harper's coven can't have gotten to him. Not at home. What if it's Luc?"

"How? Luc can't be here. We wouldn't miss him. You'd be able to tell if he broke your spell protecting Harper's building."

Pain seared through Ash's throat. He gritted his teeth, breathing ragged, and dug deep into his magic, searching the city for any sign of Luc's magic.

Power flared like a beacon.

"He's here," Ash growled, his demon fire flaring and vaporizing the sweat clinging to his skin.

Dante's white eyes cleared, his black fire burning. "How the hell did he get past us?"

"We can figure it out later. We have to go."

They launched into the sky, wings pumping at full speed.

"I'll send my birds ahead. Where is he?" Dante called.

"The Docks. Near the river." Ash could feel the location of Luc's magic but couldn't see exactly where it was. "It's dark. He must be in a building."

"Got it," Dante called in triumph. "The flock found his magic. He's in an abandoned warehouse."

"Why couldn't we find him before?" Ash shouted, anger the only thing keeping his fear at bay. He should have sensed Luc approaching well before he got to the city.

"I don't know." Dante's tone was filled with frustration and a hint of uneasiness. "Whatever Luc was doing to hide, he isn't doing it now."

"He'll be expecting us." Ash flew faster, even though it was likely a trap. His mate was in danger and nothing else mattered.

Ash's coughing and pain were gone. Was that good or bad? Would he feel if Harper died? He tried to grab hold of the bond and couldn't.

It didn't mean anything. Harper was still alive. He had to be.

Without Harper, nothing mattered. Ash would kill Luc. Consequences and countless years of friendship be damned. Luc could do whatever he wanted to Ash—betray him, imprison him, hunt him, torture him—but not Harper.

Ash beat his wings so hard they felt like they were on fire. He had to get to Harper. He had to fix this. He wouldn't be too late. He couldn't be.

Dante kept pace with him, and soon, a building swarmed with shearwaters came into view. The birds cried and darted around, making way for the two demons as they sped through the flock and landed behind the warehouse.

Ash ran for the back door and ripped it open, pulling it from its hinges.

He rushed inside, Dante at his back. A wall of fire greeted him, red and deep orange as Lucifer's flames always were. Ash surrounded himself in his own golden-orange fire, protecting himself as he walked through Luc's burning barrier.

Lucifer held Harper by the throat, limp and unmoving. No.

The Devil's glowing eyes fixed on Ash, and he jerked back as if in surprise. He hadn't expected Ash to come? Was this not a trap?

Fuck, it didn't matter.

Ash's fire flared. He charged forward and ripped Harper from Lucifer's clutches, his fire engulfing his mate in a protective shield.

He cradled Harper to his chest. Was he dead? A cut marred Harper's cheek. Ash whimpered, fingers trailing over Harper's blue lips. No. They were supposed to be pink.

"Harper, sweetheart," he choked. If Harper died, he might die along with him.

The faintest breath caressed Ash's fingertips, puffing past Harper's blue lips.

Ash's world stopped and restarted. Harper wasn't dead. Color slowly chased away the horrible tinge to his usually rosy cheeks, and Ash's knees threatened to buckle.

"Lucifer," he growled, fixing a deadly stare on the demon he'd once called a friend. "I'll flay you and feast on your fucking heart for this."

Luc seemed recovered from his momentary surprise, glancing mockingly between Ash and Dante, who'd crossed Luc's flaming circle behind Ash. "For what? Hurting your fuck toy?"

Ash roared. He'd have ripped Luc's head off if he hadn't been consumed by the need to hold Harper close. He'd never let go of his mate again.

Maybe he could chew Lucifer's head from his shoulders. He wouldn't need to set Harper down to do that.

Lucifer laughed. "So touchy. What's happened to you, Ash? Telling little witches lies about mates and obsessing over them. You've lost your senses since I last saw you."

"Harper is my mate." Ash held his flower tighter against his chest. "You'll pay for laying a single finger on him. We may not be in the Eternal Realm, but this is still a punishable offense."

"Then make me pay," Luc taunted, spreading his arms wide. "What are you going to do about it? Or are your threats nothing but more lies?"

Dante stepped forward, his nostrils flaring. "Ash isn't lying. Harper is his mate. Luc, what are you playing at? Did Harper tell you he was Ash's mate? And you hurt him anyway? Mates are sacred. You know that."

"Give it a rest, Dante," Luc snapped.

"No," Dante shouted. "What are you doing? Destroying everything in your path whether you need to or not? I don't know how you got past us and into the city but come for us if you want. Leave the innocents alone."

Lucifer chuckled. "Innocents. Your temper's gotten worse. Did looking for me send you over the edge?"

Dante growled, baring his fangs.

Luc shook his head like a disappointed father. "Calm down, Dante. You're going to pop a blood vessel."

Taking advantage of Luc's distraction, Ash pierced his wrist with his fang. Blood trickled from the wound, and he pressed it to Harper's lips.

The magic in Ash's blood would enhance Harper's healing magic tenfold. Harper seemed to have been strangled, and since he was breathing, Ash's magic should heal him faster than the injuries could kill him.

Ash got here in time. But only just.

Harper's breathing was so weak.

A tear ran down Ash's cheek. Witches were so fragile, not much stronger than humans. If only they'd mated, Harper would have recovered quickly, all on his own. Luc could have killed Harper, and as long as he didn't drain all of Harper's blood or cut off his head, Harper would have come back.

"Let me guess." Luc's snide voice pulled Ash back into the conversation. "You were searching for me by tracking my magic?"

Dante's black-flamed eyes narrowed. "Not just your magic."

"No? I guess I'm just that much more accomplished at illusions than the rest of you. Invisibility is so *basic*." Lucifer's lip curled.

Harper stirred in Ash's arms. He sucked in a deep breath and his eyes popped open, instantly finding Ash's.

Ash pressed a finger to Harper's now-pink lips, and Harper stilled. The cut on his cheek was already gone and the bruise on his neck was fading fast.

"I've been wearing an illusion of you three," Luc continued, glancing around as if looking for Onyx. He didn't seem bothered not to find his brother. "You couldn't find me because I cloaked myself in your magic, making mine undetectable and masking me against any tracking. I still have some of your power. I never used all of what I stole. Never realized that, did you? Even your winged pests couldn't find me, Dante. All they detected when they saw me was your own magic, a complete illusion making them think I was you. It was perfect. However..." His gaze landed on Ash. "I made a mistake."

A mistake? Dante caught Ash's eye, brows raised. Luc *never* admitted mistakes. It was like a punch to the face.

Luc went on as if his admission had been nothing. "I must have broken my illusion by revealing my true self to Harper. He'd seen me before, which was fine because he mistook me for human, but when he realized I was a demon, something must have changed. I suppose my spell was no longer all-encompassing. I should have realized a small crack was as good as shattering the whole thing."

Harper turned in Ash's arms and faced Lucifer, who wrinkled his nose at the sight of Harper conscious again. "Seems like you wasted your big advantage," Harper snarled, almost as growly as a demon.

Ash's chest swelled. His fierce mate. Fuck, Harper was perfect.

Luc sneered. "Like I'd make a move with only one advantage."

Ash had enough of talking. He released his hold on Harper even though it was like letting go of a piece of his soul, his body cold and empty without his mate. He stepped in front of Harper, shielding him from Luc's unworthy gaze and encasing Harper in his protective fire.

"It's not an advantage to be caught off guard." Ash bared his fangs and launched into the air.

He came down on Lucifer hard, knocking him onto his back. Ash gripped his throat. Luc raked his claws down Ash's arms, drawing blood, but Ash felt no pain. He beat his wings, using the force to press Luc into the cement floor.

Dante appeared at his side, pulling a glowing vial from his pocket.

Lucifer shot a bolt of red lightning into the center of Ash's chest. Ash's heart stopped and his body jolted, his grip tightening on Lucifer, crushing his throat. He couldn't move.

His magic raced to repair his heart. Fuck! At least he hadn't lost consciousness.

Luc pushed Ash off him, sending another bolt of lightning at Ash's chest and stopping Ash's heart just as it started to beat again. It wouldn't kill him permanently, but Ash was completely incapacitated while his heart healed.

Luc turned on Dante, his lip curled back in a snarl as his crushed neck healed itself.

Movement flashed behind Luc. Harper stooped to the ground, blazing bright with Ash's fire. When had he circled around them all? Ash caught a determined look on his flower's face.

His unbeating heart swelled with affection.

Harper gathered dust from the floor and threw it at Luc, muttering a spell. The dust sparked, hitting Luc in the back of the head.

Lucifer screamed and whirled around, only for Harper to hit him in the face with more dust. The flesh on Luc's face burned as if the dust were acid, but his rapid healing closed the wounds quickly.

Luc lunged for Harper just as movement returned to Ash's body. He grabbed Luc by the wing and pulled him to the ground. As he fell, Luc hit Ash with another lightning bolt.

Ash's teeth clenched so hard they almost cracked. *Fuck.*

Luc turned on Dante, not bothering to get up, his hands sparking as he prepared another blast. Dante threw the glowing contents of the vial in Luc's face.

A flash of white light filled the room.

Ash's retinas burned, and he saw stars. Once his vision cleared, he took a staggering step forward, heart beating slowly.

Luc was frozen, his eyes open and unmoving.

Dante pocketed the empty vial. "It won't last long."

"What was that?" Harper asked.

Ash released his protective fire, and Harper rushed into his arms.

"A sedative potion. I've been strengthening it with my blood for years." Dante nudged Luc's shoulder with his foot. "It won't work as well as it would have if he'd swallowed it. We have to act fast."

"I didn't know demons could brew," Harper said, words coming out in a rush.

Dante gave him an affectionate grin, temporarily banishing the harsh furrow in his brow. "Witches got their powers from demons. I don't think there's anything a witch can do that we can't. But we can discuss that later."

"Yes, later." Ash folded one of Luc's wings against his body. "He's going to be a beast to transport in his full form."

Dante grunted in agreement. "We need to get him to Onyx so we can open the prison."

They'd crafted a cell for Lucifer weeks ago. The prison wasn't tied to a location on Earth, so a gateway to the inter-realm cell could be opened anywhere, but they didn't have enough power to open it without Onyx.

If only the petulant demon hadn't stormed off.

"What about Harper?" Ash's gut twisted. "We can't carry him and Luc all the way to Onyx." It would take both Ash and Dante to carry a deadweight demon with his full wingspan.

"I'll be okay." Harper pulled out his phone. "I'll book a ride home and stay in the apartment. Unless Lucifer broke your protections? I don't know how he got onto the roof of my building."

The roof? What the hell? How had Harper ended up on the roof with Luc? "Lucifer must have been able to get past my protections using his illusion. He wouldn't have had to break my spell. I set it to allow me, Dante, or Onyx in without trouble."

"Shit, his disguise was almost foolproof." Harper looked up from his phone. "The car is two minutes away."

"Great. We can wait for it to arrive, but then we need to go. I'll call Onyx." Dante pulled out his phone and pressed it to his ear.

Ash pulled Harper close. "I'm so sorry, sweet. I let you down."

Harper met his eye. "No, Ash, you saved me."

Ash's chest tightened. He'd almost lost his flower. "It was too close a call. Luc broke my tracking spell, and I almost didn't get here in time."

"But you found me. You *did* get here in time."

Ash ran a hand through Harper's hair. "Yes, but if Luc hadn't broken his own illusion, I wouldn't have been able to. Here, let me recast the tracking before you go." He hurried to redo the spell so he wouldn't lose Harper again.

"The car's here." Harper showed Ash the notification on his phone.

He nodded, taking the extra few moments to complete his spell before releasing Harper.

Dante picked up Luc's legs. "We need to go. Onyx isn't answering."

Fucking typical. Ash grunted, clasping Harper's shoulder. "Go straight home." Harper nodded, and Ash pulled him into a crushing kiss. "I'll be there soon."

"And I'll be waiting for you." Harper smiled softly.

Ash's chest swelled, his feathers ruffling. He was so proud of his mate. Even after facing the Devil, Harper hardly seemed shaken.

Dante blinked, his eyes going white, then clearing. "The coven members haven't moved. You should be good to go."

Ash held Harper tight. Not dealing with Luc would be a grave mistake, but how was he supposed to let Harper walk away?

"Go." Harper pushed Ash toward Dante, extracting himself from Ash's hold. "I'll be fine at home. Promise." With a wave, he rushed out of the building.

Ash grabbed Lucifer's upper body, getting hold of his wings as best as he could, and together, he and Dante dragged him outside.

With a glance to ensure Harper got into the car, Ash and Dante launched into the air.

29

HARPER

Harper hurried to the car idling at the curb. The license plate matched his booking on the app, so he threw open the back door and slid inside.

The driver pulled away as soon as the door shut. Harper quickly buckled his seatbelt.

"Thanks." Harper twisted around, glancing out the back window and trying to catch a glimpse of Ash. Where were they?

Oh. Duh, they'd have an illusion making them invisible. Obviously. But the way Harper's pulse pounded, his whole body vibrating with adrenaline, it was no wonder he wasn't at his sharpest.

Harper squirmed in his seat, facing forward but unable to stop moving. His gaze darted around the clean car. At least the ride would be short. Lucifer hadn't taken him far.

"I really should be thanking *you*," said the driver.

Harper's body locked up. *That voice.* His heart beat at double speed and dread turned his stomach. No, it couldn't be. He looked at the driver, his face in profile as he watched the road. Recognition cut Harper in two. Fuck. No. He blinked, but there was no erasing what was right there.

His father's eyes met his in the rearview mirror.

Harper reached for the door handle. He'd throw himself from the moving car. His hand clasped the plastic, and searing pain scorched his palm, burning like a hot iron. With a cry, he yanked his hand away, his palm scorched red.

"No, no. I'm not letting you out of my sight." His father hardly glanced at the road as he drove, beady eyes fixed on Harper in the mirror. "Don't try anything, or I'll set the whole damn seat on fire."

As if to prove his point, heat flared along the seatbelt, singing Harper's shirt and burning his chest. He screamed. The heat was gone a second later.

"H-how did you find me?" Harper willed himself not to cry. Showing emotion would make this worse. It only egged his father on.

There was no time for fear. He had to escape.

"You stopped suppressing your magic. I was ready the moment you let your guard down. Did you think I wouldn't notice? Ha. It was lucky I was at the port trying to figure out what you did to my men. From there, tracking you was easy."

Harper hadn't stopped suppressing his magic. He'd never skipped his potion. Whatever Lucifer had done to strip him of Ash's tracking spell must have broken his suppression spell too.

Fuck, he was such a fool to think he was safe just because Ash found him.

"But the car?" It still didn't add up. His father didn't do rideshares, and he'd booked this through an app. He'd checked the plate.

"I stole the car." Arthur shrugged, eyes back on the road. "I knew you were inside the warehouse, so I took a gamble that you were about to get in when the car pulled up. It was the only one around. The human is slumped in the gutter, where he belongs."

Damnation. Hopefully, the driver wasn't dead. It would be all Harper's fault.

Harper shook with rage, and okay, fear too. He was ice cold. He *had* to escape. So what if he burned his palm off.

Harper eyed the door handle, placing his hand on the seatbelt clip, ready to unclick it as soon as he opened the door.

The plastic handle melted down the door, gone in a split second. *Fuck!* Harper's seat burned, pain along his back and ass flaring, and he screamed.

He'd be cooked alive.

"Do as you're told and stay still," his father growled, slamming on the brakes and twisting around in his seat.

The burning stopped abruptly, but the pain didn't. Harper's breaths came in harsh, rapid pants, yet no air seemed to reach his lungs. He needed to move. Get out of here, but his back seized. Could he even walk?

It hurt, fuck, it hurt.

His father began chanting, and magic swirled around Harper. No, not a spell. He hated his father's spells.

"*Please*," Harper begged. He didn't want to, but he hurt too much already.

Every muscle in Harper's body was locked in place.

He couldn't move. *He really couldn't move.* His eyes were frozen open. He couldn't blink. What the ever-loving fuck? Even his eyeballs were locked in a forward-facing position.

Harper wanted to scream and couldn't. His mouth was sealed shut, breaths coming in and out of his nose of their own accord. He couldn't even suck in more air or hold his breath.

His body wasn't his.

No.

Harper was trapped. Helpless. He had no control. No choice. He couldn't even cry. Couldn't react. Fuck, it was like he didn't even exist.

Hatred burned in Arthur Nightingale's eyes. Had his father ever had another emotion toward him, or had he been hated since he was born?

"You're coming home with me, son, and things will be different this time. Forget marrying Miss Thornfield. You ruined that alliance. You're useless, so you might as well be nothing. I mean, you couldn't even find the Hounds. What have you ever accomplished in your life?" Arthur paused as if waiting for Harper to answer.

He tutted disapprovingly, gaze shining bright, promising violence. "You better get used to this feeling, Harper, because you'll never have control of your body again. Once we're back at the compound, I'm hooking you up to a bunch of new toys. We have a new coven member, a doctor who promises he can keep you alive while brain-dead. That way, I can finally take your blood without having to deal with you."

No. No, no, no-no-no-no. The world seemed to drop out from under Harper, his stomach swooping as he went into freefall. The car and his father disappeared. His vision blacked out. There was no sound.

No.

His eyes burned and the car rushed back into focus, moving once again. He was still here. Still trapped. Not even terror could take him away from this. He couldn't even faint. *No, no, no, no!* He screamed inside his head, ears ringing, his head spinning as his insides ripped themselves to shreds.

He should have asked Ash to kill his father. Regret almost swallowed him whole. Why couldn't he go back in time and do this all over?

This couldn't be his destiny. He was Ash's mate.

Ash! Ash, please! Harper called for his mate inside his mind, the impulse overriding all logic. *Please, Ash! Ash!* But Ash couldn't hear him, his call as silent as the dead.

Ash, please come find me! Track me! But Ash wouldn't be looking. Not when he thought Harper was safely on his way home.

Where was his father taking him? How were they getting back to the compound? Would he hurt Harper before they left the city? Harper's soul screamed with the agony of his confinement.

How long until Ash realized something was wrong? Too long.

No. Ash! Please, I need you. I don't want to lose you. Come find me. Don't let him do this to me. Ash!

Even if his father got him out of the city, there was no way he'd get Harper all the way back to Colorado and to that evil doctor before Ash caught up with them. Right? But what if his father didn't wait? He could render Harper brain-dead now.

Lifeless and left to molder in a bed while his blood drained.

Pain vibrated deep within Harper, eating him from the inside out. This wasn't meant to be his fate. But what if Ash never found him? What if Arthur worse than killed him in this car?

Harper saw no end but his own.

Ash!

A blur fell from the sky and crashed onto the car's hood. The windshield exploded, glass spraying everywhere. Metal screeched and crumpled, and Harper jolted forward as the car came to an abrupt halt.

Ash crouched on the smashed hood, wings towering behind him, his eyes glowing. He bared his fangs with an ear-splitting snarl.

The savage sound soothed Harper more than sweet words ever had. He melted, relief so intense it would have sent him to the floor if he had control of his body.

Something crashed onto the car's roof, denting it, and Harper's pounding heart skipped. Arthur Nightingale spluttered behind the wheel. He glanced wildly around, and the spell holding Harper captive broke, snapping like a taut rubber band.

A scream tore from Harper's lips, the pleas from inside his head finally breaking free. "Ash, please. Help me!"

Ash was at his door in a flash. He ripped it clean off the car and pulled Harper out, tearing the seatbelt in the process.

"I've got you," Ash rumbled, strong arms enveloping him.

Harper clung to Ash, face pressed into Ash's bare chest. Tears streamed down his cheeks like a river. He shook so hard his teeth chattered. He wanted to crawl inside Ash and never come out, but he made himself meet Ash's glowing orange gaze. "My father... my...he's...the driver...going to put me in a coma...drain me."

An inhuman roar erupted from Ash. Dante echoed it from the top of the car, a limp Lucifer at his feet.

Arthur slowly emerged from the driver's seat. Harper would give his father this: the man seemed to have no fear. He turned to face Ash and Dante, an agreeable smile pulling at his lips. "Do my eyes deceive me, or am I in the presence of the great Hounds of Hell?"

"Do not *dare* speak to us," Dante growled, tone icy enough to burn.

Arthur's gaze zeroed in on Harper, seeming to register he was in Ash's protective embrace, and his eyes widened, lip curling in disgust.

Ash must have noticed Arthur's reaction. He snarled, the sound reverberating through Harper.

Arthur smoothed his face, but it was too late to hide his hate.

Movement on top of the car tore Harper's attention from his father. Lucifer stirred, eyes spinning around wildly until they landed on Harper. The Devil's hand shot out, grabbing Harper's face. He growled, hitting Dante in the back of the knees with one of his wings, sending Dante to the ground.

"Fuck," Dante grunted, scrambling to his feet.

Ash tore Lucifer's hand away from Harper, twisting Lucifer's wrist until the bones cracked. Harper winced, but Lucifer barely reacted.

Lucifer got to his feet and surveyed the scene. "Seems like I missed some of the fun. Dante, you're going to pay for that little trick."

Dante closed his hands around Lucifer's throat and squeezed, a static boom cutting through the air as he shocked Lucifer with lightning.

Lucifer twitched, momentarily frozen.

"I don't have any more potion," Dante warned before blasting Lucifer with lightning again.

Arthur slowly made his way around the car. "Is this...?" His eyes fixed on the red-winged demon, reverence lighting his face. "Lucifer?"

Luc glared down at Arthur as he was shot with a third lightning bolt.

Arthur's face hardened. He raised his hands, chanting in a language Harper didn't recognize.

Ash swayed against Harper, and Harper steadied him. What the hell? Did his father have some secret spell to work on the demons? Was this what he'd planned to do when Harper found them?

Dante faltered, stumbling back from Lucifer. The Devil stood, his stopped heart healed. He spun and punched Dante square in the chest, sending Dante flying down the street.

Oh shit.

Ash reached for Arthur, but his coordination was off, and he missed. Would Ash even be standing if Harper wasn't holding him up? Harper strained under Ash's weight. If only he could use magic against his father and stop this.

"Lucifer," Arthur called, his awestruck gaze fixed on the Devil. "I am your most loyal servant and have been working to bring your dogs back to you."

Lucifer threw his head back and laughed. "I don't want you to serve me, witch. Crawl back into whatever hole you slunk out of."

Hurt flashed across Arthur's face, giving Harper a sick satisfaction. Harper hated Lucifer for what he'd done to Ash and the others, but he hated his father more and loved seeing him realize he'd devoted his life to a Devil who didn't give a shit about him.

"I'm on your side," Arthur explained, a pleading note bleeding into his usually hard tone. "I've incapacitated your dogs so you can take them back. Everything I do is for you."

"What do you know about what I want with my demons?" Luc snarled, baring his fangs, his cheeks burning red with anger. "I can't stand witches like you. When you get to Hell, there will be no special place for you. You'll be the same as every other wretched soul there. A nobody."

Arthur stumbled back like he'd been slapped, and Harper grinned.

Ash's weight lifted from Harper. He straightened and stepped forward, no longer incapacitated. Whether Arthur let his spell fail, too hurt by Lucifer's rejection, or he'd lost concentration, it didn't matter.

In a flash of motion, Ash grabbed Arthur by the back of the neck and slammed him face-first into the car. There was a sickening crack. Blood splattered. Ash released the witch as if he was tossing away something putrid, his nose wrinkled in disgust.

Arthur Nightingale slumped to the ground, body unmoving. Blood poured from his nose, forehead, and mouth.

Harper looked away, only one thought echoing in his mind: *good*.

Maybe he wasn't a good person for thinking that, and that was okay. Harper had no loyalty to his father. No affection for him. Family meant nothing if they didn't treat you right. Being Arthur's son was just an unfortunate roll of the dice.

Blood wasn't thicker than water, and Harper liked seeing Arthur's spill for once.

"Ash, get Luc!" Dante shouted.

Harper whirled around. Dante ran full speed toward them, nothing but a blur, but he was still more than a block away.

"Thanks, Ash. I appreciate that." Lucifer peered down at Arthur from on top of the ruined car, seemingly amused by the bloody witch, his eyes bright like he wanted to laugh. "But I'm not going to stick around. I don't fancy getting put to sleep again."

Ash launched onto the car, wings spread and arms outstretched, but just as he was about to close in on Lucifer, the Devil disappeared.

Ash whirled around, eyes wide.

"Shit!" Dante skidded to a stop next to him. "That's a new trick."

Ash bared his teeth. "Did he just leave this Realm? Fuck, we're not chasing him down in Hell."

"He t-teleported? To Hell?" A giggle rose from the depths of Harper's hollow chest. It didn't sound right. He sucked in a deep breath, prompting another harsh laugh to escape, his whole body shaking.

Ash wrapped an arm around him. "Harper, sweetheart, I'm so sorry. I never should have left you."

Harper choked on another laugh, managing to stop the strange sounds at last. "You got to me in time. That's all that matters."

"No, it isn't. You never should have had to see this man again." He nudged the unconscious Arthur with his foot.

Harper didn't look at his father. Exhaustion swept over him and he gripped Ash for support. "Then take him away and make sure I don't see him again."

Ash nodded, his gaze serious but not uncaring. "Let's get you home first."

"I hate to interrupt, but we need to deal with that." Dante pointed across the street where a small crowd of humans had gathered.

"Dammit," Ash grumbled.

The street was mostly deserted, but it looked like some of the buildings were full of workers, who were now out on the sidewalk staring, along with the drivers of several stopped cars. Every single one was filming.

Dante strode over to the crowd and gathered phones from everyone.

"They just handed them over?" Harper blinked slowly, like his eyelids weren't working properly. He leaned harder against Ash. Who'd give away video footage of winged men? That could be worth something.

"Just like your potion brewing powers come from us, vampires' illusion and hypnosis powers do too," Ash said, keeping Harper pressed close and, most importantly, upright. "Dante, Onyx, and I don't use mind control lightly, but we can't have word of demons being real spreading among humans, and we don't need the magical community in the city aware of our presence. Dante will wipe the crowd's memories and delete anything from their phones."

Harper nodded. "Given my dad's reaction to you, I can imagine there are other witches you don't want knocking on your door."

"No." Ash squeezed Harper, nuzzling his cheek.

They watched Dante deal with the crowd, who all meekly returned to work or drove off like nothing had happened.

"I'll drag this away and cast an illusion over it." Dante gestured to the ruined vehicle beside them. "We can get rid of it later."

Once that was done, Dante picked up the limp Arthur.

"Let's get you home, sweet." Ash hoisted Harper into his arms.

Harper wrapped his arms around Ash's neck and pressed their foreheads together. "Thank you," he whispered.

Ash rubbed his nose against Harper's, his spiced scent soothing. Harper closed his eyes and Ash launched into the air.

They flew to the apartment building. Dante hovered above the building, holding Arthur, as Ash landed. He was likely trying to give them some privacy.

"How did you know I was in trouble?" Harper asked as Ash carried him inside and down the stairs.

"The mating bond." Ash opened Harper's front door and slipped inside. "Dante and I suspect it's started forming, even though we haven't fully mated. I knew you were hurt when we found you with Luc. Feeding you my blood to heal you must have strengthened the connection even further."

Ash set Harper down on the couch, an agonized look bringing countless worry lines to his face. "I could feel you calling for me." Ash's voice broke, and he stroked Harper's cheek like it was the most delicate thing in the world.

"I was so scared." Harper shivered as an echo of fear washed over him. "Logically, I knew you'd find me before we got back to Colorado, but he might not have waited to hurt me. What he was going to do to me was..." Harper couldn't finish.

Ash let out a strangled whine. "What he was planning was evil. I'm so sorry, Harper. No one deserves that, especially from their father."

Harper clenched a fist. "I don't care that he's my father. I just want him gone."

"I'll take care of it," Ash said without judgment. "He won't ever bother you again. Will you be okay here while I dispose of him?"

Relief swept over Harper. "I don't know. Are we sure Lucifer can't get into the building?" Harper didn't want to go with Ash while he dealt with his father, but separating wasn't easy after what had just happened.

"Yes, I'm sure. Now that Luc's illusion is broken, he won't be able to get in without penetrating my defenses, and he can't do that stealthily or quickly. The only place safer than this building is Dante's house, but I'll get the other two to strengthen the protections here so both will be equally guarded from now on."

Harper clenched his hands. "Okay, good."

Ash sat on the couch and took Harper's hand. "I can stay. Dante will take care of your father if I ask. He won't mind."

Harper rubbed his thumb over Ash's knuckles. "Will you be gone long if you go?"

"No. I want this over and done with." Ash's gaze hardened. The look might have terrified anyone other than Harper, but Ash would never turn his power against him.

Harper was safe and cared for. An unexpected calm settled over him.

"You should go. I want you to ensure it's taken care of, but come right back." Harper gave Ash a small smile. "I think Ollie will be home soon. So maybe don't come in with your wings out."

Ash chuckled. "Sounds like a plan." He rose from the couch. "Be back soon."

Harper couldn't quite put into words why Ash had to be the one to finish his father. He just needed it to be this way. Maybe he couldn't bring himself to ask Dante for something like this, no matter how much the demon might willingly do for him. Dante cared. There was no doubt about it.

Harper's heart clenched.

Hopefully, Dante found his mate. Harper was so lucky to be Ash's fated love, especially when being a mate gave him so much more than a partner. With so many years ahead of him, Harper was sure he'd love Dante like a brother one day. Onyx too. They deserved a future where they all had their mates. That way, they could be one big family.

A real family. The kind Harper had always longed for.

30

ASH

Ash ended what was left of Arthur Nightingale's life quickly and sent him to a watery grave. There was no point lingering over the task. Returning to Harper's side was more important than punishing his father. The afterlife could have him.

Ash and Dante returned to shore and dealt with the rest of the coven. Mind control was easiest, even if it wasn't the most moral way to approach the situation. Ash could threaten and intimidate the witches, but the Nightingales had been hunting demons. They might attack rather than run scared, even without their leader.

Ash wanted them gone. Away from Harper forever, without any risk that they might regroup and come back to Shearwater Landing.

He banished the Nightingale Coven from the city, forcing the members to run home. Their leader was dead, and they were no longer welcome on the West Coast.

He'd keep tabs on the coven. Whether he'd share that with Harper, he wasn't sure. He might keep that plan to himself, at least for now. Moving on was most important for his flower. But if Arthur was replaced with someone just as bad, further intervention might be necessary. If the Nightingale Coven ever caused trouble in the magic world or among humans, he'd deal with it.

After disposing of the destroyed car and checking on the driver—who only had minor injuries—Dante flew back to the apartment building with him.

Harper's faint presence prickled in the back of Ash's mind the whole time they were apart, a newly formed awareness telling him his mate was safe. He wouldn't have left otherwise, regardless of the apartment's protections.

Now that Ash was nearing his mate, the connection flared, as if welcoming him home.

How had he not realized the mating bond was this complex or dynamic? For thousands of years, he'd seen the mating ritual as the singular event to bind him to his mate, but he and Harper were already weaving together.

Ash and Dante landed on the roof and headed down to the apartment, their wings, tails, and horns tucked out of sight.

"I just want to see he's all right before I go," Dante explained as if he needed an excuse.

Ash smiled. Dante was attached to Harper already. "I'm sure he won't mind if you want to stick around."

"No, probably not, but I need to track down Onyx. He completely ignored my calls."

Ash grunted. If Onyx had helped, maybe they wouldn't have lost Luc. But he'd worry about that later. He knocked on Harper's door.

There was a scurry of movement within the apartment before the door swung open.

"Hi." A frazzled Ollie stood before them, his hair disheveled. "Harper said it would be you, Ash." Ollie looked him over, gaze catching on Dante behind him. "Um, hi to you too." A slow smile curved Ollie's lips, and he ran a hand through his hair.

"May we come in?" Ash asked.

"Oh." Ollie shook himself, tearing his eyes away from Dante. Maybe he was surprised that neither Ash nor Dante wore shirts, but it was too late to do anything about that now. "Yeah, of course. Harper was just telling me all about the cult he escaped and how his dad tracked him down today. He seemed so off when I got home, I had to ask, but I never thought... Fuck. I'm so glad you were able to help him, Ash."

"Me too." Ash studied Ollie as they walked to the living room. Harper probably hadn't told his friend the full story, but it was good Ollie knew Harper had a traumatizing day. Saying the Nightingales were a cult wasn't too far from the truth. "I'm glad he has you to talk to."

Ollie flashed him a sweet smile. "Yeah, of course." He flopped down in an armchair, his gaze returning to Dante.

Ash joined Harper, who was slumped on the couch. "Hey there, flower."

"Hey." Harper hugged Ash tight. The moment dragged out. When Harper finally released him, he pulled away slowly, as if he didn't want to. Harper's cheeks darkened as he registered Dante standing in the doorway, like he was embarrassed the other demon saw him be so clingy. "Hey, Dante. Come sit. There's plenty of room."

Dante jolted like he'd been caught by surprise. His eyes flicked from Ollie to Harper, then back again. "That's okay. I can't stay. I just wanted to check on you."

Harper gave him a tired smile. "I appreciate it."

What was with Dante's expression? It changed too quickly to be sure.

"Anytime, Harper. I'll see you soon." Dante nodded to Ollie, gaze lingering, then turned and left.

Ollie shot a meaningful look at Harper. "You should definitely invite him over again."

Harper gave a nervous laugh, body vibrating against Ash. "Yeah, maybe."

Was Ollie interested in Dante?

Ash had to tell Harper not to get Ollie's hopes up. Dante was waiting for his mate, and while he'd reacted to Ollie, Ash didn't think it was more than general appreciation. Ollie was attractive. Anyone could see that.

Unless... What if Dante was reacting to Ollie's scent? To Ash, Ollie gave off a faint typical but not unpleasant human aroma. Nothing like Harper's bluebells.

Ash's heart rate picked up. No. It was too much to hope Dante would find his mate so soon after he had.

Harper and Ollie chatted idly, then ordered food and put on a show they'd been watching together. It was nice to be along for the ride. Anything that made Harper smile was good in Ash's book, especially if he could hold Harper close while it happened.

After they ate, Harper's eyelids started to droop. "I think I need to lie down."

"Of course," Ollie said softly, his brows coming together. "Are you sure everything is wrapped up with your family, and they won't keep bothering you? I'm happy to send anyone buzzing into the building away."

"Thanks." Harper got up and walked over to Ollie, squeezing his shoulder. "They won't be coming around." He shot a look at Ash.

"No, they won't. It's all taken care of," Ash confirmed.

"Okay, good." Ollie's posture relaxed. "I'm glad you got away from them, Harper. You'll always be welcome here."

"Perfect because I'm not leaving." Harper grinned, the light not quite reaching his tired eyes. "But I seriously need to lie down. I think the day's catching up to me."

Ollie patted Harper's arm and let him go.

Ash rose and followed Harper into his room.

"It's all done?" Harper asked as soon as the door shut.

"Yes, your father is finding out firsthand what the Realm of the Damned is like, and your coven won't be back."

Harper shifted restlessly from foot to foot. "Is it terrible that I don't feel bad about it?"

"About your father's untimely end?" Ash clasped Harper on the shoulder. "No, not at all."

Harper's hand fisted the hem of his shirt. "But you said I was a good person for not wanting to kill him."

"And I still think that was very good of you, but it's okay to want justice. You're still a good person, Harper. Your father hurt you in despicable ways. He deserves what he got." Ash's hatred for Arthur Nightingale simmered, heating his blood. Maybe he should have punished the witch just a little. He shook himself. "I'd say Arthur deserved worse, but that's just my angry side, the one that rages at an unfair world and wants to make it right even when I can't."

Harper nodded hesitantly like he wasn't convinced, so Ash went on, "Do you think I'm a bad person, or demon, for wanting to kill your father?"

"No," Harper said automatically.

"Then neither are you. You don't have to feel guilty about your reaction." Ash squeezed Harper's shoulder, and he relaxed under Ash's touch. "His death won't undo what happened, but it'll stop him from hurting you or anyone else, and you're not wrong for wanting that. Besides, the magic world doesn't play by human rules. There's no 'right' way to deal with someone like your father. What would we have done? Gone to the human police?"

"No, you're right. When you put it that way, anything else

would have left me looking over my shoulder for the rest of my life. My father was power-hungry and abusive. He believed it was his right to take what he wanted, and I'm glad he's gone." Harper released a breath and seemed to unwind as he wrapped his arms around Ash. "You've destroyed all my monsters."

"All of them? You mean your coven?"

Harper buried his face against Ash. "One of the men you killed at the port was the one who assaulted me. It was such a relief. He'd caught me, but then I woke up, and you'd taken care of it."

Ash squeezed Harper tight. His pulse spiked. If he'd known... But no, it didn't matter. It was done. "I'm glad I was there. I'd been following you around since the club."

Harper pulled back. "I know, Luc mentioned you'd been stalking me." He bit his lip. "I probably shouldn't think that's romantic."

Ash grinned. "But you do?"

Harper nodded. "And not just because of how bad it'd have been if you weren't at the port with me. You were drawn to me. What we have is that strong. Don't know if it gets more romantic than that."

Ash chuckled softly. "Agreed. You captivated me, and I couldn't stay away. It was the strongest instinct I'd ever had." Ash cupped Harper's cheeks. "I tried to fight it, and not even that worked. It took me a while to come to terms with you being my mate. I was...afraid to believe and be wrong. Afraid to want and be left alone."

Harper let out a soft whine. "You don't have to be afraid of the things you want."

He brushed Harper's cheeks with his thumbs. "No, not anymore."

Harper's tender expression broke into a yawn. "Sorry.

Killed the moment." They both laughed. "Will you stay with me while I sleep?"

Ash ran a hand through Harper's hair. "Of course I'm staying. You couldn't get rid of me if you tried, sweet."

"Good. I need you with me." Harper held him tight for a long moment before whispering, "I don't want to wait to mate. I get why you do, but after today, I don't want anything coming between us."

"Neither do I." Ash's heart was so full his chest twinged. "But I want you to rest first. Put this day behind you. Then I'll claim you as my mate."

Harper sucked in a breath. "Please, Ash. I want to be yours."

Ash laid a gentle kiss on Harper's lips. "You are mine. The bond is already coming together. So take a nap, knowing our connection draws you closer to me every second."

Harper returned Ash's kiss. "Okay."

Ash undressed him, shoes first, then shirt and pants. "Just so you know, we aren't mating here. We need a lot more privacy than this." He glanced at the door, the sounds of Ollie moving around only slightly muffled.

Harper's cheeks bloomed with color and his scent intensified. "True."

Ash pulled off his own pants and climbed into the bed, holding the covers back for Harper. His mate slid in and curled against his side.

"I've never felt as safe as I do with you," Harper whispered. "It shouldn't be possible to feel at home or secure after today, but I do."

Ash hummed, nuzzling into Harper. "I feel it too. You know, I think my time living in the mountains felt so good because they smelled like you. I just didn't know it." Ash laid a kiss on the top of Harper's head. "I didn't realize how lonely I was until I met you. You changed my world, and I'm here to change yours."

Harper slept the rest of the day and night. Ash dozed, mainly keeping an eye on his mate, waiting. When Harper finally opened his eyes, heat crackled between them.

Harper pressed his lips to Ash's chest, wiggling against him. "I'm ready."

Ash's heart fluttered. "Hold that thought, flower."

They dressed quickly, and soon, Ash had them up on the roof.

He scooped Harper up, carrying him bridal style. "Come with me, mate. It's time to claim what's mine."

Harper moaned and buried his face against Ash's neck.

Ash took off and flew toward Dante's house, his pulse thrumming to the beat of his wings. The fresh air filled with the scent of Harper's bluebells. His sweet mate.

Mine. Ash laughed at the possessive voice in his head. How had he ever doubted it?

He landed on Dante's deck and set Harper on his feet.

Harper glanced over his shoulder toward the house. "Is Dante here?"

Ash gripped Harper's chin and turned him to face him. "No, he messaged to say he was out for the day. We have the place to ourselves."

Harper's cheeks pinkened. "Then mate me, Ash. Fuck me and make me yours forever."

Ash growled and crushed Harper into a kiss. He almost took Harper right there, bending him over the rail and spreading him wide, but he didn't want this to be over in a rush.

"Come with me." Ash tugged Harper's hand and led him

inside, all the way to his bedroom. When Harper made for the bed, Ash pulled him in the opposite direction. "In here."

He guided Harper into the bathroom and turned on the luxurious waterfall shower, big enough to accommodate a winged demon.

Harper grinned. "Ooh, I've never had shower sex."

Ash chuckled. "Strip."

Harper's clothes practically disappeared. Ash got himself naked and followed Harper into the shower.

Ash's cock stood at attention, demanding entrance to his mate. It could wait. He closed his fist around Harper's hard length and stroked him, eliciting a chorus of beautiful moans. Ash's tail thrashed and his wings flexed. What music his mate made.

"You're going to make me come too soon," Harper gasped as Ash twisted his fist around Harper's precum-slick tip.

"Not too soon, sweet," Ash murmured in his ear. "I'm going to make you come so many times you won't know your own name."

Harper let out a strangled wail and thrust his hips. Ash wiggled his tail between Harper's ass cheeks and pressed against his hole. Harper came on the touch, jerking in Ash's hand and covering Ash with his cum.

"My eager mate," Ash cooed. "So desperate for me."

"Yes." Harper clutched Ash's shoulders. "Please mate me, Ash. *Please*."

Dropping his head back, Ash groaned. "I've got to get you ready first." He grabbed a washcloth and soap and got to work.

Ash caressed every inch of Harper's skin, from his soft cock to his toes, then up to his face, washing his mate like he was the most precious thing in the world. Because he was.

Harper moved with him like he was drunk on lust, pliant and unsteady on his feet, trusting Ash to do whatever he wanted. He let out a symphony of soft sounds, and Ash kissed each one from his lips.

When almost all of Harper was clean, Ash turned him to face the tiled wall. "Brace your hands here." He positioned them above Harper's head, and Harper complied.

Ash rubbed the soapy cloth over Harper's round ass, then delved between his cheeks. Harper sucked in a breath and pushed back, arching his spine. Ash cleaned him and rinsed the suds away before kneeling behind his flower and spreading his cheeks.

Harper's exposed hole twitched, and pleasure coiled in Ash's core.

"Ash," Harper groaned, pushing his ass farther back.

"I'm right here." Ash leaned forward, pressing his face between Harper's cheeks, and kissed his sweet hole, the scent of mountains, bluebells, and sex as intoxicating as the feel of his mate against his lips.

Harper groaned, long and low, as Ash lapped at him.

Ash squeezed Harper's ass and worked his tongue like it was his purpose in life. But wasn't it? He lived to please his mate, to connect with him. To give everything to this sweet, strong man.

Ash pressed his tongue inside Harper, one of his hands finding Harper's cock hard and leaking. He fucked Harper with his tongue, jerking him off as more of those perfect sounds filled the room.

"Oh fuck, Ash." Harper thrust back into his face, then forward into his fist. "Ash, please. *Please.*"

Ash groaned, and Harper came, his hole dancing against Ash's mouth.

"Holy fucking shit." Harper sagged against the wall, looking over his shoulder with heavy-lidded eyes.

Ash stood and pulled Harper against him. "You taste sweet, flower."

"Fuck," Harper groaned, lips twitching. "You broke me. That was so good."

Ash lifted his chin. He was pleased with himself, but so what? He'd earned it. "Seems we'll be doing that again."

Harper's damp lashes fluttered. "Oh, we definitely are."

Ash grinned and quickly washed himself. Harper grasped Ash's aching cock and stroked, teasing his slit and playing with his balls.

Ash's orgasm threatened, and he caught Harper's hand. "Not until I'm inside you."

Harper shivered. "Okay."

Ash shut off the water and toweled them both dry. He led Harper to the bedroom, pausing in the doorway. His fingers tightened on the doorjamb, shaking slightly. He was about to claim his mate. He'd thought this would never happen.

Harper slipped past and filled his vision, cupping his cheeks. "Are you okay?"

Ash nodded, his throat tightening. "I never thought I'd find you. Harper, I...I want everything for you."

"I want everything for you too, Ash. I'm your mate, but you're mine too. I'm going to take care of you and love you for the rest of time. We're in this together."

Ash cleared his throat, blinking away the moisture in his eyes. "I convinced myself I didn't need anyone, but it was always a lie. I needed you. I needed someone to turn to and share my most private thoughts with. I don't want to be alone anymore."

"You won't be," Harper promised. "You're mine, Ash. I'm here for you."

"Are you ready for this?" Ash had to check one last time, his pulse suddenly racing. "There's no going back. You'll need to feed on my blood, and I'll need to drink yours."

Harper's brow furrowed. "There better be no going back. I'm all in. And it's fine. I had your blood yesterday."

"But you were unconscious. This will be different. I understand if exchanging blood is hard or makes you uncomfortable."

A shadow fell across Harper's face. "I hate the idea of anyone taking my blood, but you aren't taking it." He gripped Ash tight. "I'm giving it to you. We're coming at this as equals, and I trust you. You won't hurt me."

Ash's heart swelled. "No, I won't. I'll do you one better and make sure my bite feels as good as my mouth on your hole."

Harper's eyes widened. "You can do that?"

"Mm, you'll see." Ash picked Harper up and tossed him on the bed. "My lips will only ever feel good against your skin, my fangs too." He let his fangs drop, climbing onto the bed and spreading Harper's legs so he could settle between them.

"Show me," Harper panted, his skin rosy all over and his soft cock starting to fill.

Ash hummed. He hitched one of Harper's knees, took hold of his aching cock, and rubbed his precum-slick tip against Harper's tight hole. Harper clenched against him, and Ash groaned.

He rubbed his tip harder against his mate, purring deep in his chest. "I'm going to fuck you, Harper. Fill you with my cum, my magic. Then I'm going to feed you my life force, and when I taste yours, you're going to see stars."

31

———

HARPER

"Yes, Ash, please," Harper begged like Ash was denying him and it was the only way to get what he wanted, even though that was far from the truth.

Harper's cock stiffened as Ash rubbed his cockhead against his sensitive hole. Fuck, Ash should just shove inside, pry him open with that velvety tip, and take him. He wanted it now.

Luckily, Ash had more patience. What Harper's lust-drunk brain wanted would hurt, and he wasn't ready for that kind of roughness. Ash leaned over Harper and grabbed the lube from the side table, coating his fingers.

"This hole is mine," Ash rumbled as he slathered Harper's rim, slicking him obscenely. "Mine to touch and fuck."

Harper grabbed his hardening cock and stroked. "Yes. It's all yours."

Ash spread his wings, eyes glowing, and pressed a finger inside Harper. His muscles were relaxed from being rimmed in the shower, and Ash slid right in, all the way to his last knuckle.

"So hot for me, mate." Ash swirled inside Harper, and he squirmed. "My cock belongs in here. Fate made you to take me."

Pleasure raced down Harper's spine. He threw his head

back on a groan and released his cock before he came. "Fuck. Yes, your cock belongs inside me. I want to be yours. I need you to own me."

"You're already mine, Harper." Ash pumped his finger before adding a second. "I know you can feel it. Look inside."

Harper gasped as Ash stretched him, but as he adjusted to the sensation, he looked inward.

Feelings of home and safety burned stronger than ever, but beyond that was something else. He felt a loving presence, a warmth so deep he didn't think he'd ever be cold again. He felt Ash, and the more he opened himself to Ash's presence, the stronger the link became.

"I feel you," Harper whispered. Ash's presence seemed to intensify, bursting with love and pure joy.

"I feel you too, sweet." Ash gazed down at Harper like he hung the moon.

Harper clenched around Ash's fingers. He wanted more. More of the connection between them and more of Ash's body. He wanted to be consumed by it.

Ash worked him open more urgently, like he knew Harper needed it. Given their connection, he probably did. Just as Harper knew Ash's desire to claim him was soul-consuming.

"Now," Harper begged when he couldn't take any more of their combined need. "Claim me now."

Ash moaned, the sound vibrating at the end as it turned into a growl. He pulled his fingers out of Harper and slicked his cock. He lined up, and Harper wrapped his legs around Ash's hips.

Ash's gaze lifted from Harper's hole and settled on his face. "Put your arms around my neck. Hold me close."

Softness flooded the bond, and Harper's heart pounded. He wrapped his arms around Ash and pulled him into a kiss. Ash whined and thrust forward.

His cock stretched Harper wide, pushing Harper to his limit. He gasped as Ash's cockhead made it past that tight ring of muscle, sending a thrill down his spine.

Ash purred against Harper's mouth. He pressed his hips forward, giving Harper just enough time to adjust, but not so much that he lost the feeling of Ash taking him over.

"Yes, Ash." Harper thrust, taking Ash all the way inside. "*Ugh*. Yes. Perfect."

"I couldn't agree more, sweet. I want to stay like this forever."

"Deal." Harper rubbed his cheek against Ash's and tightened his arms around his neck.

Ash hummed. He pulled back before thrusting forward, jolting Harper up the bed. Harper swore, and Ash captured his mouth, working him over, his kiss commanding and hips relentless in their sensual, unhurried rhythm. Harper's pleasure built, and the bond strengthened, his awareness of Ash increasing until it filled his soul.

Harper cupped his demon's cheeks and stared deep into his glowing eyes. They may only be starting to get to know each other, but Harper could feel what the bond could become. They were going to grow into something wonderful together.

"I love you, Ash."

"I love you too, Harper." Understanding radiated along the bond as Ash rocked his hips, holding Harper's gaze.

Harper had never felt so claimed. Ash owned his body, but it went beyond that. Ash claimed Harper's emotions, good and bad, all aspects of who Harper was and who he'd become.

He bared himself to Ash, showing Ash all of himself, and Ash accepted him, loved him, and wanted it all. And in return, Ash gave himself over to Harper.

Harper sensed the depth of Ash's heartache caused by so many years alone. Ash had been numb. It broke Harper's heart because he knew that feeling. He'd been numb too. They'd both shut down. It was how they'd survived.

But Harper could do more than survive with Ash. He had so much to give. Life sizzled between them. Ash's joy at finding Harper shone bright. Together, they had a home.

"Ash..." Harper wanted to put it all into words, but his body trembled with pleasure, and he couldn't figure out how.

"I know, sweet," Ash whispered. "I feel it too. It's time."

"Yes. I need you."

Ash murmured words in a melodic language, the sounds dancing across Harper's skin. Magic flared, electrifying the air, and the mating spell brought everything together.

Harper whimpered, Ash echoing the sound. He picked up his pace, snapping his hips against Harper's ass. Harper cried out. It was too good. Pleasure tightened inside him, and he exploded, cum spilling onto his stomach.

Ash growled and stiffened, heat flooding Harper as Ash filled his body. "*Mine*," Ash groaned, pumping his hips. "*Mine*."

"*Yours*," Harper echoed, deep satisfaction washing over him as his pleasure rolled on.

Ash brought his wrist to his mouth and bit down, drawing blood with his fangs. His eyes flashed golden, a hint of red lingering on his lips.

Harper reached for Ash's wrist. He didn't think twice. He had to connect with his mate, give and take everything he possessed. Harper pressed Ash's wrist to his mouth hungrily, latching on. Blood filled his mouth, Ash's spiced, smoky flavor bursting on his tongue.

He drank deeply, moaning as Ash fucked him, the magic of their connection keeping them hard and needy even though they'd just come.

"You're mine, Harper," Ash grunted, hips smacking against his ass. "Make me yours."

Harper sucked on Ash's wrist. He'd never get enough of his mate. The bond sparked and drowned his senses with pleasure and possessive need.

Ash growled. His hips faltered, and he came again. Harper released Ash with a groan. He ground his ass against Ash, keeping his cock buried deep.

"Please, Ash."

Ash knew what he needed. The bond telegraphed it loud and clear. He turned Harper's head to the side and pierced Harper's neck with his fangs.

"*Oh, Ash.*" Harper's back arched. He grabbed Ash's horns and fucked himself on Ash's cock.

Pleasure radiated from his neck, pulsing in time with the pounding in his ass. *Fucking hell.* Each gulp Ash took felt like getting his cock sucked.

Ash rumbled, drinking deeper, and Harper came, spilling bursts of cum onto his belly as his orgasm turned him inside out.

He saw stars, and nothing had ever been more beautiful.

32

ASH

One week later.

Ash pulled a tray of pastries out of the oven. Look at that golden-brown color. He'd fucking nailed the recipe.

He set the homemade berry Danishes on the counter beside Harper with the air of a demon who'd conquered impossible odds for his mate.

"Wow, these look amazing." Harper beamed, his appreciation worthy of Ash's not-at-all-inflated view of his baking skills.

"I think you'll find I can make all your favorite treats." Ash set the oven mitts down and puffed out his chest.

Harper giggled. "I'm sure you can. But how are we going to eat all these?"

"Dante will hoover them up if you're not careful. His sweet tooth is revolting."

Harper nodded, no doubt having noticed Dante's preference for candy and cake over real food. "Maybe I should take some for Ollie when I go home."

"By all means." Ash plated a pastry and slid it over to Harper. "Am I still coming over for dinner tomorrow night?"

Harper rolled his eyes. "Yeah, obviously." He paused. "Ollie was wondering if Dante is coming with you."

Ash sensed hesitance through the bond. "Do you not want Dante to come?"

"No, I do. I like hanging out with him." Harper turned his plate in idle circles. "What does Dante think of Ollie?"

"He hasn't really said."

All Ash managed to get out of Dante was that he was pleased Harper had a trusted friend. It was odd.

Harper bit his lip. "I want us all to be friends, but it could get messy with Dante looking for his mate and Ollie having no idea that's a thing and flirting with him."

"Dante will let him down kindly if he has to." Unless Dante's strange avoidance was because he'd sensed something in Ollie and was trying to figure out what it was.

Would Dante hide it if he suspected Ollie was his mate? It was hard to imagine Dante not shouting it from the rooftops immediately. Ash pushed the idea to the side. He wouldn't pester Dante for an explanation. At least not yet. If Ash had this all wrong, he didn't want the reminder to hurt Dante.

After all, what were the chances Ollie was Dante's mate?

Harper took a bite of his pastry, and his eyes rolled back. "Oh fuck, Ash. This is so good."

Ash purred, brushing sugar from Harper's chin.

Pleasure zipped down the bond.

Ash wrapped an arm around Harper, warmth blooming everywhere they touched. They'd spent most of the last week in bed, except for the evenings when Harper went home to hang out with Ollie.

The bond grew between them, strengthening with each

passing day. Ash wasn't sure he'd ever get used to the way their connection heightened physical intimacy.

A burst of happiness hit Ash straight in the chest. Had it come from him or Harper? Not knowing was an even better feeling than anything they'd achieved in the bedroom.

Ash had his mate. Everything was better shared with Harper.

"We should get going," Harper said once he finished his treat.

"You've got your potions?"

"Yeah. I'll go grab my bag." Harper hopped off the barstool and headed down the hall toward Ash's room.

Harper had a long talk with Nico the other day. He hadn't been surprised to learn Harper wasn't working for anyone. He'd known Harper was a witch after thoroughly assessing him on his first visit, when Harper had only worn the bracelet as a disguise.

"We'll have to come back for the pastries," Harper said as he reappeared. "I don't want them getting crushed in my bag while we fly."

"I'll tell Dante not to eat them all." Ash took out his phone and shot off a stern text.

"Where is Dante?"

"I'm not sure. I think he's been spending time with Onyx." Ash hadn't seen much of the blue-haired demon, which was perfectly fine.

"Have they had any word of Luc?"

"No." When Luc disappeared, he escaped the Human Realm, returning to Hell, but there was no way he wouldn't be back. "Dante is working on a spell to break illusions like the one Luc used, so there'll be no more hiding in Shearwater Landing for him. We'll be able to sense when he reenters this world, and if he can't mask himself, we'll find him."

"Good." Harper adjusted his bag with a sense of finality. "I can't believe after all that sneaking around, he just ran off to hide."

"I'd say he's regrouping, not hiding. He won't try anything until he thinks he has the upper hand."

Harper's jaw clenched. "He won't fool me so easily next time."

"No, he won't, but don't worry. He's fooled all of us at least once. If not more."

Luc's return wasn't as concerning now that Ash and Harper were mated. It was still a problem. Luc would hunt Ash, Dante, and Onyx until he dragged them back to the Realm of the Damned. But as his bonded mate, killing Harper would be no different from killing a demon or an Eternal, and that was a line Luc had never crossed. Harper wasn't vulnerable like he'd been before.

Luc still had to pay for hurting Harper, but Ash could be patient. He'd get Luc back for that along with everything else. He, Dante, and Onyx would make their stand in Shearwater Landing. Ash almost welcomed the inevitable confrontation.

"Come." Ash led Harper out to the balcony.

"Can we fly all the way to The Herb Emporium?"

"Sure thing, sweet." Ash hoisted Harper into his arms.

Harper's magic sparked with excitement.

Being near Harper was even more intoxicating now that he wasn't suppressing his power. Their magics danced together in an echo of the mating bond. Ash loved the tingle of Harper's power playing with his.

Ash soared over the city, catching a sea breeze and riding it inland.

He had to hand it to Dante. This place wasn't bad. It beat his isolated lodge in the mountains by a long shot. He had all he needed from the mountains right in his arms. His sweet flower.

They landed on a deserted side street near The Herb Emporium, where Ash removed his illusion of invisibility.

Harper led the way down the street. "Come in the shop with me this time?"

"Sure." Ash nudged Harper's shoulder with his. "I'd like to see you brew sometime."

"Yeah? I guess I can set up my stuff at your place rather than brewing in the middle of the night at the apartment. I should make you something." Harper's brow crinkled. "Do witch potions even work on demons?"

"The ones in your bag wouldn't, but if you enhanced something more powerful, it would affect me. You're strong enough."

Harper bit back a smile. "Interesting. We won't do that in front of Nico though."

"No."

They'd decided not to try and pass Ash off as human to Nico, partly because he was already suspicious of disguises around Harper. Ash wasn't suppressing all of his power like he normally did. He let enough come to the surface that he seemed like an average witch.

Nico needed to know Harper had magical beings in his corner. Harper wasn't sure it mattered, but it did to Ash.

He entered the shop behind Harper, gaze zeroing in on the man behind the counter.

"Harper." Nico smiled warmly at Ash's mate. "And who's this?" His lips thinned as he took in Ash.

"This is Ash." Harper laid a hand on Ash's shoulder. "My boyfriend."

"Boyfriend. Right." Nico narrowed his eyes slightly before turning his attention back to Harper. "Let's see what you've got. Then, Kat and Melanie are ready for you out back."

Was Nico upset Harper had a boyfriend? Were his sights

set on Ash's mate? If so, it was good to clear that up before Harper took the in-house job.

Ash better not have steered Harper wrong by encouraging him to get to know this man.

Harper unloaded his bag, bouncing on the balls of his feet, joy and excitement radiating down the bond as he detailed his potions to Nico. Harper wanted this job so badly. Nico's intentions better be good.

Ash clenched his fist.

But the shop owner seemed pleased with the new array of potions Harper had brewed. "Thanks, Harper. These are great. Really high quality and so creative. Let's introduce you to Kat and Melanie." He opened a curtain blocking off the back of the shop, beckoning Harper over with a friendly air.

Maybe he wasn't disappointed Harper was taken.

Harper rounded the counter and followed Nico into the hidden room.

Soft voices murmured back and forth. Ash concentrated his demon sense until he could hear what they were saying.

"Is he really your boyfriend?" Nico asked in an urgent whisper.

"Yes," Harper replied, sounding confused.

"It's just that you said your coven was tracking you, and then *he* shows up glued to your side. Are you okay, Harper?"

Ash raised his brows. Nico was worried for Harper's safety? Seemed he wasn't bad at all.

"Yes. I'm fine, Nico. He really is my boyfriend. Ash is the one who helped me get away from my coven. I really don't need you to do anything. I have it all under control."

"Okay. But you can always come to me if you need anything."

Harper thanked Nico, their voices growing louder as Harper was introduced to the others.

After a few minutes, Nico reappeared in the main part of the shop, pulling back the curtain to reveal Harper talking to two women.

"He's one of the best brewers I've ever met," Nico said as he tidied the potions away.

"Lucky for your shop."

Nico snorted. "Yes. And lucky for my customers." Nico paused, tapping a notebook lying out on the counter. "If that coven gives him more trouble, call me." A hint of venom laced Nico's tone.

Ash crossed his arms. He flexed only a little. "They won't be an issue, but thank you."

Nico nodded. "So, you here to keep an eye on me, or what?"

Ash's lips curled in a sly smile. "Maybe. Harper asked me to tag along. Otherwise, I'd be scoping you out some other time. Just to be sure."

Nico chuckled. "You seem all right."

Ash let out a good-natured huff. "So glad you think so."

Nico shrugged. "I look after people who need it. My employees. My friends." A distinct warning crept into Nico's tone.

"Noted." Ash could have laughed—this witch had nothing on him—but his protectiveness came from a good place and wasn't something to sniff at.

Harper had a knack for finding good people. There almost had to be some magic in it rather than blind luck, but Ash wasn't sure how. Whatever it was, Harper deserved to be surrounded by people who only lifted him up.

Anyone else would have Ash to deal with.

Harper returned to the front of the shop with a wide grin. The two women followed, quizzing Harper on custom brews. He seemed energized by the questions, clearly happy to talk about potions.

Ash melded into the background as Harper brewed tonics for Kat and Melanie and one for Nico, though only after some prodding.

"I love making new things," Harper said, handing Nico a vial.

Melanie sipped her potion. "Perfect. You have more than enough knowledge to personalize your brews, and enthusiasm is the next most important thing."

Harper's eyes widened as he looked between the three of them. "So you think I'm a good fit?"

Kat and Melanie nodded.

"Definitely," Nico added. "While I'm sad these two are leaving, and I'll miss Kat's flair, I'm glad this worked out."

"Me too." Harper made arrangements for taking over the in-house position and led Ash out of the shop.

Ash grabbed Harper's hand. "You're excited to work here?"

"Yeah, you should know. I'm sure you can feel it." Harper bit his lip and sent a jolt down the bond.

Ash grinned. "That felt a little sultry, Harper. Are you trying to tell me brewing potions turns you on?"

He laughed. "No. I just can't help feeling a little riled up around you, no matter what we're doing."

Ash hummed. "I like that." He dropped his voice to a deep purr. "Let's stop by your place before we pick up those pastries. You need to unwind if you're this riled up."

Harper released an adorable squeak and picked up his pace, dragging Ash along.

At the apartment, Harper threw his bag onto the new chair occupying the corner of his bedroom and pulled Ash into a kiss. Heat flared as their lips collided.

Harper had gone shopping the other day after talking to Nico. Once he was confident his income wasn't about to disappear, he'd felt comfortable spending some of the money he'd saved.

As a result, his bedroom was starting to look lived in. The thrifted chair matched a small rug, and Harper had hung a string of lights above his bed, where more pillows than anyone needed were carefully arranged. Ash's favorite piece was the seventies-esque lamp on the side table.

"Ash," Harper groaned, breaking the kiss and running his hands through Ash's hair.

Ash let his horns free, and Harper caressed them reverently. "I love seeing you happy, sweet."

"You too." Harper's lust-hazed eyes cleared. "I can feel how happy you are. But there's so much more to it. To us. That's not all I feel."

"I know." Ash tapped Harper's chest. "There's a bitter-sweetness there too."

Harper splayed his hand over Ash's heart. "And here."

"But that's why I feel so much joy now. When I longed for my mate thousands of years ago, I'd have been thrilled to find you, but I wouldn't have taken joy in every little thing. It wouldn't have been the same, and I wouldn't change what we have, not even to have found you sooner."

Harper's eyes widened. "Even if it meant you didn't have to be alone?"

"No, because I got through it. And it brought me here."

"I don't know if I'd say the same." Harper looked away. "I'd trade the time with my coven if I could."

"Of course." Ash let Harper's sadness find a home in his chest. "I'd wish it away for you too."

"But we don't have to. I can feel how well you understand me, and loneliness is part of that. That's what I was trying to say. It's something we shared while we were apart, which makes it easier to move on and start a new life with you."

Ash cupped Harper's cheek, his chest expanding. He felt more alive than he ever had. "I can't wait to see the man you become, Harper, and who I become with you. Together, we're going to thrive, and for the first time in a long time, I'm looking forward to my eternal existence."

Ash sank to his knees. "Hold on, sweet. I'm going to take care of you."

EPILOGUE
HARPER

TEN YEARS LATER.

HARPER OPENED the Center's front door and stepped into the dark foyer. A light shone in the hall beyond. He knew he'd find his mate here, not just because of the bond.

"You're supposed to be closed for the night," Harper called.

"I just have to finish one more thing," Ash shouted back.

Harper entered the small office. "What are you doing?"

Ash pointed to the computer. "I just needed to order a few extra things for the community night next week."

Harper inspected the screen. "More food?" He rolled his eyes, pretending to be annoyed, even though he knew Ash could feel how warm and gooey he was inside.

"Just a little more food. We didn't have a great variety. Onyx would've complained if everything on offer was 'kid friendly.'"

Harper bit back a smile. "So the vegan truffle tarts are for Onyx?"

"The vegan truffle tarts are so I don't have to hear Onyx whine all night."

It wasn't the worst idea, and way better than letting Onyx plan the event like it was an opening at the gallery. "All right. Onyx better share though." Harper paused, glancing around the office. Ash always kept it pristine, his files color-coded to match the wall calendar. "How are the new mentors doing?"

Ash swiveled in his chair, turning away from the screen. "Good. Stacy and Milo are ready for their first mentee, and Kara's started running group sessions alongside Michelle."

Harper nodded. Everyone was settling in great. The Center had grown beyond his wildest dreams. Five years ago, he'd never have pictured this.

He and Ash had created a sanctuary for witches from abusive covens, a place where they could come for help or to get away from bad situations. The Center did everything from being a first point of contact to helping with housing, accessing counseling, helping find employment, and rebuilding social networks and community after witches left their covens behind.

It was the kind of place Harper would have killed for when he'd left his coven. No one should have to go through what he did alone.

Since they opened, they'd helped witches from the wider Shearwater Landing area and across the state. Harper had even started planning a second center when one of their counselors moved and offered to head a new location.

It was work Harper had never seen himself doing. Somehow, he'd never imagined he could help people beyond what his power and potion mastery offered.

He'd loved brewing for Nico, but this felt like what he was meant to do. When Ash first suggested creating a place for witches to turn to when they needed help, Harper knew it was where he wanted to put his energy. Of course Nico had been one hundred percent on board and had helped almost as much as Ash to make their dream a reality.

"Dante texted, asking when we'd be home." Harper ran a hand through Ash's hair. "Are you almost done?"

"Yes, we can go." Ash's eyes fluttered closed. "He'll forgive me for being late when he hears I ordered those crystal candies he likes."

Harper massaged Ash's scalp. "Our community nights are going to get a reputation if you keep ordering treats like that."

He shrugged. "I bet you the candy doesn't even make it to the event. Guaranteed, Dante will coincidentally be hanging around as it's delivered, and it'll disappear."

Harper snorted. "You could just buy him some and bring it to the house. Save everyone the trouble."

Ash's eyes popped open. "And encourage him? Never."

Harper tugged Ash's hair, and he purred. "You ordered those fruit platters Michelle likes?"

"And garlic bread for Zack. The pizza order seemed adequate, so I left that alone."

"Oh good."

Ash snaked his arms around Harper's waist. "Just be glad I haven't insisted on cooking everything like I did for Thanksgiving."

"You're right. I am glad. That was way too much work." The Center hosted holiday meals, usually potlucks, but last Thanksgiving, Ash had made everything himself.

Ash huffed. "I'm a demon. If I can't manage to cook one meal for thirty-five people, then I'm losing my touch. Super speed in the kitchen really is a game changer."

Harper shook his head. "I'm still surprised you've never cut a finger off."

Ash gasped like he was offended, but amusement tickled the bond. "I'm very careful."

Harper kissed him on the forehead. "Come on. Let's not keep Dante and everyone waiting."

Ash shut down the computer and stood, taking off his shirt. "Why don't we see how fast I can fly? I think I can beat Dante's record."

"Even carrying me?"

He grinned. "You better believe it, sweet."

Harper laughed. "Okay, you're on. But if you can't beat Dante's time, you have to admit it to him."

Ash grumbled. "Fine, fine. But then all his gloating is on you. He'll never know if I lie, so if you want to spare yourself..."

"Then you'll just have to fly faster. I didn't think it'd be a problem for you to beat him."

"Correct answer." Ash's eyes flashed golden.

Harper grabbed his hand, joy sparking in his chest, down the bond, and in his mate. "I love you, Ash. Now take me home to our family."

The End

Looking for more Harper and Ash? Don't miss *Sweet & Lacy*, a steamy bonus epilogue available for free to my newsletter subscribers. Join now and see what pretty underwear Ash buys Harper after they're newly mated.

Will Dante get his happily ever after? Find out in *Lovers of the Damned Book Two: Demon's Heart*.

Want to keep in touch? Join my reader group on Facebook, Colette Rivera's Coven. You can also find me on Patreon for monthly bonus ficlets, weekly WIP chapters, and behind the scenes updates.

THANK YOU FOR READING DEMON'S MATE

I hoped you enjoyed Harper and Ash's story.

Reviews are invaluable to authors. Please consider leaving a review for *Demon's Mate* on your favorite review site or the site where you purchased this book to help others find magical books they'll love.

DEMON'S HEART

Fated to a broken heart.

Dante never gave up on finding his fated mate. For thousands of years, while the rest of the Fallen lost hope, he was the demon who believed he'd find his man.

And when Dante sees Ollie, he knows.

His mate. His human. His Ollie.

Ollie Hudson doesn't do relationships. Not even the spark he feels for his roommate's friend Dante can change his mind. History taught him not to trust anyone in love, even himself. But that doesn't mean he and Dante can't be friends.

And why can't fated mates form a bond through friendship? Dante won't push for something Ollie doesn't desire. With Ollie unaware of magic, there's no rush to explain the draw between them and no pressure to mate.

Until Lucifer returns and everything goes to Hell.

Dante is forced to cement the mating bond or lose Ollie forever, tying them together before they're ready. Will Ollie ever accept what they have and choose Dante, or is Dante's fate a mating bond forever marred by the pain under which it was formed and a mate who wants to undo it all?

Order Now

ACKNOWLEDGMENTS

I had so much fun writing this book and love Harper and Ash to bits.

To everyone who was excited about this story as I wrote it, responding to teasers and hints, you helped me look forward to *Demon's Mate's* release. It's always nerve wracking beginning a new series, so thank you!

Thank you Abbie Nicole, for your wonderful editing and attention to detail. I'm so glad you enjoyed this story. It's always a pleasure working with you.

Thank you to Molly from We Got You Covered Book Design for the amazing cover. It's so demon-y and perfect. Ash's glowing eyes are my favorite.

Angki.s_ thank you for the beautiful illustrations of Harper and Ash. I really enjoyed working with you and can't wait to share all the other *Lover's of the Damned* commissions you've created for me.

Thank you to TK for supporting all my magic worlds, reading all my books, and encouraging me. Couldn't do it without you.

Thank you to all my readers. I'm grateful for every single person who reads my stories. You make this job magical.

ABOUT THE AUTHOR

Colette is an author of queer paranormal romance novels. She loves to write couples who take care of each other and show their soft sides in love. Sugar and spice are key ingredients in all her books. She's an avid PNR reader and loves all things magic. Colette once lived in the US but now calls New Zealand home. As a bisexual she has to resist making all her characters bi. When she succeeds, you'll find a variety of representation in her books.

Colette can be found on Instagram @colette_rivera and on Facebook under Colette Rivera Author. She can also be found on her website coletterivera.com where you can sign up to her newsletter for bonus epilogues and updates.

ALSO BY COLETTE RIVERA

Moonlight Falls

The Fall of Elijah Gray

The Seduction of James Gray

The Cursed Sebastian Storm

The Heart of Moonlight Falls

Love & Magic

Give a Witch a Chance

Keep Your Witches Close

One Wicked Night

Witch Boyfriend Wanted